AWAKENED

CIARA DUGGAN

THE PARLIAMENT HOUSE

ISBN: 978-1-956136-90-6

Edited by Kassie Metivier, Cindy Kilbourne, Malorie Nilson, and Sophia Desensei

The Parliament House

www.parliamenthousepress.com

To my husband for surrendering the office.

CHAPTER ONE

H-a-n-n-a-h...

As Hannah Fenwick walked by the historic Bellcliff University Library, she heard a voice whisper her name. It was beautiful and soft, like the warm, amber sunset over campus, yet unsettling. Even a little eerie. Her skin chilled. She stopped, searching for its origin, but there were only excited students ready to start a new semester. A group of boys flying a frisbee back and forth. Some girls gathered around the library railing, cooing over one of their phones. All unaware of the voice whispering on the breeze.

H-a-n-n-a-h...

Goosebumps crept on the back of her neck, beneath her mass of curly, chestnut hair. She knew this wasn't real; the wind didn't whisper. Despite the cool weather, tiny beads of sweat gathered along her hairline and dampened her neck. Hannah squinted her eyes shut, hoping that not seeing might equate to not hearing. This had worked sometimes when she experienced memories of her past. And even though Hannah could recognize an oncoming anxiety attack, it didn't make her distress any less real.

She reminded herself to breathe in for a count of *one, two, three, four, five...* She held her breath for another second, and then exhaled. *Five, four, three, two, one...* She paused, inhaled again, decelerating her racing heart. As her breath steadied, she touched her thumbs to her fingertips, over and over. She subtly looked over her shoulders, trying to gauge whether other students were taking notice of her symptoms—something she desperately didn't want. That was all she needed...to be the freak here too.

A silent breeze refreshed her clammy skin, and Hannah slowed each tap of her fingers. The grass was littered with red and yellow leaves. It was all so normal. The commonality of it all reminded Hannah of her resolution: This year would be different.

It wasn't a coincidence that Bellcliff University was on the opposite coast from California—3,000 miles away from the people who looked at her like she was about to break.

She was no longer going to blame herself for what happened to her parents or search for some explanation of what really transpired that night. She vowed to leave all that behind and live an ordinary college life.

She would try, at the very least.

And because of this resolution, she did her best to act like nothing was wrong. She pinned a smile on her face and continued to walk, tapping her fingers less and less. She knew there was no voice. Everything was fine.

Thankfully, the farther she walked away from the library, the more normal she felt. Crisis averted, moving on. Crisp air brushed up the autumn leaves. Distant waves were loud, but pleasant. The cold was sharper here. It cut a little deeper.

Hannah clutched at the sleeves of her blue-knit sweater and quickened her pace on the cobblestone pathway.

The students she passed on the short journey back to her dorm building were smiling, waving, and full of energy as they reunited with old friends or faced the prospect of new friends and newfound independence. Uncle Paul said that college was where you could redefine yourself or discover who you truly are. Or uncover who you've always been.

Hannah arrived at her dorm building: dark red brick, white stone trim, and a black shingled roof that oozed collegiate charm. The inside of the building was equally aged with grey stone and dark wood.

When she walked into her dorm room, she was greeted with all the boxes she had yet to unpack. The room was already small for two people. She didn't need all her baggage clogging up the limited space. Thankfully, the high ceilings with dark wood beams kept it from feeling too claustrophobic.

Amelia entered the room, wrapped in a towel with her perfectly arranged shower tote, the bottles lined up in order of height. As soon as she closed the door, the smell of her lavender shampoo wafted in with her.

"Hannah, hi!" she said, cheerful and refreshed.

"Hey, Amelia," Hannah said. She sat on her bed, mismatched with a beige comforter and navy-blue pillowcases, and attempted to tame some of her flyaway curls.

Amelia looked Hannah over. "Why aren't you getting ready?" she asked, high-pitched and energetic. She shimmied her underwear up her legs under her towel and struggled to put on her bra with the towel clenched beneath her arms.

"Ready for what?"

"You said you'd go to the party with me. Fisher Hall? That boy from my orientation group invited me." Amelia hung her towel on the back of the door. She sauntered back to her bed, confident in her tall, slender, physique, making Hannah feel frumpy in comparison. Amelia combed through her long blonde hair and smiled to herself.

Hannah didn't remember agreeing to a dorm party. Maybe the invitation got lost in the rapid flurry of words Amelia spewed when they first met. But she did remember the promise she made to herself. "I'll go for a little while," Hannah said, hoping it sufficed. "I'm supposed to arrive at my first anthropology class on Monday with a research topic picked out, so I'm planning on an early start at the library tomorrow."

"You know there's this thing called *the internet?*" Amelia took her tote and placed it neatly under her bed. Everything on Amelia's side of the room had been neatly unpacked and arranged in a color scheme of blush pink and white with accents of rose gold. While Hannah's side of the wall was blank, Amelia's was filled with photos of loved ones and strategically placed twinkle lights. It looked like a dorm room straight off Pinterest.

"I know, but there's something about libraries that the internet can't replicate." The wooden desk at the end of her bed was piled with books she had come to cherish over the years.

"Ugh, homework already." Amelia cut Hannah off. "Remind me never to major in anthropology."

"Oh, that's not my major," Hannah said. "I'm actually undecided." After two years of therapy and mourning, Hannah wasn't quite sure what interested her. How was she supposed to decide what she wanted to do for the rest of her life when she just got back on her feet?

"Something else we have in common," Amelia smiled. "This must be the building where they toss the kids who can't make up their minds."

"So, what's this boy's name again?" Hannah asked, challenging herself to keep up the social interaction.

"Bryce." Amelia swooned. Hannah, on the other hand, grimaced. "What's with the face? Did you meet him? Oh no. What's wrong with him?"

"No, no, no," Hannah reassured Amelia. "I've never met him. Just the name."

"What's wrong with the name Bryce?"

"I don't know." Hannah leaned back against the headboard of her bed. "If Bellcliff had fraternities, I'm sure there'd be a bunch of Bryce's rushing. All with the overarching goal be to become the frat president."

"And what's so bad about that? If Bellcliff had sororities, I'd probably go for it. And I bet you would too," Amelia said. She pointed her brush at Hannah and shuffled her toes against the white shag rug that bordered her bed. "Then we could be sisters." Her voice reached a piercing note on the word "sisters."

Hannah winced. While she vowed to have a fresh start, she was definitely not the sorority type. She had her small group of friends, and that was all she needed. That was before she pushed them all away. But as far as roommates went, she could have been paired with someone far worse than Amelia.

"Well, then maybe you're perfect for each other." Hannah offered a smile and readjusted herself against her pillows.

Amelia slid a flowing floral top over her head. Her whole demeanor was breezy and effortless. Hannah wondered why she couldn't be like that. Maybe she could, one day. She could care about boys and makeup and parties. Life could be simple.

"Come on, get dressed. We should go soon." Amelia gazed at her reflection in the magnifying mirror that sat on her desk and applied a pale pink lip gloss.

"What's wrong with this?" Hannah asked. She pinched the plain navy-knit sweater she wore.

Amelia eyed it suspiciously, her gaze then falling to Hannah's jeans and black Chelsea boots. "Nothing, it's just not very...chic."

"Not sure if I brought anything...chic."

"Let me see." Amelia barged over to Hannah's cramped armoire and perused its contents. Blazers, button-up shirts, turtlenecks, jeans, sweaters, and the rest were just gym clothes. "So, you're either a professor here, or you're on some type of athletic scholarship." Amelia pulled out a blazer and a pair of track pants. "This one has elbow patches, and this has snap-buttons all the way down the leg," Amelia exclaimed.

Hannah shrugged. She liked what she liked.

"What about something in these?" Amelia pointed to an unpacked box.

"More of the same."

"Then you can borrow something of mine." Amelia opened her own wardrobe and flipped through her clothes.

"Do you think any of your clothes will fit me?" she asked. She'd never experienced the sharing of clothes or makeup or anything else, for that matter. Hannah was an only child. "You're a lot taller."

Amelia ignored Hannah and pulled out a light blue shirt with off-the-shoulder long sleeves. "Wear this. It will bring out your eyes."

"It looks tiny." Hannah protested, holding up the shirt. "It'll be a crop top on me."

"You can pull it off," Amelia said. "I know you have a slim frame under that oversized pullover."

Hannah imagined sharing clothes with your college roommate was part of the whole normal college experience, so she didn't fight it. Hannah slid off her bed and changed out her sweater for Amelia's shirt. It smelled like hyacinth.

She approached the long mirror that hung on the side of her wardrobe and didn't totally hate what she saw. Amelia was right. The shirt made her light blue eyes appear brighter than usual.

You have your mother's eyes, her father used to say. The more Hannah stared at her reflection, the more her mother appeared. Bright blue eyes and rosy cheeks contrasted her coarse brown hair. Perhaps it was her mother's voice she had heard earlier.

"See!" Amelia said. "You love it."

Hannah looked away from the mirror and forced a smile. Maybe if she could fool everyone else that she was happy, then she'd start to believe it too.

"Now, about your hair—"

Hannah cut her off. "It's a lost cause. Trust me."

As soon as Hannah and Amelia arrived at the party across campus, a boy who smelled of weed handed them each a red solo cup. Hannah sniffed the unidentified dark liquid; it reeked of cinnamon, vanilla, and something resembling wood varnish. Her stomach reeled. If it tasted as awful as it smelled, she was guaranteed a hangover tomorrow. She held it, however, so that no one else would offer her a drink.

The room was filled with both eager and awkward college freshmen. One boy couldn't decide what to do with his hands while flirting with a girl, while another continuously propped up his overly-gelled hair when he didn't think anyone was looking. There were already two girls crying, and one who had clearly drank too much, swaying and babbling to no one in particular. Others were slowly testing the waters, taking small sips while observing their fellow classmates. Hannah wondered if any of them were doing the same thing as her—pretending.

Overplayed pop music streamed from the speakers and was accompanied by the smell of various perfumes and colognes. Between that and the stench of the fuel-like alcohol, Hannah's nose stung.

A troupe of girls, all holding hands, pushed by Hannah and Amelia, giggling and only paying attention to each other. They all wore tight mini dresses with the aim to squish their boobs as close to their necks as possible.

Hannah tugged at her borrowed cropped top, still feeling underdressed.

"Bryce," Amelia shouted over the music. She took Hannah's hand and dragged her across the room. They pushed and shoved their way through the crowded hall into the living room where a boy stood beside a fireplace.

"Bryce!" Amelia said. She thrust her arms around his neck and balanced the solo cup in her hand. "This is Hannah. My roommate."

There was nothing about Bryce that was too exceptional. Medium-length blond hair, light grey eyes, and tan skin, as if he had been at the beach all summer.

"Nice to meet you," he said, extending his hand to

8

Hannah. She couldn't remember the last time she shook someone's hand, especially with people her own age. He nodded, then redirected his attention to Amelia. "So happy you came." His grin grew as he gazed at Amelia.

On first impression, he came across as a decent guy. Like maybe he should have been named Peter or Robert.

"This is my roommate, Landon," Bryce said. He nodded to the boy beside him. Landon was a bit taller than Bryce, but dressed similar in khaki pants and a button-down with the top few undone.

"Nice to meet you," he said. He shook Hannah's hand. Everything about him was warm. His light brown eyes, sandy brown hair, his smile, his voice, and even his grip.

"Yeah, you too," she said.

"Would you like a drink?" Bryce asked Amelia.

And even though Amelia held a full cup in her hand, she eagerly agreed. Together, they disappeared into the party.

Hannah shifted in place, transferring her gaze between Landon and over her shoulder to where Amelia had abandoned her. She pressed her sweaty palms together as her shoulders climbed towards her ears.

"You okay?" Landon asked.

"Yeah, fine," Hannah said. "It's just—she basically dragged me here..."

"You didn't want to come?" Landon asked.

"No. I did. Of course, I did." Hannah bobbed her head up and down more times than necessary. "Just haven't been to many parties lately. Feeling a bit rusty."

"Well, you're doing fine." Hannah wondered if Landon was actually interested in talking to her, or if he was trying to figure out a quick exit plan. Part of her would be okay if he left her alone. She could slip out without anyone noticing and escape to her room for some peace and quiet.

However, that was not what normal college kids were supposed to do. They were supposed to be social, meet new people, and drink. Hannah took a sip of the mystery liquid and immediately regretted it. Her face twisted in agony.

"Not good?" Landon chuckled.

"What is this? It tastes like gasoline and cinnamon."

"Not a big drinker?"

"No, that's not it," Hannah said as she struggled against the awful taste in her mouth. "I'm from Sonoma, so I was raised on wine." Despite fearing whether her taste buds would ever survive such an attack, Hannah relaxed her shoulders.

"I suppose drinking shitty alcohol is like a college initiation," Landon said, grinning at Hannah's repellent expression. "Here, take this." Landon handed her his drink.

"You didn't drug this or anything, did you?" She forced a suspicious smile.

"My own drink? I would hope not."

Hannah took a sip, and it dulled whatever acid-like substance coated her tongue. "Is this...lemonade?" she asked.

He scratched the back of his neck, slightly embarrassed. "I rather not puke at my first college party. But don't tell anyone, okay? Just let everyone think I'm really good at handling my liquor."

"So much for being initiated," she said. "My lips are sealed."

"You keep that," Landon said, referencing the lemonade. "I'll go get another one and get rid of..." He took

Hannah's cup of mystery liquid. "Whatever this is." He paused and looked back at Hannah. "Don't go anywhere."

Hannah turned towards the fireplace and allowed the flames to warm her cheeks. As she waited for Landon to return, a sense of pride washed over her. This time last year, she was holed up in her bedroom, refusing even to talk to some of her friends. And here she was, at a college party, talking to a boy—a handsome boy.

Hannah drifted through the room and took in all the care-free college kids getting gradually more inebriated. Her pride devolved into guilt.

For a moment, she had forgotten all the darkness and guilt that surviving had plagued her with. She shouldn't be here. She should be dead, just like her parents. Before those negative thoughts could siege her mind completely, a random guy stumbled toward her.

"Why's a pretty girl like you standing here all alone?" His slurred words were accompanied by glazed-over eyes and the stench of bile.

Hannah released a tuft of laughter. "Just enjoying my own company," she said.

"You look sad."

Hannah straightened. "No, I don't."

"How would you know? You can't see yourself." His flimsy grip on his cup caused a splash of liquor to cascade down his arm.

"You make a good point," Hannah said. "You must be very intelligent." Her deadpan tone was completely lost on his intoxicated state.

"I am," he said, proud of himself. He wrapped his arm around Hannah's shoulders. "You like that, don't you?"

Hannah was quick to crawl out from under his sweaty arm. He faltered toward her and clumsily slammed his forearm against the fireplace, steadying himself close to Hannah. Too close. His stale, bitter breath assaulted her face.

She stepped back, careful not to brush her skin against his sweaty arm hair. She would rather shove her nose in the gas-cinnamon combo than be that close to his mouth ever again.

Before he could set his humid, hairy arm back around Hannah's shoulders, Landon walked up beside her.

"You okay?" he asked.

"Yeah, fine." Hannah exhaled, relieved that she no longer had to endure this drunkard alone.

"I think you'd feel better if you went back to your dorm and drank some water," Landon said to the blasted guy who swayed in place.

Hannah wanted easy, breezy fun—not sloppy drunk encounters at her first college party. Though, maybe that was too much to ask. It was college, after all.

"Only if she comes with me." He groped at Hannah's hand.

Her skin blazed.

She yanked her hand back, but the boy's clammy grip tightened, crunching her knuckles.

Her heartbeat pulsed in her ears. Anxiety pricked at her arms like tiny needles, spreading from her shoulders to her fingertips. She focused on her breath, but her temperature rose. Her temples dampened with perspiration.

Landon stepped forward. "Let go of her." He shoved the boy's shoulder.

Hannah jerked her hand once more. A spark shocked between her palm and his. The white flash thrust Hannah into an unwelcomed memory.

She sat in the backseat of the jeep while her dad drove. Rain thrashed against the roof and windows. Her mom looked back at her from the passenger's seat—concern in her blue eyes. The tiniest white flash sparked across Hannah's hands before a strike of lightning pierced the roof of the jeep. Loud. Bright. The car flipped off the bridge. Crashed into the lake. Water everywhere.

Hannah squinted hard as the guy ripped his hand out of hers. "What the hell? That fucking hurt." Hannah looked down at her reddened palm and rubbed it until the sting disappeared.

"Get lost, man," Landon said, stepping in front of Hannah.

"My pleasure," he slurred. He walked away, swaying, and looked back at Hannah. "Freak."

As soon as he disappeared, Landon turned and looked Hannah over. "What a jerk." His gaze was serious, but his tone was light.

Hannah felt the blood drain from her face. Her eyes glossed over with tears. She promised herself that she wouldn't do this.

"Hey, are you okay?"

"I'm sorry," she said, clearing her throat. "I think I just need some air." Hannah rushed through the party to the door while tapping her thumb to her fingertips in her left hand. When she got outside, the cold air brushed against her hot skin, and her heartbeat slowed.

She walked to the center of the courtyard that graced the entrance of Fisher Hall, quickly turning away when she noticed a couple kissing on one of the nearby benches. No longer able to hear the music from inside, she focused on the soothing sound of the ocean in the distance.

"That guy was just wasted," Landon said, following behind. "He won't bother you again."

Hannah crossed her arms to keep warm and tried to

keep her face stern. "I know. It's not that." She thought of what to say next, but came up empty. She didn't want to dive into a discussion about her anxiety and PTSD. That would only lead to a conversation about her parents and how they were gone while she was still here. She looked down at her palm and rubbed it over and over.

"Just a bit of static shock," Landon said. Hannah had heard this before. She nodded at him, placating his attempt to make her feel better. They stood awkwardly a few feet from each other. Landon swayed from side to side, his hands in his pockets. "I've been meaning to go down to the beach," he said, breaking the silence. "Want to come with me?"

"Now?" Though Hannah could hear the waves lull in the background, it was on the other side of campus, closer to her dorm building.

"Yeah, why not?" He fidgeted in place.

Hannah shrugged. "I guess honing my partying skills will have to wait for another time," she joked.

"You made a strong first effort." There was something about Landon's voice and calm demeanor that was appealing to Hannah. He didn't look at her like she was wounded or damaged. He made her feel normal.

"Okay. Let's go."

WAVES CRASHED AGAINST THE SAND BENEATH the moonlight. The sea foam fizzled and shushed before the next wave methodically arrived, keeping to the ocean's soothing rhythm. The beach was pretty much empty other than a couple of other students surrounding a bonfire a few yards ahead of Hannah and Landon. It was quiet and removed, stretching along the base of the tall cliffs where the campus sat above. Hannah held her boots in her hand and let her toes squish into the soft sand. The crackling of the fire against the hushed ocean sent a shiver up her spine.

"Do you want my jacket?" Landon asked.

Hannah's initial reaction was to decline the offer, but she realized that that was old Hannah's thinking. Old Hannah never accepted help from anyone. While her therapist claimed that it was a natural instinct to isolate herself, Hannah thought she simply didn't deserve any help after the accident. But this was just a jacket. "You sure?"

Landon didn't even bother to answer before shaking off his jacket and draping it over her shoulders. Hannah fit her arms into the large sleeves and allowed the warmth to envelop her.

As they moved further up the beach, the white noise of campus-life faded away. They were alone now and seemed small against the looming overhangs. Hannah looked ahead and noticed a small opening at the base of the jagged cliff.

"So, Hannah of Sonoma, what brought you all the way to Bellcliff University?" Landon tucked his hands into his pockets.

Hannah's uncle had given her applications for colleges all over California—USC, UCLA, Stanford, Pepperdine, San Francisco, San Diego. He didn't think it was a good idea to stray too far from home while she was still recovering. But how long was Hannah supposed to recover? It was something that she would carry with her for the rest of her life, and a fresh start on the other side of the country could be just what the doctor ordered.

"Honestly? It was one of the only East Coast schools that had a later application deadline. And it was prestigious enough to appease my uncle. He especially liked the part of the University's mission statement that read, *A secluded campus promotes focus, education, and engagement in one's collegiate community.*"

"What, is he paying your tuition or something?"

"Uh, no. I mean, he'll help, but he was who I lived with after my parents..." Hannah's voice trailed off, and she cleared her throat as she searched for a way to change the subject.

"Oh, sorry. I didn't mean to pry..."

"You weren't prying." She swallowed and kicked a shell in the sand. "It's weird starting at a new place." She forced a smile. "Can't just assume that everyone knows everything about me."

Landon frowned. "What happened to them, if you don't mind me asking?"

Hannah's lips pursed and her smile disappeared. "Now you're prying," she said through nervous laughter, trying to make it seem like she was joking, but Landon's expression squirmed with discomfort.

Even though Hannah really didn't want to talk about it, she didn't want Landon to feel uncomfortable either. He was just trying to get to know her better, and Hannah should have been making the same effort. "My parents died a long time ago. Paul, my uncle, basically raised me," she said. Hannah knew this was a lie—it had been less than two years since her parents died—however, making it sound like it happened when she was little typically garnered less sympathy.

"Oh, I'm so sorry," Landon said—the safe and standard response.

Hannah nodded, like she had done so many times

before, but was desperate to change the subject. "How about you? Why Bellcliff?"

"The pre-med program here is good. That, and they gave me a pretty sweet scholarship. I want to be a pediatrician."

"Ah, nice," she said, but she couldn't tear her eyes away from the opening at the base of the cliff. "Does that look like a cave to you?" Hannah pointed to the ragged rocks up ahead.

"I'm pulling out all the big guns, Hannah," Landon laughed and gave her an incredulous smile. "Most girls would swoon when I tell them that I'm going to be a doctor —a children's doctor, no less—and you're more interested in rocks?"

Hannah was definitely not most girls. "Sorry. But I think I read somewhere that only 20% of premeds actually become doctors. Still early days, Landon." Hannah chuckled, smiling. "Come on, let's take a look." Hannah ran up the beach and slowed down as the sand transitioned into pebbles. Landon followed after her.

There was something compelling about the formation in the cliff. It was as if something magnetic pulled her toward the opening. The closer they got, the faster the adrenaline pumped through her. But when she arrived at the small stone archway, the air she had been holding in her chest deflated. There was a relatively smooth stone wall just behind the craggy arch. Landon jogged up behind her.

"Weird. Definitely looks like it was an entrance at some point," he said, tracing his hand over the border of the protruding stone arch.

"Yeah, this wall looks man-made. Like it was placed

here on purpose." Disappointment swirled through Hannah, and she wasn't quite sure why.

"These cliffs are hundreds, if not thousands of years old. Rocks can shift, crumble…wind currents could account for its smoothness." He nodded his head while observing the rock shelter as if he were trying to portray confidence in his assessment.

"So now you're an expert geologist?" Hannah asked, trying to not make her fascination for the structure seem so strange and her disheartenment so obvious.

He turned toward her and took a step closer. "Well, according to you, my medical career doesn't seem too promising." Hannah smiled and looked up at him. His body was only inches from hers when his charming smile faded, and his gaze grew more intense. He tilted his head forward, his lips parted.

"Oh wow, it's getting late." Hannah pulled her phone from her pocket, stepping away. "Maybe we should head back?" Hannah wasn't sure why she rejected his gesture, but it was a knee-jerk reaction. Landon seemed nice and was easy to talk to—traits she knew she should cherish. Still, something was holding her back. Maybe it was because her mom wasn't around to tell; her dad wasn't here to jokingly threaten his life.

Landon stepped away from her and took her casual avoidance in stride. "Your carriage going to turn back into a pumpkin?"

"It just might," she said.

He pointed to her phone. "Then I should at least give you my number."

She offered him her phone, happy that she could give him some kind of affirmation. Landon smiled, typed in his number, and handed it back to Hannah. They turned and headed back toward campus.

As they returned up the beach, Hannah couldn't help but look back at what she thought was a cave. Something stirred in the pit of her stomach—that feeling when you think you've forgotten something. She looked forward and tried to be present, sinking her toes into the cool sand with each step and smelling Landon's sweet cologne. But she couldn't shake that gnawing sensation deep within her gut. Perhaps she was just trying to distract herself by fixating on a mysterious rock shelter that wasn't actually so mysterious. After all, Hannah had experienced this feeling before, nearly one year ago on her birthday. And with her eighteenth birthday approaching, it was no wonder she was out of sorts. Not only does it mark the day she was born, but will also be the two-year anniversary of the accident.

CHAPTER TWO

$\mathcal{T}$he library was old and grand and overrun with mahogany bookcases and desks. Black iron staircases spiraled to the higher levels. It was musty and desolate, with stale air hovering over the rows of elegant manuscripts. Hannah proceeded with caution, hoping she wouldn't hear the voice from yesterday. As her footsteps echoed through the empty space that reached high into the vaulted ceilings, she indulged in the silence. Aged stained-glass windows allowed hazy strips of light to stream in, highlighting floating particles of dust. Hannah crossed into one of the streams and felt the dull warmth on her freckled face.

"Can I help you?"

She jumped at the voice that spoke behind her—gliding to the open pockets of the library.

It was just a boy. No reason to be startled.

"I need to find a research topic for my Anthropology class," she said.

"Well, that narrows it down a bit." He was young,

maybe a freshman or sophomore, but he dressed like an aged librarian in Chinos and a bowtie. "Anything in mind? A particular culture or time period?" he asked with a melodious timbre.

"Was just planning on moseying about. Hoping to find some inspiration."

"Suit yourself. Most literature is on the first floor. Second floor is math and sciences. And the third and fourth floors are a hodgepodge of everything else—different cultural rooms, geography, periodicals, languages, law, theology, philosophy, etcetera," he rattled off. "Just be careful. This library is older than your grandparents' grandparents. The stairwells could crumble just as fast as the parchment pages." He laughed. "Kidding, but the building is quite ancient."

"Thanks, I'll be cautious." She gripped a notebook to her chest.

"My name is Edwin if you need any help," he said as he turned away, leaving Hannah to her own devices.

She skipped the first and second floors and climbed the spiraled staircase to the third floor. She walked by a historic map room, Celtic art room, a section on World War II, and an entire corner dedicated to modern marketing and advertising. Edwin was right—quite the assortment of topics. Hannah wasn't sure what she was looking for, but so far, nothing had grabbed her interest. The further she ventured into the jumbled third floor, complete with narrowing aisles and off-kilter rolling ladders, something fluttered within her. It was a similar sensation to what she had felt last night, approaching what she thought was a cave in the side of the cliff—some magnetic pull or luring force. Or maybe it was just some manifestation of her PTSD, trying to fantasize the mundane.

It didn't take long before she came upon a very small room in the back corner. A tarnished plate read, "The Occult and Mysticism Sector." Hannah stopped in her tracks, and her throat went dry. She knew she shouldn't go in, but it was the first area of the library that sparked any sense of interest or curiosity.

For a time after her parents' deaths, Hannah was constantly searching for answers. Pouring over books, scrolling the internet, talking to priests, therapists, or anyone who might have been able to provide an explanation. If there were answers, Hannah was determined to find them. She explored varying religious beliefs and even mystical traditions that strayed away from conventional churches and bibles. Could some kind of god or supernatural force have intervened that night? She made the mistake of posing this theory to her friends, and as so happens in high school, word spread that she was losing her mind. She garnered odd looks and passing comments like *freak* and *cracked*. But at that time, she didn't care. She kept to herself and researched the occult and neopaganism. All that mattered was finding answers.

Hannah stepped forward, but hesitated. Her hand hovered over the doorknob. She had left this all behind. This was supposed to be her new beginning. She could write about the evolution of feminism. Something else. Anything but this. Still, she couldn't shake the feeling that something was waiting for her inside the room. Hannah had come a long way in the past few months. She'd be fine. Her hand finally twisted the knob and pushed open the door to the Occult and Mysticism room. It offered a foreboding *creak*.

It seemed older and forgotten in comparison to the rest of the library. It was as if Hannah had stepped into a different building or time all together. The wooden shelves were thinner and somewhat warped with books crammed against each other in no particular order. The floor was covered in a musty and frayed maroon area rug that she might have found in her grandmother's house. While the room was not too impressive, it was the information inside the books that piqued Hannah's interest.

She scanned the shelves and gently picked out book after book until the crook of her elbow stiffened. She brought the stack over to the small, square desk in the corner of the room, and dropped them onto the surface. Dust billowed from the wood. She delicately flipped through their stained pages, trying to absorb as much information as possible. She could get lost in these books for hours and hours without getting bored. She didn't consider herself a religious person, but the incredible amount of faith and devotion different people throughout history put into their specific beliefs made Hannah wonder if there was some truth to it. Some worshipped singular or multiple gods, the earth, magical creatures, darkness, light...the list went on and on. It was amazing that the core of so many cultures was imbedded in mysticism or some unknown supernatural force. And though she rationalized that there was no such thing as magic, part of her wondered if it could explain what happened to her the night of the accident.

She fanned the books out on the desk. A symbol or etching of some sort peeked out from beneath the others. She shimmied it out, careful not to tear its soft binding. This one was flimsy and handwritten in old script. Hannah's skin tingled.

She blew the dust off the cover. The symbol was a scale that balanced two unfamiliar sigils. Her temples pulsed as the image flared across her mind, like a fleeting memory. It appeared more vibrant than its appearance on the manuscript; one of the sigils glowed white, and the other throbbed behind shadow.

Hannah couldn't identify why the symbol felt familiar. She gasped and clutched her head, shaking the image away. Though Hannah assumed these flashes were a symptom of her PTSD, she didn't always know what triggered them.

Hannah took a photo of the symbol, zooming in on the details with her phone. She carefully opened the book and read the first lines: *Magic can be gracious, vengeful, rewarding, punishing. Depending on the intention of the spell, the caster may owe magic gratitude, commitment, or blood. Some magic is love, some is hate, and some is indifference. The greatest knowledge we have of magic is that it is unknown.*

Through Hannah's brief studies and exploration of religion and mysticism, she had never come across a passage like this one. Most known cultures believed their mysticism to come from somewhere—a god, a mythical creature, the earth—but this seemed to insinuate that magic was an entity unto itself; that magic was personified in some way.

She continued to peruse the manuscript and came across a passage that stated: *For a witch who breaks the cycle of his/her own spell or curse may face the consequences of committing themselves to that fate.*

Hannah assumed this text must be Wicca or a magical sect of paganism. Though she continued to flip through the book, she couldn't seem to find an origin—year, location, or even an author.

The handwritten manuscript appeared more like a personal journal than an academic document. And for that reason, it sparked her interest even more. As her fingertips brushed the brittle pages, her nerves stood on end. It was a feeling that Hannah recognized, and she was dangerously close to backsliding into old ways. She couldn't allow herself to obsess like she did after her parents died.

She closed the manuscript. This was research. A homework assignment. Nothing more.

She gathered the books to take with her, but noticed a small plaque on the inside of the door that read, "Due to the age and condition of books in this room, they may not be checked out of the library."

Hannah scoffed and neatly piled the books on the small desk. She doubted anyone else would be in this room for a while, so she didn't see an issue with leaving her stack as it was.

She placed her hand on the doorknob, but paused. The hairs on her arms and neck pricked on end.

H-a-n-n-a-h...

She whipped her body around to locate the voice, but no one was there. It was louder this time, almost like someone stood directly behind her.

"Who's there?" Hannah demanded, her voice raspy with fear.

No one answered.

She raced out of the room and slowed her steps as she descended the spiral staircase, trying to maintain composure. She knew the voice wasn't real. It couldn't be. Every couple of steps, she forced herself to suck in a deep breath. She reached the main floor and noticed that the natural light streaming through the windows had dimmed. Only the eerie glow from the yellowing bulbs illuminated the floor. The wall sconces flickered.

Edwin sat behind the circulation desk, consumed by a book wrapped in protective plastic covering.

Hannah rushed past the desk.

He lifted his head. "Did you find everything all right?"

She nodded, glancing over her shoulder.

H-a-n-n-a-h...

She startled at the noise. It was fainter now—as if the voice resonated from deeper within the library.

"Did you hear that?" Hannah asked Edwin, no longer trying to control the panic on her face.

"Hear what?" he asked, his tone bored.

She waited another moment and listened for the whisper, but the open space was silent and still. She inhaled through her nose, closed her eyes, and exhaled as she shook her head back and forth.

Edwin surveyed her as if she was a little deranged. "You all right?"

Hannah nodded. "Must be hearing things," she said, gripping the strap on her bag and shoving it farther up her shoulder. She tucked a curl behind her ear and nibbled on her lower lip.

"It's an old library. Things creak and moan. You get used to it." He shrugged, picking up his book.

Hannah nodded and relaxed her shoulders as she walked through the detector, toward the library door. Her blood pumped, and her skin prickled. Hannah knew that if she didn't get herself under control, she would spiral.

The library door clattered behind her.

HANNAH RETURNED TO HER DORM ROOM AND changed into running pants. Whenever she felt an episode coming on, running always seemed to help. And that was all this was. Her anxiety. Her PTSD. Nothing more. Exercise released her excess adrenaline and managed to calm the tiny sparks across her skin.

Amelia still hadn't returned from the night before, so Hannah assumed that she was having a late morning with Bryce. Before she left for her run, she shot Amelia a text to see if she was okay—proper roommate protocol, Hannah decided.

Amelia texted her back in record time with: *I'm great. I <3 College,* followed by a winking emoji and a thumbs-up emoji. As long as Amelia was safe, Hannah didn't need to know the details.

She pulled out an old Sonoma Valley High sweatshirt from an unpacked box and threw it over her sports bra. It was oversized, thin from age, and reached down to the middle of her thighs. She tied her hair back as best she could, a few curly strands managing to escape, and pushed her headphone in her ears.

Hannah headed for the cliffs on the sea-side edge of campus despite the looming clouds. She ran along the dirt path that was surrounded by wild yellow and green grass. When her feet pounded the ground, it was as if any extra agitation crawling beneath her skin released into the earth. Though the air was humid, the cool breeze from the ocean billowed over the ridge and cooled the sweat that gathered on her forehead and neck.

The rocky brim seemed as though it could go on forever. She stopped at a high point on the trail and looked down on the beach. She was high above the rock shelter where Landon tried to kiss her the night before.

A streak of lightning flashed across the sky. Thunder roared a few seconds after. She jolted. It was as if her organs felt the pain of two years ago. The memory of streaming white electricity piercing her parents' car flashed in her head.

Rain broke through the humid air and poured down on Hannah. She swallowed the familiar fear, burying it deep. Her jaw tightened, and her knuckles turned white through clenched fists. Though she knew it wasn't smart to run in a storm, she didn't care.

This was her fresh start. She wanted to prove that she wouldn't be afraid of lightning forever. She couldn't be. She gritted her teeth and ran, pushing her muscles to move faster 'til they stung.

Hannah ran down the path towards the beach, dirt turning soggy beneath her feet. Rain drenched her sweatshirt, but she wouldn't ignore this burst of determination.

Her vision blurred as she fought against the rain. She arrived at one of the lowest points of the cliff side and started down a steep path toward the beach. The dirt turned to slick mud. She slipped. Her limbs flailed, and she tumbled down the hill.

She grappled for anything that would stop her fall—a patch of roots, a stone, but her fingers skated past each. Sludge smeared her skin and she plunged against the pebbles that lined the beach. Her face ground against their rough edges.

Her forehead stung as she laid against the tiny rocks. Something wet dripped down her lip. It tasted like iron. Covered in mud and scrapes, she lifted herself up. She extended each arm and rotated her wrists, followed by slanting her neck from side to side. Nothing was broken. Taking a hesitant step forward, her legs ached, and her heart raced. She placed one hand against her chest, willing the rapid thump to ease.

The rain pelted harder, and she felt the vibration of the

thunder beneath her feet. Despite her will to overcome her fear, her hands shook; adrenaline pumped through her veins.

She thought of the rock formation she visited the night before and the deceptive way it appeared to be a cave. But upon closer inspection, it was nothing but a shallow enclosure that was part of the cliff wall. She decided that if she could make it there, she'll have won.

Hannah ignored the ache in her legs and ran, unable to see her next step through the rain. She passed the day-old bonfire from the night before—long pieces of torched wood piled against each other, soaked by rain—and another image flashed in her mind.

Large planks of dark wood stacked against a charred stake in the middle of a dirt clearing. Smoke wisped from the deadened fire. The sound of sorrowful cries in the background.

The image was quick, but Hannah didn't let it slow her down. She jumped every time the lightning cracked against the rolling gray sky. Beads of water rushed down her cheeks, though she couldn't tell whether they were tears or the rain. Probably both.

She swiped the water from her eyes and sucked more air into her lungs. The fresh scent of dampened earth filled her nostrils. The rock shelter loomed before her. Lightning struck, illuminating the jagged stone that surrounded the smooth blockade.

Hannah stood in front of the stone that filled the arched entrance. The ragged edge of the cliff hovered a few stories above and provided a bit of respite from the torrential rain. She drifted her hand over the stone and took a deep breath.

A cool breeze brushed rain against her neck. Every hair on her skin prickled.

Shaking, she flatted her palm against it. A shock jolted her backward and she hurled to the ground.

A shriek escaped her, and her spine throbbed in pain. Her chest ached for the breath torn from her body. Hannah was now certain that tears were streaming from her eyes. She sucked in a breath as a lightheadedness took over and black splotched her vision.

The car filled with water. Hannah wrestled to unlatch her seatbelt, but her fingers slipped, weak and growing limp. She yanked at the belt and pounded her fists against the window. As the car sank deeper and deeper into the lake, Hannah's parents looked at each other, fear filling their wide eyes... They gripped each other's hands beneath the water's surface and looked to Hannah, panicked. She too knew what was about to happen.

Hannah winced and tried to pace her breathing, but she couldn't stop the images from blazing against her mind.

Hannah mouthed 'I love you' to her mom and dad, bubbles escaping from her mouth. They kept eye contact as long as they could, knowing this was it. Her father's arms drifted above his head, and his limp fingers grazed the roof. The creases in her mother's forehead disappeared as her pale eyes became vacant. She felt her own life slipping away...

Hannah's thumbs tapped ferociously against her other fingers. She laid against the sand, paralyzed for what seemed like eternity. She tapped slower as her breath relaxed. The pricking against her skin steadied and gradually disappeared.

Hannah shook her head to herself. What was she trying to prove? The storm wasn't letting up and she was scraped and bleeding. She rose to her feet, and her body trembled like the aftershocks of an earthquake. She raised her hands in front of her face, remembering the shock that catapulted her to the ground. Hannah had felt them before, but nothing this intense—nothing that had literally knocked her off her feet. Except for—

A loud boom struck her parents' car, and bright light invaded her vision.

She snapped her hands into fists and shoved them to her sides. Hannah fastened her eyes shut and sucked in another deep breath to keep herself from reliving the worst moment of her life all over again. It was all a bit too much to wrap her head around. She stepped out from under the edge of the cliff and let the rain wash her tears away.

That was the difficult thing about starting over. Even though no one knew of Hannah's past, it was impossible for her to forget.

HANNAH ARRIVED AT THE DORM BUILDING AND took solace from the rain under the arched brick entrance. Her eyes stung from crying. She wrung out her sopping sweatshirt before going inside.

She walked into her room and was greeted by a cheesy aroma. Amelia, Bryce, and Landon were gathered around a massive pizza, oozing with sauce, topped with sizzling pepperoni. While Amelia's legs were swung over Bryce's lap on the edge of Amelia's bed, Landon sat at Hannah's desk. Hannah looked like a wet dog, and she certainly didn't feel like small talk after her meltdown on the beach.

"Hannah, oh my god, what happened?" Amelia squealed, her high-pitched voice impaled Hannah's ears.

"I went for a run and it's raining," Hannah said, stating the obvious. She kept her head down to keep them from seeing her bloodshot eyes.

"Was it a mud run?" Bryce said under his breath.

Landon was quick to jump out of Hannah's desk chair and stood uncomfortably close to her face.

"You're bleeding pretty bad," he said.

Hannah touched her finger to the corner of her forehead and felt it sting. A small amount of blood stained her finger. "I tripped," she said. "It's no big deal. Really. I'm fine."

"Tough guy," Bryce announced and raised his fist into the air as if saluting Hannah's bravery. She feigned a tepid smile.

"You should let me help you get this cleaned up," Landon said. He moved closer to inspect the cut, but Hannah turned her head and avoided his gaze. Landon immediately stepped back and softly clapped his hands together. "I clearly need the practice if I'm going to defy your premed success rates."

"It's nothing," Hannah said, stepping away. She forced another smile. "Just going to take a shower." She gathered her shower tote and towel. "I'll see you guys later," she said, making sure her smile was apparent to everyone. Despite her strained sunny demeanor, Hannah knew that she wasn't fooling anyone, especially herself.

ON MONDAY MORNING, HANNAH ARRIVED AT HER first class. The massive lecture hall was in an ancient stone building. The room was round with stone walls and high-reaching rafters. It smelled of old parchment and chalk dust.

Hannah was one of the first students to enter the class-room. She climbed the stairs to sit in the back of the lecture hall at a curved, rich redwood table. Other students trickled in, most in gym clothes and pajamas—probably taking advantage of the fact that there was no dress code. Hannah must have missed the memo. She tugged at her white cable knit sweater.

Promptly at 9:00 am, the professor took her position in front of the podium. "Hello, everyone. My name is Professor Nina Cruz, and this is Intro to Anthropology." Her powerful voice echoed through the lecture hall. She was petite, in her mid-forties with long, straight black hair and tawny beige skin. "Why do people study anthropology?" The class was silent. "Don't be shy. It's not a trick question. Why are you here?"

Generic answers flew across the classroom: *To understand people; to observe how people act; to learn the difference between cultures; to find reasoning behind certain human behavior...*

"Yes, yes...good, good," Professor Cruz said, unsatisfied. "While you're hitting on all very relevant aspects of anthropological studies, we can go a bit deeper. Anyone?"

"To learn about ourselves," Hannah said, too quiet for anyone to hear.

Professor Cruz perked up and located her in the back of the classroom. She pointed at Hannah.

"Expand on that," she said.

Hannah shifted in her seat, uncomfortable at all the heads in the room turning to look at her. She felt her face heat up, and rogue static danced on her skin. "I guess if we are able to study and understand other cultures across the world, we might be able to discover where we, ourselves, belong."

Professor Cruz smiled. "Yes. While it is interesting to explore people on an individual basis and as a member of society—which we will be doing lots of this semester—a lot of it boils down to our natural desire to belong."

Hannah *belonged* with her parents. After they died, she drifted through self-imposed isolation. She felt an emptiness that could only be filled by answers. She wanted reasons for something unreasonable—explanations for something inexplicable. But she knew it was time to leave old quests behind. It was time to find her new place in the world.

She allowed a small smile to form. She straightened in her seat and intently listened to Professor Cruz's every word.

"Whether you look at familial units, community groups, religious organizations, or political parties," Prof. Cruz said, "this is a common theme. Everyone wants to find their people. To find their truth. To find their home."

She continued with her introductory lecture and outlined what the semester would look like. The class reviewed the syllabus, and Professor Cruz discussed the most important part of the class grade.

"Your final paper will be a research study of any element within a culture. It is up to you whether you want to research the role of women in a given culture, economic systems within a specific society, or religious beliefs or practices. However, choose wisely, because it will account for fifty percent of your final grade." The class gasped and groaned at the weight of one assignment. "And because you were all supposed to come to class today prepared with a topic in mind," she continued, "why don't we use the rest of the class to share and workshop ideas."

Hannah gulped. While she had decided to further research a topic in the Occult and Mysticism room in the library, that was before she heard the voice whispering her name. If she could avoid going back there, she would. Thankfully, as other students pitched an array of topics—

body modification in sub-Sahara Africa, the role of women in Norse society, Islamic cosmology—class time ran out.

Hannah joined her classmates in filing toward the exit of the lecture hall. Hannah walked down the stairs and she passed Professor Cruz's podium.

"Insightful comment today. You are…"

She was so close to an unnoticed escape. "Hannah Fenwick," she said, letting other students pass her by.

"I'm sure you have an interesting paper topic in mind, Ms. Fenwick." Professor Cruz waited, and Hannah paused.

"Uh, possibly," she said.

"Well, go on. Don't be shy. Hit me with it." Professor Cruz's eyes widened with enthusiasm.

Hannah offered a feeble smile as she searched her mind for a topic—one that didn't involve a belief in magic or the supernatural. When she came up empty, however, she sighed and delivered the idea she had originally intended to present. "Um, I was thinking of tackling something like the personification of magic throughout history and in different cultures, but…"

Professor Cruz cut Hannah off. "Interesting. May need to be more focused, but please, continue."

"I found an old manuscript in the library yesterday that suggests a belief that magic, in itself, has elements of consciousness—that magic as an entity behaves like a human does. It can be rewarding, forgiving, punishing…" Even though Hannah wasn't sure if she wanted to continue with this topic, she found herself intrigued as she pitched it.

"And where does this manuscript come from? Where is this believed?" Prof. Cruz leaned an arm against the podium.

"I don't know."

"You didn't look?"

"It didn't say." Hannah tried to read Professor Cruz's expression, but it didn't sway one way or the other. "I might choose a different topic. I'm not sure if..."

"I like it," Professor Cruz interjected. "Both your topic and your initiative. Not many freshmen would have already visited our library."

Hannah wished she hadn't.

"For a comprehensive research paper, you'll need to find additional sources that support your claim. More proof. And don't forget a thesis—some sort of analysis you can derive from your findings. I can't wait to see what you come up with."

Hannah's stomach hardened. "I will. Thank you, Professor." She turned to leave the lecture hall and tapped her fingers.

Hannah was going back to the library.

CHAPTER THREE

*B*ack in the library, Hannah staggered into the Occult and Mysticism room. She paused in the doorway, waiting to see if she heard a voice.

"Hello?" she asked. When she didn't hear a response, she felt silly for thinking that the books might talk back. She sighed in relief and hoped that she didn't hear any voices today...or any other day.

Her books were exactly where she left them. Her next class wasn't until later in the afternoon, so she settled into the cramped and musty room. She returned to the fragile manuscript and skimmed her fingers over the old penmanship. The paper felt crimped and excited the nerves in her fingertips. She picked up from where she left off and continued reading through passages—those she could make out, at least. Whenever something related to magic being an independent source with its own behavior, desire, or will, she made a note of it in her journal.

She came across a section that scrawled about light and dark magic. Light magic was described as good, and dark was described as stereotypically evil—both equal in power. *While most magic is believed to be neutral or indifferent, there is some magic that prefers a certain extreme. That magic searches for those who are most susceptible to channeling either light or dark and settles within them, creating magical prodigies. These are witches who have been granted great power in the name of either light or darkness.*

She scribbled this entry as fast as her hand would allow into her notebook. Whatever culture or religion this author described, it believed that magic lived within certain people —witches. And just as some humans are born with incredible talents for certain subjects—mathematical geniuses or musical prodigies—certain witches were also capable of exceptional power.

Hannah turned the page and paused on the last sentence written in the chapter: *I believe magic has chosen me as a prodigy for light.*

This was the first time the manuscript wrote in the first person. Hannah's suspicions were right. This was a personal document—a journal or diary, perhaps. She realized how valuable and rare it was to come across a primary source, this old, of any kind.

H-a-n-n-a-h…

Hannah launched herself out of her chair. Her wild curls blocked her vision. She tore them out of her line of sight, but didn't see anyone. Immediately, she slapped her notebook shut and shoved it into her bag. Abandoning the open manuscript on the table, she slung the strap of her bag over her shoulder and moved to the door. She'd either tell Professor Cruz that she would choose a different topic or simply default to the internet. There was no way she'd come back here.

H-a-n-n-a-h…

She tripped on the rug, and the contents of her bag scattered across the floor. Her pen rolled and rolled to the back of the room.

A breeze blew through Hannah's hair and whirled through the thin pages of the open manuscript on the table. Goosebumps erupted all over her skin. She froze. The impossible breeze from inside the windowless room crept behind her neck and over her shoulders. She had a difficult time believing that this wasn't real. She couldn't possibly be imagining this.

H-a-n-n-a-h…

The whisper surrounded her, and her breathing accelerated into short, shallow gasps. Then suddenly, something shifted within her. Her temperature cooled, and the prickling softened. Tranquility washed over her, and she was overwhelmed with this curious sense of satisfaction.

Hannah didn't understand. She didn't do any of the exercises that typically helped her calm down, but even when she would, she never felt this good. Though she knew she should question it, she didn't want to. She couldn't remember the last time she felt this at peace.

H-a-n-n-a-h…

Her name was sung in a soothing, airy tone. It was alluring and called to her, wanting to be found.

Leaving her belongings scattered on the ground, Hannah lifted herself to her feet. She walked to the back-right corner of the room, where the voice sounded loudest. The long-ignored bookshelves carried books on Haitian Voodoo, Feri Tradition, Brazilian Quimbanda, and Seidhr and Galdr from Norse Tradition, but none of them were the source of the voice. When she stepped backward, she faltered over the aged, maroon carpet. It dipped lower than the rest of the floor.

She pulled back the carpet and found a stone slat embedded in the creaky wooden floor. That was where the voice was coming from. She could feel it.

Hannah tried to use her fingernails to pull the square slat loose, but it was no use. She ran to her bag and rummaged through it for something that might be helpful. She pulled out a steel ruler and a pair of scissors from the front pouch and rushed back to the stone in the floor—still feeling at ease and even exhilarated.

She wedged the ruler between the wood and stone, then crammed the scissors beneath the stone slab, prying it upward. She shifted her instruments back and forth, and the slat moved. It was much thicker than she thought. It took all her strength to push it out of the way, revealing a deep pocket beneath the floor.

H-a-n-n-a-h…

The voice was sweet and intoxicating and she was so close. She dug through debris of rocks and dirt, and finally, a leather bind peaked out from behind the dirt. Hannah removed the cobweb-covered rocks and dug until she could wrap her hands around the book. It was large, beautifully bound in old, black leather with pewter edges and clasps. She blew dust off the cover.

An odd sensation, like warm liquid, ran through her. While the feeling was unfamiliar, she didn't question it. She couldn't quite put her finger on how she was feeling. Tranquil? Empowered? Entranced? Either way, she knew what she wasn't feeling: anxious. Though she knew that something bizarre was happening, she didn't want it to stop.

She brought the book to the table. The book's energy, or whatever it was, felt like silk against her skin. She ran a finger along the spine and let it trail across the pewter clasp. At her gentle touch, it unlocked, and the book flipped open. The pages were similar in consistency to the one she'd been taking notes on, yet it was more organized and purposeful than the random notes scratched in the soft-bound journal.

Awaken him, the book sang.

The book's breath swirled through the dust in the air. The pages rose and fell like lungs. Her mind raced with endless, yet impossible, possibilities of what could be happening before her.

Was this magic?

The pages flipped to a page titled, *An Incantation of Awakening.*

Awaken him...

Hannah slammed the book shut. She stood and shoved it in her backpack, completely ignoring the rules to not checkout these books.

As Hannah made her way down the spiraling staircase of the library, she felt invigorated. Something was happening, and though she didn't know what, it felt important.

"Leaving so soon?" Edwin said while re-shelving books on the first floor. Hannah blew past him, unwilling to slow down.

He followed her. "You all right? You seem..."

"Just lost track of time. Running late to my next class." She quickened her pace and clutched her bag. She didn't want to be caught removing a potentially valuable book from the library. Holding her breath, she walked through the library detector.

"Okayyy..." Edwin said, his voice trailing with suspicion.

It didn't matter, though, because the detector didn't go off. She doubted the book in her bag was even in the library system; no one probably even knew it existed. The silence of the detector only justified her stealing it. No one was going to miss it or even realize that it was gone.

Hannah stepped outside and inhaled the cool air. It felt fresh against her face and smelled like salt. She instinctively headed for the beach. It was where the book wanted her to take it, and she willingly followed its command.

THE BEACH WAS EMPTY. HANNAH KNEW FULL WELL that she should have been sitting in her Irish Literature class admiring the works of James Joyce and Jonathan Swift instead of walking on the beach with a spell book, but at the moment, it didn't feel like she had a choice. The beautifully-bound book directed her here, and she felt deep within her bones that she had to follow through with the book's command.

She was not surprised when it led her to the shallow cave-like opening. She pulled the book out of her bag and placed it on the pebbled sand before the cavern. Kneeling in front of it, she unlocked the clasp and allowed the pages to flip themselves. It opened to a page that read: *To Withdraw a Barrier.*

R-e-a-d, the voice instructed. Hannah took a deep breath and did as she was told.

"What once was not there," her voice shook. She cleared her throat and licked her lips, tasting salt. "Can no longer stand."

She continued in a confident tone, "Be gone this barricade." A low rumble vibrated from the rocks. "Be one with the sand."

The smooth stone wall that filled the jagged arch

cracked and disintegrated into a pile of fine sand. Darkness awaited on the other side.

Hannah gasped as a surge of electricity coursed through her veins.

Go, said the voice, smooth and reassuring. It was as if it knew what to do with the extra adrenaline pulsing beneath her skin. Since the night of her parents' death, she had never felt more in control of the anxiety that invaded her body.

She picked up the book and cautiously walked into the dark cave, crouching beneath the entryway. She took out her cell phone to turn on its flashlight. The cave was stark and cold—water dripped down the sides of the narrow tunnel. She walked a few yards and it opened into a grotto, no larger than her dorm room. She stood up straight.

H-e-r-e…

She kneeled and placed the book against the hard ground. Without touching it, the pages swept to a page entitled, *Incantation of Awakening.* The same breeze she felt in the Occult and Mysticism room brushed against her skin and twirled through her chestnut hair. Despite all that happened, she felt calm and in control.

R-e-a-d… Hannah inhaled, and once again, followed the voice's command.

"Awaken what has been lost, what has been deep in slumber.
   Come forth from thy dreams, none need to encumber.
   Reconnect to the earth and open thy soul.
   Awaken thy power, and once more be whole."

As soon as the last word left her lips, the stone wall fractured. Her chest tightened. The cracks in the wall webbed out in all directions. It was as though the stone was desperately trying to expand.

Unsure of how detrimental the blast of the cave wall would be, she scooped up the book and decided to sprint out of the cave, back to the safety of the beach. Not only did she not want to be lacerated by shards of cave rock, but she also felt an innate sense of duty to protect the book. Before she could reach the entrance, the wall ruptured and spikes of rock burst within the cave. The blast pushed her hard against the ground and knocked the wind from her chest. Her ears rang. She couldn't even hear herself gasp.

A haze of dust clouded her vision. She turned onto her back and brushed debris off her jeans.

The ringing in her ears faded away, and she heard hard footsteps stumbling through the rubble. The haze cleared. A young man walked toward her.

Hannah hugged the book tight to her chest and scrambled to pick herself up. She thought to run, but her wobbly legs refused. She gripped the book's leather bind with sweaty palms. The euphoria dissipated.

"Raven?" he asked, his voice deep and wispy.

She stared at him, frozen.

The young man appeared before her dressed in dirty, beige suspenders that strapped over a billowing white shirt. His green eyes were so bright against his warm brown skin that she actually felt her heart lunge in her chest.

Tears filled his eyes as he ran toward her. In one smooth motion, he placed his hand behind her head and brought his lips to hers.

Though Hannah felt paralyzed, her body was thrown into overdrive—hundreds of emotions barreled through her. Shock and fear molded into an overwhelming passion, longing, fulfillment. She was on fire, as if sparks of white energy floated above her skin and rippled in every direction.

As time started to move again, she was thrust back to reality. A boy, a stranger, was kissing her.

Hannah pushed him off of her. "What are you doing? Stay back. Don't come any closer," she shouted.

The boy, who didn't look that much older than her, looked deep into her blue eyes. The intensity of his gaze struck her, and Hannah felt tears build in her eyes. His scent of cedar and smoke lingered, and her chest heaved as she inhaled his distinct scent. Its familiarity was painful, and she had no idea why.

"How is this possible?" he asked.

Hannah's mind flooded with questions. Who was this person? Why was he so familiar to her? She knew with certainty that the effects of the book had worn off. Her skin crawled with apprehension. She took another step back.

The boy looked Hannah over, then fixated on the book she still held tightly to her chest. His expression switched from wonderment to horror. His brows furrowed and rage filled his eyes; he took a step back.

"What have you done?"

CHAPTER FOUR

*H*e pried the book from her hands and flung it across the cave. It hit the stone wall and thudded against the damp ground.

"What are you doing?" Hannah yelled. She lunged for the book, but he held his arm out to stop her.

Though his touch electrified her in a way she couldn't understand, that book harnessed the uncontrollable anxiety within her more than she ever thought possible. It was as if she had been thirsty for the past two years, and the spell book was her first sip of cool water. She was not willing to give it up so quickly.

Hannah pushed past the strange young man. He grabbed her wrist, pulled her back, and wrapped both his arms around her waist. She struggled against him, slapping her arms against his back, but he didn't relent.

"Prithee!" He gritted his teeth and held her tighter as she fought against his hold. "Be still despite your fight." He spoke so rapidly that his words ran into each other. "Be calm and hold your flight."

His words crawled over Hannah, rendering her immobile in his arms. He released her, and she froze in place.

"What's happening?" she asked through quivering lips.

The young man stood in front of her and closed his eyes. He wavered in place as he observed his surroundings. He hovered his palms away from his hips, either overwhelmed or trying to keep his balance. He paced back and forth, each step looking like it took enormous effort.

"You know that grimoire is pure darkness." Both his voice and eyes exuded desperation. "You read from it?

"I don't know," Hannah said. Static roared in her blood as if maddened by its paralysis. She instinctively tried to touch her thumbs to her fingertips, but they were frozen in place.

A dark thought sparked in Hannah's mind. If the book consisted only of darkness, then why did its touch feel so good? Was she evil?

"I believed you to have perished," he said, hunching over with his hands on his knees. "How is this possible?"

He clearly knew who Hannah was, and though he seemed familiar, she had no recollection of ever meeting him. All she knew was that she had to get out of here—undo whatever it was he did to her. Perhaps if she talked to him, calmed him down, he would free her.

"What is your name?" Hannah asked, thinking it was a safe place to start.

"What?" His gaze was intense and confused. "It is I. Callan."

Fire blazed across Hannah's mind. Over the flames, she heard a woman's voice scream his name. *Callan!* When the image dissipated, she stared at him.

He took a step back. "What manner of dress is this?"

Hannah had somehow broken into a secret cave and

released a man from stone…and he was asking about her clothes? She wanted to crawl out of whatever enchantment she was in. Panic bubbled from her gut and into her throat, but she couldn't run, couldn't move. She was trapped.

"Why were you buried in a cave? Why can't I move?"

"Prithee, Raven. You are acting strange." He waved his hand at her as if to dismiss her questions.

"Who is Raven?" Callan's eyes grew heavy, and he stumbled. Blood drained from his face, and gravity pulled him to the cave's hard floor. Hannah feared that he might pass out, leaving her frozen like this for God-knows-how-long.

"Callan, let me go. Undo whatever you've done. I need to help you."

While fighting to keep his eyes open, he whispered, "Move as thee will, no longer still."

Suddenly, Hannah's limbs were released. The spell book tugged at her attention. It lay beside the rubble, only a few feet behind Callan. Its lure was too strong to ignore, but she needed to help Callan first.

"Stay awake," Hannah said. She arrived at his side and supported his head. She had no idea what was going on, but she couldn't leave him helpless in this cave.

"I feel so weak," he said. His dry lips stuck together. "Who—" he cleared his throat. "Who are you, if not Raven?" His voice was haggard.

"My name is Hannah."

His eyes fluttered shut. She gripped his hand and nudged his shoulder.

"Where am I?" he rasped, eyes mere slits.

"Bellcliff University? Cape Cove?" Hannah said.

"What year is it?"

"2019."

He swallowed hard. "The last time I saw you was 1693." His eyes closed and his head fell against his shoulder.

"Callan? Callan!" Hannah shook him, but it was no use. He wouldn't budge.

She gently laid his head down. He had a pulse and his chest rose with breath.

The book lay a few feet from her. She itched to retrieve it, to touch the parchment. She shook her head. No, Callan needed her help.

She pulled out her phone and called Landon. He answered on the second ring.

"Hey! It's Hannah."

"Hannah, what's up?"

She paced the cavern. What would she tell him? That she woke a boy from the 1600s using an ancient spell? He'd hang up, thinking her insane. "Uh..." Some nervous laughter escaped her. "Remember where we walked to on the beach on Saturday?" Her mouth was having trouble keeping up with the speed of her thoughts.

"Yeah?"

"Want to meet me? With food and water. And a change of clothes." She could hear the uneasiness in her voice. She debated whether she should she just come clean? Tell him everything over the phone. No. He wouldn't believe it. He'd have to see it.

"Yeah, definitely." He sounded excited. "Be there soon."

"Great." Hannah cringed at the high pitch of her voice and hung up. Oh god. Landon probably thought she was asking him out. But that was the least of her worries.

If Callan was from 1693, no wonder he was weak. He was starving and dehydrated and should be dead. But

Hannah's reality was no longer what it used to be. Her brain raced with too many questions to count.

What if the anxiety she had been struggling through for the past two years wasn't anxiety at all?

What if it was magic?

HANNAH GAZED DOWN AT CALLAN. HIS EYES shifted under his lids. She must have paced the cave ten times over waiting for Landon to arrive. She resisted the urge to flip through the book's pages despite its allure. She eyed it over and over, but heeded Callan's warning. *That grimoire is pure darkness.*

As she stared down at Callan, another flashing image occupied her mind.

He laid next to her, the glow of a crackling fire illuminating his face. His green eyes slowly fluttered open, and he smiled when he saw her. He caressed the back of his fingers against her cheek.

She snapped out of her vision and gulped. She eyed the book. Breaking her resolve, she gave in to its allure and raced to pick it up. As soon as her fingers touched the black leather binding, her blood ran wild once again, and not in a bad way. She felt powerful when she held it. The tender breeze returned to her skin and reassured her that everything was okay.

"Hannah?" Landon's voice called into the cave, waves crashing on the beach in the background.

Hannah startled. She wanted to open the book and explore its spells, but Landon was waiting. Though it took all of her strength to resist its enchantment, she returned it to her bag. As soon as she zipped the bag shut, its enticing song muted slightly, but she would still have to actively resist its pull.

What was she going to tell Landon? Her brain didn't have enough space to process a lie to tell, especially when she wasn't entirely sure what the truth was.

"Hannah? Hello?" Landon asked.

Tears welled in her eyes and she didn't know why.

She had to keep it together. She wiped the tears away and hardened her face.

"I'll be right back," she whispered to Callan, though she knew he couldn't hear her.

But Landon was waiting.

She rushed to the cave's entrance where Landon was waiting with a backpack hanging off his shoulder along with a picnic basket, blanket and bottle of wine. *Oh no.* Landon did think Hannah had asked him on a date. Before any of today's events unfolded, Hannah probably would have found this charming—lucky to have a normal college experience with a handsome boy. Now, things were a bit more complicated.

"Landon," she said, her voice urgent. "Come on. Hurry." She waved him in.

He stepped inside, his expression stunned. "But Saturday there was a wall..."

"No time to explain," she said as she ushered him into the darkness, only illuminated by the beach's afternoon sun and the flashlight on her phone.

Landon observed the cave, his mouth open in awe. But when his gaze landed on Callan lying unconscious on the ground, he jumped back. His eyes widened, and his lips parted as if he couldn't quite find his words. "Hannah? What the hell is going on? Who is he? What happened to him? How the hell did a cave form overnight?"

Hannah grappled with telling him the truth. He would think she was crazy. *She* thought she was crazy.

"I don't know," she shouted. "I was just walking along the beach in between classes, saw the cave, and I found him like this." Panic rang through her voice. She gulped hard, hoping he bought her half-truth.

"You could have said that on the phone," he said, referencing the picnic basket and bottle of wine.

"Bring it here," she said. Landon handed Hannah the picnic basket, and she whipped it open. There was bread, cheese, cured meat, and a bunch of grapes. Beneath a checkered cloth there was a mini bottle of Poland Spring water.

"This is all the water you brought?" She didn't wait for his answer. She pulled out the small plastic bottle, uncapped it, and drizzled it into Callan's mouth.

"I brought wine. Wanted to show you that I don't only drink lemonade. It's from Sonoma." He trailed off. His cheeks flushed. "I'm sorry."

"Don't be sorry," Hannah said. "I should have been more specific on the phone." She tilted Callan's chin up as she drippled water across his chapped lips. She wanted him to be okay. She *needed* him to be okay.

Landon maintained a distance between himself and Callan, but kept a close eye on Hannah as she tilted the bottle further against his lips. Callan's eyes fluttered open, and he swallowed the water.

"It's working," she said. She poured the rest of the water into his mouth and he gulped it. She waited for the water to revive him, but his eyes closed again, and his head tilted to the side.

"Give me the wine."

"Don't you think we should get him to the hospital?

Something could be seriously wrong with him." He shifted from side to side and glanced over his shoulders.

"The wine, Landon. Now!" Hannah didn't recognize the force behind her voice.

Landon passed the wine and bottle opener to her, and she regretted snipping at him. She recognized the Buena Vista label on the bottle of cabernet.

"Good choice," she said and offered him a brief smile. He smiled back.

Hannah uncorked the bottle with ease, the *pop* echoing off the cave walls. She put the opening to Callan's mouth, and let the wine trickle past his lips. The ruby liquid seeped down his throat. As he drank, he coughed some up. Droplets sprayed on Hannah's white sweater, but she didn't mind.

His eyes opened. "Water," he said.

"That's it. I'm calling 9-1-1." Landon pulled out his phone and raised it toward the cave's entrance. "Damn, no signal."

"Just wait," Hannah yelled over her shoulder. How would she explain this to the paramedics? If it came to needing medical help, then of course they would call. But she also had an inkling that whatever was going on wouldn't be solved by modern medicine.

Landon paced, but dropped his phone to his side with a frustrated grunt. "There'll be better service on the beach," he said.

Hannah ignored him. She reached into the basket and plucked a few grapes from the bunch. "Here, eat this," she said to Callan. She popped one into his mouth and he bit down.

"Hannah?" Landon asked again. "We have to call for help."

"He's going to be okay," Hannah answered him over her shoulder, never taking her gaze from Callan.

He chewed the juicy grape and swallowed hard. He sighed, and it sounded painful.

"Are you okay?" she asked.

He nodded.

"He's okay," she said to Landon. Reluctantly, he shoved his phone into his pocket and crossed his arms.

Hannah smiled and continued to feed Callan grapes. Though Landon was there, watching in silence, it felt as if Hannah and Callan were alone—no one else existed. After a few more grapes, Hannah broke off a piece of the baguette sticking out of the picnic basket and offered it to him. He sat up, leaned his back against the cave wall, and clasped his fingers around it. He devoured the bread and opened his palm for some more.

"Did you bring the change of clothes?" Hannah asked Landon.

He opened his backpack, pulled out a pair of jeans and a Red Sox sweatshirt, and passed them to her. "I wasn't sure what you were looking for. I nearly brought pajamas."

Hannah gave him an incredulous look, but ignored what she thought was the suggestion of them spending the night together. She took the clothes and unfolded them. She eyed Landon, then Callan, then the clothes again. Callan was taller and broader than Landon. It would be a tight squeeze. "These should be fine. Thank you."

She directed her attention back to Callan. "Here. Once you gather your strength, you can change into these."

Callan chewed on the bread and looked bemused as he poked his finger through a tear in the jeans. He glanced between Hannah and Landon, and she wondered if he recognized him as well.

"Who is this?" he whispered to Hannah. Landon could clearly hear Callan; he only stood a couple feet away.

"Do you know this guy?" Landon asked Hannah.

"It's complicated," is all she could think to say. She *felt* like she knew him.

"Well, I really think he should be brought to the hospital. Even just to be checked out."

Maybe Landon was right. If Callan had been sealed in rock for over three hundred years, then a medical workup probably wasn't a bad idea. The fact that he was alive, however, told Hannah that they were beyond modern medicine. Beyond science or logic. This was something else. Something powerful. Something enchanting.

"Do you think you need to go to the hospital?" she asked him. "You might be sick."

"No," he whispered and leaned forward. "I will be all right." His eyes glimmered to hers. He smelled of incense and the earth after rainfall.

"If you're not going to call an ambulance, at least let me take a look," Landon said. "I know I'm no doctor, but I did take a summer prep course."

Hannah nodded to appease Landon. She knew Callan would be all right.

Landon knelt beside Callan. "Could you shine your phone light here," he asked Hannah, motioning just above Callan's head.

Hannah followed his instruction.

"His pupils look okay, normal dilation." He held a finger in front of Callan's eyes. "Follow my finger back and forth."

Callan obeyed. But when Landon's finger came too close to his face, he swatted it away.

Landon jolted back. "This is insane," he said. "Hannah, I know we don't actually know each other that well, but you called me to come down here, and I gotta tell ya—I'm really confused."

"Landon," she started.

Callan cut her off. "Turn away. Return from whence you came. Forget this hour past, and all will be the same."

Landon's eyes glazed over. He stood up straight and left the cave without another word.

When Landon was out of sight, Hannah turned to Callan, amazed and bewildered. "What did you do to him? Will he be okay?"

"He was not one of us. He shan't remember this."

"One of us?"

He looked at her, mystified. "You do not remember?"

Hannah slowly shook her head, waiting for him to continue—awaiting the first answer of many more she hoped to come.

"We are witches."

CHAPTER FIVE

*B*efore Callan changed into Landon's clothing, he insisted that he had to wade into the ocean. He lowered his bare body into the freezing water and allowed the waves to crash over him. Hannah's entire body chilled.

She sat on a boulder outside the cave and tried not to stare too obviously at Callan. While he was quite handsome, it was the sense of familiarity she felt around him that she couldn't quite understand. She crossed her arms and absorbed some warmth from her sweater, just as her mind tried to absorb everything that had happened—all she learned. And though she tried to grasp the fact that magic truly existed, and Callan claimed that she was a witch, one thought resurfaced:

Did magic have something to do with her parents' death?

As Callan emerged from the ocean, Hannah slid off the rock and marched toward him, determined to get her answer, once and for all. "I need to ask you something."

"You have many questions, I am sure," Callan said, his teeth chattering. "However, they must wait until I have changed and replenished." Hannah pulled her gaze from the defined muscles beneath Callan's wet shirt and focused on anything else. A bird flying above. The wind swirling the sand.

She cleared her throat. "Jumping in the ocean probably wasn't the best idea, then."

"Seemed a shame not to after all these years."

"Has it felt like years to you?" Hannah asked, still unsure how or why Callan was trapped within a sealed cave.

"Physically, perhaps. But 'twas only yesterday it feels that I lost you." He gazed deep into Hannah's eyes, and she could see his sorrow.

She wanted to ease his sadness. Even her desire to help him felt familiar. But how? She had no idea who he was. All Hannah knew was that his green eyes brought her comfort and his voice was a warm embrace.

"Lost me?"

Callan blinked, as if breaking away from a daydream. His demeanor hardened. "Prithee, may your questions be patient."

Hannah sighed and handed Callan the jeans and sweatshirt Landon provided. His fingers grazed hers. Her skin tingled from his touch, and the sensation spread up her arms and down her spine. She blushed and wrapped her arms around herself, overwhelmed by a devotion or affection that she was sure didn't belong to her.

Callan held the clothes out in front of him. "Such odd garments you wear."

Hannah rubbed her hands along her sleeves to keep warm, but mostly to wipe away the tingling from his touch. "There's a lot you probably won't be used to," Hannah said.

He nodded and returned to the cave to change away from Hannah's sight.

In Harbor House, Bellcliff's student food court, Hannah sat at a far corner table, eating an apple, while Callan slurped soup and shoved an entire piece of bread in his mouth.

"More." He stood and returned to the buffet line. Hannah jumped up after him. He heaped a mountain of food onto his plate. Chicken wings, roasted potatoes, carrots, rice, beans, corn. When he happened upon the fast-food selection, he leaned in close to observe the pizza, hotdogs, and French fries. His nose twitched and he marched past.

Hannah couldn't help but smile, especially when he seemed bewildered by anything sealed in plastic.

He poked the packets of chips and shimmied his fingers along the individually-wrapped Cinnabuns. "Strange," he said.

He barely sat back down at the table before inhaling large mouthfuls of the assortment in front of him. In between bites, he drank from plastic water bottles, squeezing them too tight at first, causing water to spill on the table.

As he finished his third water bottle, Hannah noticed some vitality returning to him. He sat up straighter, releasing small, satisfying grunts between bites and sips. He seemed more alert, observing the students around him.

A few guys from the soccer team couldn't stop staring at him as they walked by. They collided into a table of girls, but the girls barely noticed. They also seemed compelled by the new arrival. They giggled and whispered to each other, all while peering over at Hannah's table. Even though Landon's clothes fit a bit snug on Callan, he was still striking. Hannah ignored them and focused on Callan.

"Feeling better?" she asked.

Callan nodded. His green eyes brightened.

She wanted her answers, and she wanted them now.

"Why were you in the cave?" Her voice was serious and hushed.

"Right to the point, then." He wiped crumbs from his lips.

"Who put you there?" Hannah wanted to ask a hundred more questions all at once, but she made a conscious effort to hold back.

Callan took a deep breath as if to mentally prepare himself to revisit the past. "It was I."

Hannah's brows furrowed. Why would anyone ever seal themselves in a cave?

Callan continued. "After what Mara did to you, I knew I had to stop her. 'Twas the only way I knew how."

"Callan," Hannah said. She leaned in close over the table and held his gaze. "I am not this Raven person."

"I know this is difficult for you to understand. I can hardly fathom it myself. You were not supposed to be reincarnated. Mara made sure of that. But as sure as the sun rises in the morn, you are my Raven."

"Reincarnation?" Her heartbeat quickened. "That's not possible."

"You just released me from stone, experienced magic, and yet, you question reincarnation? You really do not remember a thing."

"I think I've made that quite apparent," Hannah said, her voice tight with frustration.

"'Tis a known truth among witches. At the hour a witch dies, their magic leaves their body and relocates into their reincarnated self. Magic can only exist in witches—people with the enchanted blood. Therefore, magic can only continue to exist if it finds its witch reborn."

Hannah took a deep breath and tried to understand. She pushed aside the doubts in her mind and tried to embrace everything Callan said as truth. "Is it magic that reincarnates the witch? Or is it something in their blood? Or is there a spell? Or…"

"Raven," Callan said, reaching across the table to hold Hannah's hands.

She jerked them away and tensed her jaw.

"Apologies. Hannah." He reached out again with open palms. Hannah hesitantly gave him her hands. "A truth every witch is taught from a young age—a truth that is of utmost importance to understand—is that magic is mysterious. We cannot possibly understand every element of it. We must accept that it is an unknown force. Otherwise, we shall drive ourselves mad."

Callan's touch calmed her. She embraced the tingles she felt.

"So, I'm just supposed to believe that witches, magic, and reincarnation are all real. No questions asked. It just is."

"What more proof do you require?" He removed his hands from hers and sat back in his seat.

When the warmth of Callan's hands disappeared from Hannah's, her mind raced. But she took another deep breath and made an effort to keep calm. She collected the facts in her head: A magical spell-book led her to free Callan, who by all scientific standards should be dead. Hannah had once believed that there was something else—

something inexplicable—that caused the accident the night of her sixteenth birthday. And she was finally about to find out.

"So, a witch is born with magic inside them?"

"Indeed."

"When can a witch start using their magic?" Hannah pressed her thumb to her pointer finger, afraid to hear the answer.

"They are taught the ways of magic from childhood. However, a witch's magic only emerges during the Convergence—the year of their sixteenth birth."

He provided this information as a matter of fact, but he had just confirmed Hannah's worst fear. That is what happened the night of the accident. She didn't need Callan to explain any further what the Convergence was. She experienced it. And she had never felt the same since.

It was her fault.

Hannah killed her parents.

CHAPTER SIX

*W*ithout thinking, Hannah stood, her chair screeching against the tile, and ran out of the food court.

"Hannah," Callan called after her, but he was cut off by the slam of the door.

Hannah's feet thumped against the ground as she ran across campus. Tears streamed down her face.

After all these months—hours of therapy, mourning, conjecture, isolation, anxiety, attempts to heal and move on —Hannah finally had her answer. She was responsible for her parents' death. Magic must be how she survived, and they didn't. And though she still didn't quite understand it, it was enough to make her heart ache.

With the cliff's edge in sight, Hannah slowed. Her heels dug into the earth. She stopped and balanced herself on the very edge of the cliff, gasping. She took a step back, but a familiar dark thought crept up her spine.

What if she did go over? What if she took one step too far and joined her parents? Maybe it would finally subside her survivor's guilt—the guilt that cloaked her with heavy, unrelenting remorse.

Or would she simply be reincarnated? Maybe that was her true punishment—to be bound to this earth by magic, never able to see her parents again.

She took a slow step forward, her feet skirting the edge of the cliff. The slightest gust of wind could knock her over. She'd fall onto the sharp, jagged rocks below, the vengeful waves thieving her final breath.

Would they hurt more than the guilt she felt? No matter what fate awaited her, Hannah believed she deserved excruciating punishment. She may not have asked for this, but that didn't mean she was not responsible. One foot inched forward and hovered over the edge.

There had only been one other time she felt this close to death, and she should have died that night. If she fell now, would magic protect her like it did before?

"Hannah!"

Hannah jerked her foot back from over the edge and stumbled back from the cliff.

Callan stood on the path, jagged stone and switchgrass behind him. He held her bag that she hadn't even realized she'd left behind.

Had he found the spell book? Would he be angry that she took it from the cave? What did it matter?

The sea raged against the cliffside. Her shoe scraped loose pebbles. She shook her head back and forth. What was she doing? Hannah collapsed to her knees on the mossy ground. She sobbed, and a whole new surge of tears streaked her face.

Callan rushed to her side and wrapped his arms around her. She pressed her face against his chest and heaved.

"It was my fault. I'm the reason they're dead," Hannah cried.

Callan held her tight. "You are okay. I need you to breathe." There was a lull to his voice, like a song. "All is right. You shall be fine. There is no need to be filled with such woe."

Hannah felt the same way she did when their hands touched in the cave—overcome by an immediate sense of devotion and affection. His words were commandments she had to follow.

"Stop your tears," he instructed.

Hannah sat up straight and wiped her eyes with her fingertips. She sucked in a deep breath and released.

Callan appeared disappointed and relieved all in the same glance. He gazed at the ground and then back at Hannah. "Now. Tell me what happened."

"On my sixteenth birthday, a flash of light pierced through my parents' car and struck deep within me." Hannah recalled what happened that night, like a robot reciting code. "The car went off the bridge and crashed into Lake Sonoma. My parents died. I survived and now I know that it's my fault."

"Fault may only be linked with intention," Callan said. "The Convergence was not something you had knowledge of or control upon."

"I killed them." Hannah felt tears swell at the back of her eyes, but she gritted them back.

Callan put both of his hands on Hannah's shoulders. "The fault was not yours. I pray you believe there was nothing you could have done. You are not to blame."

His words filled her, and she felt compelled to believe him. Still, she wasn't ready to forgive herself. Hannah resisted whatever compulsion he cast over her and she snapped out of the haze.

"Stop it," she yelled at him. "Whatever it is you're doing, just stop." She stood up and backed away from him.

He rose to his feet. "You can resist it," he said. A pleased grin emerged.

"What is *it?*"

"There is much I have to tell you. First, there is something we must do."

CALLAN WALKED ALONG THE EDGE OF THE CLIFF, determined in every step. Hannah paced behind him with her bag slung over her shoulder, trying to keep up. Every step was heavy with the burden of knowing she was responsible for her parents' death.

"Where are we going?" she asked.

"The caster of a spell is linked to the spell itself. I was the one who locked magic away, knowing full well that I would be buried along with it. But when you awakened me, you broke my spell. You awakened all magic my spell sent to slumber." Callan's voice had an urgency that sparked a sense of doom within Hannah.

The spell book tugged at Hannah from her bag. She pressed it to her chest, feeling a trickle of warmth. While Callan warned against its darkness, Hannah couldn't deny that reading from it felt amazing. She was relieved that he hadn't discovered it in her bag.

"Why would you want to stop magic?" Hannah asked. She still couldn't quite wrap her head around the fact that she was having a casual conversation about magic in the first place.

"My aim was not to stop magic. It was to stop Mara. I *needed* to stop her."

"Who is this Mara you keep mentioning?" Hannah quickened her pace to keep up with him.

"Have you heard of a creature called the Devil, in this time?"

"You're kidding me, right?" Hannah stopped. "The personification of all evil? The monster who lives in Hell and prays on hostility and destruction? The representation of sin in nearly every religion or popular media?"

"Time truly does distort truth," Callan said.

Hannah sighed with relief.

"A close depiction, however," he said against his long strides.

Hannah jolted forward to keep up.

"She is a witch who possesses an affinity for dark magic. Feeds on the fear of her victims. And is gifted beyond any witch a soul has ever encountered."

Perhaps that was what Hannah had—an affinity for dark magic. Maybe that was why reading from the grimoire made her feel so good. Maybe that was why her parents died. She shook the thoughts from her mind.

"You're talking about her in the present tense," Hannah said.

"I could not kill her. No one could. She is far too power-ful. Therefore, I did the only thing I could think. I cast a spell to seal all magic away in stone—a spell that could only be broken by magic. If I succeeded in trapping all magic, then it could never be reawakened, or so was the plan. 'Twas the closest thing to death I could inflict."

It sounded like he was describing a horror movie, not reality. "Then how was I able to release you?"

"Only after I cast the spell, you must have been reborn.

Your magic was not bound to a witch, therefore, it would not have been affected by my spell."

Hannah stopped again and drank in the information he delivered, trying to get the facts straight in her mind. "So, Raven died? Is that why you wanted to stop Mara? She killed Raven?"

Callan turned, his expression tense with frustration. "You are Raven. You may not possess the memory, but you are she. Mara killed *you*. You..." Callan bit down on his lip. "I apologize," he said. "My only wish is that you remember."

It made Hannah uncomfortable that this familiar stranger knew more about her supposed past life than she did. She wished she could remember too, if only to appease Callan's frustration and the blindness she had to her own life. A matter of hours ago, magic was a thing of fairy tales and popular TV shows—not something that actually existed or lived inside of her.

"Maybe I could remember," Hannah said. "Is there some kind of spell that you could..."

"I know of only one book that possesses such a spell, and it shall never be opened again."

Hannah gripped her bag, the corner of the leather binding pressed to her chest. "You never answered my question." Hannah chased after him, still resisting the spell book's lure and the self-blame she felt. Despite her fatigue, she kept up with this quickened pace.

"There is not time."

"Where are we going?"

"We must find Mara's grimoire and destroy it," Callan said, clenching his fists. "We've wasted enough time already."

Hannah paused, knowing full well that they didn't need to return to the cave to retrieve the spell book.

"Why must it be destroyed?" She tightened her grip around her bag. Even though Hannah heeded Callan's warning, she didn't want to be parted from the book.

"The longer we delay, the better chance she has of locating it," Callan said. "I should have taken it when you first revived me, but my mind was lost in a fog." He focused on the path ahead. "It is bound to her blood. Once it is destroyed, Mara shall be vulnerable. She may be tracking it at present."

"What happens if Mara finds it?" Hannah could tell that she was frustrating Callan with all of her questions, but she needed to know. Was she going to be responsible for even more deaths by reawakening magic and leading the Devil to Bellcliff? Hannah focused on the sound of the waves below.

"She shall continue to use her dark magic to seduce witches, turn them wicked, and tip the scale toward evil. Before I sealed myself away, she created a horde of magical creatures to strengthen their magic and do her bidding. She will continue to do the same now."

Hannah's jaw fell. She stumbled over the jagged ground. She had only just started to absorb the revelation of witches, and now she was being bombarded with other magical creatures? But if witches existed, then why wouldn't other supernatural beings?

As her mind debated with itself, she concentrated on turning her thoughts into words. "What kind of creatures? How do you know all of this?" The pitch of her voice rose.

Callan stopped so abruptly that Hannah nearly ran into him.

"Because I am one of them."

CHAPTER SEVEN

$\mathcal{H}$annah stepped back. Since she released Callan from the cave, he had only spoken against evil; he physically knocked the spell book out of her hands to keep her from accessing its darkness. Now, he stood before her, revealing that he was one of the Devil's evil henchmen?

Callan's sorrowful gaze pleaded with Hannah. He stepped toward her, but she maintained space between them.

"What are you?" Hannah asked.

Callan looked to the sky, then back at Hannah. His jaw tensed; his nostrils flared.

"Mara's darkness seduced me," he admitted. "I craved the way the book's magic made me feel. My weakness allowed her to turn me into something despicable." His throat tightened, and he swallowed hard. The young man who was urgent and determined moments ago now stood, shoulders slumped, and head cowered low. "She turned me into a Siren."

Pinpricks stung Hannah's skin and static danced between her fingers. She sucked in a deep breath, cool air filled her lungs, and she shakily exhaled. "Like, the people from the sea? The mermaids who call to sailors?"

"Another distortion made by the passing of time, I am sure. Though, I would not doubt that Mara could create such a beast." Callan looked carefully at Hannah. "My touch has the power to influence others. If I give a command, the other shall have no choice but to obey."

Disgust emerged on Hannah's face. She had already fallen victim to his sorcery. "That's what I felt? That's what you were doing to me?"

"My aim was only to calm you when you were full of despair."

"You take away people's free will. That's supposed to make me feel better?" Her heart raced in her chest and its thud vibrated in her ears.

"Only two souls have ever been able to resist my compulsion. Because Mara transformed me, my influence obviously does not affect her. And Raven was the other. *You.* You resisted."

Should she be flattered? Proud of herself? Did the fact that she didn't listen to his Siren's command absolve his crime?

"How do I know you're not evil...? That you didn't help Mara create all her dark followers?" Hannah couldn't believe they were discussing such strange things—things that were now her reality.

"I am evil. I aided her." Tears welled in Callan's eyes.

Hannah should have been scared by his admission to being evil, but the agony on his face was sincere. It matched the anguish and guilt burrowing within her own body.

"I was weak," Callan continued. "I allowed myself to be taken by her darkness. She was my creator—my master. Just as I could compel the wills of others, she was the only soul who could compel me. She commands all her creations—her servants.

Silence brewed between them. Hannah struggled between the choice of running away or comforting him. If she ran, she may have been able to put this behind her. She could get back to her resolution for a fresh start and live safely in ignorance. Even though this option had some appeal, it was no longer a choice.

Hannah would always wonder about the magic that lived within her, the grimoire she was enticed by, and Callan—the young man who made her feel both at ease and completely terrified.

Hannah took a step forward. His emotion was too raw and tormented to be fake. "I think I believe you," she said, still wary of the supernatural boy before her. "But how do I know you're not compelling me?"

"My touch is not upon you."

She remembered the odd sensation that came over her back on the beach and just moments ago when she was inconsolable. She remembered the impulse to do whatever he said and her sudden undying devotion. It was strong and unnatural. She didn't feel that now.

"And you never wanted this?" Hannah asked, taking another step toward Callan.

"I willed myself away for eternity, not only to stop Mara, but to thwart myself from her compulsion. I do not regret my choice."

Hannah's heartbeat slowed and the tickle on her skin dulled.

Just as Callan caused harm by becoming something he

never asked for, Hannah caused the death of her parents because of the Convergence—the moment her magic was activated within her. She recognized his pain and felt it overwhelmingly within herself.

"I need you to promise me two things," she said.

Callan nodded.

"First, you have to be patient with me and answer all my questions. This is all completely new and I'm still not sure I believe it."

Callan straightened his posture and raised his chin. "I shall."

"Second, you have to promise never to compel me. *Ever.* I don't care if I can resist it or not, and I don't care if your intentions are good."

"Sometimes 'tis difficult to control," Callan said. "A simple touch might influence your behavior, even if it is not my intent. 'Twas why I was pleased to see your ability to resist..."

"Promise me," Hannah scrutinized.

"I promise."

Hannah took a few steps toward Callan and stood inches from him. She brushed her arms around his waist and hugged him, squeezing tight.

He stiffened, then hugged her back. His heat cloaked her, and she tucked her chin against his chest. Though she sensed the Siren's enchantment like a distant hum, she pushed it aside and melted into Callan. He flexed, pressing her to him. His comfort dismantled any suspicion or fear she may have had.

Callan pulled away from her, cleared his throat, and straightened his sweatshirt.

"I thank you for your understanding," he said. "But now we must retrieve Mara's grimoire. With haste."

Before Hannah could tell Callan that the spell book sat in her bag, she heard her name being called from up the path along the cliff.

"Hannah!"

Landon, Bryce, and Amelia walked toward them. Hannah stiffened at the sight of Landon, afraid that he'd remember what transpired in the cave. The closer they got, the harder Hannah tried to relax and act natural.

"Funny bumping into you here," Landon said to Hannah, looking Callan up and down.

"Small campus," Hannah murmured.

"Hey, roomie," Amelia smiled, her long blonde hair tucked into her sweater. "Who's this?" Her eyes lit up at the new man standing next to Hannah.

"Uh, this is my friend Callan." Hannah kept an eye on Landon, who was still sizing Callan up.

"Nice sweatshirt, man," he said. "Think I have one just like it. Red Sox fan?"

Hannah was relieved that Landon couldn't remember him. Callan's spell had worked. Callan looked to Hannah, confused, and she realized that Callan had no idea who the Red Sox were.

Before she could intervene, Callan said, "I have never owned a pair, however, I am sure the color does not have an impact on their comfort."

Hannah forced herself to laugh. "He has a dry sense of humor."

"Right," Landon said, his voice trailing off.

"How long have you two known each other?" Amelia asked.

Hannah was quick to answer before Callan. "Met him in my Anthropology class this morning." Hannah observed the sun beginning to set over the ocean and couldn't believe all that had transpired in the matter of only one day. Simply trying to remember all that she had learned—how drastically her reality had changed—was leaving her light-headed.

"You make friends fast," Amelia said with a cheeky smile.

Hannah shrugged, uncomfortable at Amelia's implication.

"She makes a great first impression, doesn't she?" Landon said. "We couldn't stop talking at the party last night. And then the beach after that." He offered Hannah a smart smile.

It was obvious to Hannah what Landon was doing. If this had happened yesterday, Hannah probably would have been flattered and even enjoyed the fact that Landon was getting defensive over her. It would have fit in perfectly with her plan for a fresh start and a nice, normal college experience. But after today, that resolution had been put on the back burner...indefinitely.

Right now, all she wanted was to be alone with Callan, so she could ask the millions of questions that burned in her brain. She desperately wanted a clear picture of every-thing that happened over 300 years ago, and everything that was happening now. She wracked her brain for an excuse to leave.

Callan spoke up. "It feels as though I have known her for my whole life." Callan smirked; only the two of them understood the depth of his comment.

Landon cleared his throat.

"I'm Bryce." He offered his hand. "Landon and I are roommates in Fisher Hall. Which dorm are you in?"

"He's a commuter," Hannah said, proud of her quick thinking.

"I'm Amelia." Amelia offered Callan her hand, palm down, in the way a princess might greet a suitor.

He shook it. Amelia gasped, wide-eyed. Callan swiftly dropped her hand. She must have felt his Siren's sensation.

"Oh my," she said under her breath. Thankfully, Hannah didn't think Bryce heard Amelia's swooning remark.

Callan didn't notice. His gaze was fixed on something in the distance. His eyes squinted farther up the path along the edge of the cliffs. Hannah followed his gaze and saw a man in a long brown, leather coat. Callan's eyes enlarged with horror.

"We must depart," he whispered.

"What's wrong? Who is that?" Hannah asked.

Landon, Bryce, and Amelia looked up the edge of the cliffs. The figure moved down the cliff path toward them. At first, his steps were slow. Then, the man broke into a sprint, his long coat trailing behind him. He ran faster than anything Hannah had ever seen before. His shape even blurred.

Callan quickly placed one hand on Amelia's shoulder and the other on Landon's. He gazed at them, his eyes glowing green against his golden-brown skin. "Run with great haste to your rooms. Lock the doors and do not trust the entrance of strangers."

Landon and Amelia inhaled at his touch and nodded in agreement. Without hesitation, Landon and Amelia raced away from the cliffs toward campus.

"What the hell?" Bryce watched Landon and Amelia run away and jolted backward when Callan reached for his arm. "What are you doing? What did you do to them?"

"There is no time to explain," Callan said. "You must leave. Now." The man racing down the cliff was getting closer with every second. "You should go too," he said to Hannah. He didn't try to touch her, keeping his promise never to compel her.

"I'm not going anywhere," Hannah said. She didn't know who this man darting toward them was, but she was not about to bolt when she was so close to getting the answers she wanted, whether she liked them or not.

"Same here," Bryce yelled. "Not until you tell me what the hell you did to them." Bryce raised his hands defensively in front of his chest.

The blurred figure slowed and came into focus. He was only a few feet away from them. His hair was a muddy brown that limply fell to his shoulders. His eyes were the palest grey Hannah had ever seen—almost white.

"Callan," Hannah warned.

The stranger displayed a sadistic smile.

Callan lunged for Bryce, but the man broke into his unnatural speed, allowing him to reach Bryce first. He grabbed Bryce from behind and wrapped his cloaked arms around him.

"Stop!" Hannah shouted. She wanted to intervene, but her body was too stunned to act.

Though Bryce struggled, the man was too strong for him. "What the fuck," Bryce shouted. "Let me go. Who are you? What's..." The man placed his large hand over Bryce's mouth.

"Let him go," Callan said.

"It's been a long time, my friend," the man said. Hannah detected some sort of rough English accent. What looked like blood was smeared on the collar of his worn brown leather coat. The skin beneath his eyes were dark grey in comparison to the rest of his pale complexion, ashen and cracking like an old painting. He must have only been a year or two older than Callan. But because of his abnormal speed, she wondered if he was human at all.

"Raven," he shouted, turning his attention toward Hannah. "I thought you dead."

Hannah stepped back. Callan reached his hand out to Hannah, stopping her from stumbling off the side of the cliff. He guided her to stand behind him.

The man smiled even wider than before, revealing a set of long, sharp teeth, resembling fangs. "Mara will be interested to know that her spell failed."

Bryce's eyes widened at the word *spell*.

"What is it you want, Nathaniel?" Callan asked.

Hearing Callan say his name prompted a series of images to flash across Hannah's mind: *She sat in a small cottage, in front of a fireplace with Callan sitting behind her. She rested her head against his chest as they watched the fire wisp and crackle against the burning kindling. The old, wooden door opened, and Nathaniel took a step inside. Callan abruptly stood up. "What is it you want, Nathaniel?"*

Hannah snapped out of her vision—the most detailed one she'd ever had. And then something clicked. The images she had received since her sixteenth birthday weren't symptoms of her PTSD at all. They were memories from a past life. Raven's memories. They must have been.

"You know what I desire, Callan," Nathaniel said.

"You do not have to do what she commands," Callan pleaded with him.

"Have to? I want to. I should die before disappointing her."

"That is not how you truly feel, Nathaniel. You can be free of her."

"What, like you? Look at you," he shouted. "Trying to help humans like this?" Nathaniel tightened his grip over

Bryce's mouth. His chipped, yellowing nails dug into his cheek. Bryce moaned and struggled against him. "What's the fun in that?"

"You never even attempted to resist," Callan said. "You surrendered to the darkness, and now you revel in it. Even though you must know how wrong it is."

"Rich coming from you. You introduced me to Mara, remember? We both reveled in it." Nathaniel ran his tongue over one of his fangs like a nervous tick.

The muscles in Callan's neck tightened.

"Besides," Nathaniel continued, "right and wrong, black and white...it's all a bit relative, don't you think?"

Bryce bit down on Nathaniel's hand. Nathaniel hissed. "I'm the one who's supposed to do the biting." He opened his mouth and fangs protruded over his lips. He sank them into Bryce's neck. Bryce screamed. A chill reverberated down Hannah's spine.

Hannah lunged forward. Callan was quick to hold her back.

"Get off me," she yelled. Hannah looked for help, but the cliffs were barren.

Bryce's face turned stark white, and the light in his eyes dimmed. Nathaniel retracted his fangs from Bryce's neck and let him collapse onto the moss-covered ground. Hannah's stomach dropped with him.

She broke past Callan and rushed to Bryce's side. Blood dripped down his neck and was bright against his pale skin. She held his face in her hands. He was cold to the touch and his head limped to the side.

Nathaniel wiped blood from his mouth and licked his fingers. "Did I just do you a favor, mate? She seems quite shook up over the lad."

Hannah placed her fingers against Bryce's neck, but felt

nothing. "You killed him," Hannah cried. When she looked over Bryce's dead body, she couldn't help but remember assaulting images of her father's blank face floating underwater. Hannah gently closed Bryce's eyes.

"Move away from him, now," Callan shouted. Hannah wasn't sure if he meant Nathaniel or Bryce.

Nathaniel crouched next to Hannah. A smell of birch tar wafted from him. "Oh, come on, Raven. You know how this works."

Hannah stumbled back, crawling against the dirt. Pebbles scraped against her palms. Callan helped her up and stepped in front of her. "She does not," Callan said, standing between her and Nathaniel. "This is not Raven. Just similar features. Your eyes must be failing you, Nathaniel." Callan clearly didn't want Nathaniel to know that Hannah was Raven reincarnate. Simply thinking those words sent Hannah's mind into a frenzy.

Nathaniel laughed. "Give me some credit, mate. I may not be as bright as you, but I'm not some halfwit. I remember Raven like it was yesterday. The same curl of the hair, same freckles, and the bluest eyes I've ever seen. Which means, she was reborn." Nathaniel stepped back, a proud grin on his face. "We knew you were powerful, but this is very impressive," he said, observing Hannah. "Mara won't like it one bit."

"Enough, Nathaniel," Callan warned.

"I'm surprised you haven't used the memory spell on her yet. I know you have it."

"We do not have it."

Hannah eyed her bag, which was still strapped across her chest, and she immediately regretted it.

Nathaniel noticed her glance. "I sense a lie," he said. He ran his tongue in a circular motion under one of his fangs.

Callan looked behind him and noticed the bag they were both looking at. "You took it?"

Before she could answer, Bryce jolted upward and gasped for air. His eyes matched the eerie, pale glow of Nathaniel's. His nose sniffed the air and his lips twitched.

Bryce was dead. Hannah watched the life fade from his eyes and felt nothing when she checked for a pulse. She couldn't even muster relief to see that he was awake. She was too disturbed at what he had become.

"Welcome back, my new friend," Nathaniel said to Bryce. "Hungry?"

Bryce nodded.

"Go for the girl," he said. "You don't want pesky Callan here laying a finger on you."

Without further instruction, Bryce scampered for Hannah. Her blood surged through her veins so quickly that it felt as if her skin was moving. Static tickled at her palms and her fingers shook uncontrollably.

Callan guarded Hannah, but Bryce was too quick, like an agile dog on the hunt. He dodged Callan and leaped at her. Though she could hear Callan shout for her to run, there was no time.

His eyes were wild, and his mouth was agape. Drool slipped off his new fangs. She put her hands in front of her face to brace for impact.

Bryce collided with her, and a bright white shock blasted him off the cliff. The force of the spark even knocked Hannah to the ground. She gasped at her burning hands.

"And you wish me to believe that she is not Raven," Nathaniel said to Callan, not even blinking an eye that Bryce, his new creation, was just thrown off a cliff. He flung his chin upward and released a blustering cackle. The wind roared along the cliffs.

Callan ran to Hannah's side. "Are you hurt?"

Hannah stared at her hands, eyes wide and mouth agape. They were foreign to her, acting upon their own volition, separate from the rest of her body and mind. She continued to stare at her trembling hands, while trying to comprehend everything that just happened.

Bryce fell off the cliff. Hannah sent him off the cliff. She killed him. Her hands killed him. Whatever inside her killed him.

Hannah's eyes watered.

Callan brushed her shoulder. She gasped. She hadn't realized that she had stopped breathing.

"I'm fine," she said. She wasn't fine, but she couldn't allow herself to fall apart. Not now. She tilted her head up and blinked a few times to keep her swell of tears from spilling over.

Callan couldn't even help Hannah to her feet before Bryce propelled himself back over the cliff, posed on all fours, his fingers clawed into the dirt.

Hannah's heart dropped back into her stomach. She couldn't manage to scream or even move at Bryce's resilience.

Nathaniel clapped his hands, thoroughly entertained. "Takes more than a little shock n' fall to kill a Vampire." His stringy hair danced upon his shoulders.

Vampire. Though it was obvious, hearing the word out loud was a different story entirely. Bryce licked his lips and leaned forward, his gaze set on Hannah. She backpedaled against the weeded path, too flustered to lift herself to her feet. Bryce pounced off his back feet and outstretched his dirt-covered hands, already in formation to strangle her.

Callan charged in front of Hannah and shoved a hand against Bryce's chest. He gripped his other hand around Bryce's arm. His heels thrust against the gravel as he halted Bryce's momentum. "Stop," he commanded.

Bryce obeyed. His flailing limbs quelled. He still looked rabid and thirsty, focusing his eyes solely on Hannah, but he was frozen beneath Callan's spell. "You shall never drink from any human, animal, or blood source, ever again. You shall never reveal what you are or what happened here, today. Do you understand?"

Bryce looked to Callan and nodded. "Go. Now."

Callan removed his hand and sighed. Bryce walked away.

Hannah was relieved at Callan's intervention, yet horrified at Bryce's fate. Despite the mayhem in front of her, she couldn't help but think of his budding relationship with Amelia, his friendship with Landon, and the future he would now probably never have.

Callan offered Hannah his hand. She held on and let him effortlessly pull her to her feet.

Nathaniel released a theatrical sigh and cocked his head to one side. "Pity." He licked the tips of his fangs. He hopped from foot to foot, then stormed toward them.

Callan pushed Hannah out of the way and collided with Nathaniel.

Hannah toppled to the ground, and the grimoire slid out beneath the flap of her bag. She army crawled toward it and wrapped her fingers around its binding. Before she could shove it back into her bag, goosebumps erupted up her spine.

H-a-n-n-a-h. The book called to her again. *Give him the book. You don't need me anymore.* Hannah paused in a trance. Callan and Nathaniel's struggle faded into the background.

She picked herself off the ground and brushed dirt off the black leather. The soothing sensation slipped over her skin. It slowly relieved the staggering shock and disbelief that had overwhelmed her and gave her the hope that everything would be okay.

"Hannah, no," Callan screamed, a tenuous grip around Nathaniel's neck. "I know the temptation, but you must fight it. Resist her compulsion just like you resisted mine." Nathaniel broke free of Callan's hold and thrust his elbow into his chest. Callan stumbled back.

While the grimoire's voice held a similar sensation to Callan's Siren gift, its lure was much more powerful. Its soothing song calmed Hannah's worries, yet an all-consuming sense of power washed over her—captivated her.

"She can't resist, mate," Nathaniel said, laboring for air. "That book misses its mother, and it wants to go home."

Hannah calmly strode toward them. The wind rolled against the ground, brushing debris over her feet.

Callan obstructed her path to Nathaniel and yanked the book from her arms. But she didn't let go. *Senties dolorum*, the book whispered to Hannah. Without giving it a second thought, she repeated the words. "Senties dolorum."

Callan flew backward and crashed to the ground. His entire body seized in pain. His teeth grinded against each other. He squinted in agony, a few small tears slipping out from under his eye lashes.

Hannah's chest constricted at whatever she just said. Her eyes shifted between Callan and the book that sat harmlessly in her hands.

"Mara may not be pleased that you were reborn, but she'll be happy to know that you can no longer resist her persuasion." Nathaniel chuckled to himself and rubbed his hands together.

The closer Hannah stepped toward Nathaniel, something didn't feel right. She looked back at Callan and felt sick at the sight of his body thrashing on the ground. And *she* did that to him, by simply speaking some words—words the spell book provided her.

She snapped out of her trance. She chose to ignore the book, no matter how compelled she felt to comply. She threw it back to Callan, and his body relaxed.

Nathaniel's eyes narrowed. His hands balled into fists at his sides.

Callan opened his eyes and breathed heavily, a frail smile appearing on his face.

Hannah took his hand and helped him to his feet. "I'm sorry. I'm so sorry."

"Do not apologize. You repelled the book's charm—*her* charm. I knew you could." Callan smiled down at Hannah, both pride and affection in his gaze. Empowerment overwhelmed her. While she had felt helpless for so long, this was the first time she noticed a glimmer of strength within herself.

She couldn't fixate on this for long, however, because Nathaniel was already racing toward them—rushing for the book. It sat on the ground next to Callan's feet.

Hannah swooped it up in her arms, laid a palm against the black leather, and positioned herself in front of Callan, determined to block Nathaniel's path.

"Senties dolorum," she declared, but nothing happened. Nathaniel slowed and broke into more laughter. Hannah's sense of empowerment disappeared.

"The book accessed your power for that spell—Mara's spell," Callan explained. "You shan't be able to replicate it on your own. Not without the book's say-so."

"What about you?" Hannah asked, urgency in her voice. Nathaniel tauntingly stepped closer.

"I've never been strong enough for one of Mara's old language spells," he whispered from behind her.

Hannah didn't know whether this meant that she was exceptionally powerful, or if Mara's grimoire could compel any witch to do its bidding. If Hannah was truly powerful, however, she would have been able to perform the spell without the book's help. Her mind burned with questions and thoughts about magic that seemed completely illogical.

Nathaniel was mere inches from Hannah when he bared his fangs and lowered his gaze to the book. Hannah threw it down the cliff path behind her and Callan, putting as much space as possible between Nathaniel and Mara's spells. She thrust her palms against Nathaniel's chest, hoping her hands would spark, but nothing happened. Nathaniel shoved Hannah into Callan. As Callan steadied her, Nathaniel blurred with speed to the book.

He reached the grimoire, picked it up, and smiled. "I wonder how Mara will reward me for rescuing her most prized possession," he said.

Callan lunged behind him and placed his hands on the sides of Nathaniel's head. "Be still. Drop the book," he commanded.

Nathaniel released a deep growl from low in his throat. "Her compulsion is stronger than yours, Callan. You know I can't disobey."

"Try," Callan urged. "Drop the book and flee this place. Get as far away from Mara as possible. Remember a time before her—before I brought you to her. You were good. You still can be."

"I can't," Nathaniel hissed, his pale eyes shifting back and forth.

"Yes, you can." Hope filled Callan's eyes, but his conviction didn't last long.

"I don't want to."

Nathaniel fought against Callan's compulsion, too far gone to be saved.

Callan's face fell. In one swift motion, Callan twisted his hands and snapped Nathaniel's neck with a loud *crack*.

Hannah gasped as he fell to the ground.

"Come," Callan said. "Grab the book. We must leave."

Hannah didn't move. She looked at Callan in horror. "You killed him."

"He shan't stay dead for long."

CHAPTER EIGHT

*H*annah and Callan sat on a shuttle bus that took them from the Bellcliff campus to the Cape Cove town center. The sun was almost set, causing the clouds to streak purple and pink across the darkening blue sky. Callan kept his jaw tight and sat up straight. Hannah could tell that he didn't trust the contraption they rode. He jolted every time the bus went over a bump or made a sharp turn.

"It's safe, I promise," Hannah said.

He nodded and kept his hands firmly gripped to the seat. "It moves very quickly."

"We'll be there soon." Hannah tried to find amusement in Callan's first interactions with modern technology, but she was too overwhelmed by everything that had happened. "Why do we have to leave Bellcliff?" she asked. Though she assumed the answer, talking was a better alternative than letting her mind go wild in the silence between them.

"Nathaniel would be sure to discover us. Or find Mara and disclose our whereabouts."

"How did he find us in the first place?"

"Magic can sense magic," Callan said. "When I locked magic away, he mustn't have been too far afield. He could have followed the pull of our magic or the magic of the book. There is also a tracking spell. There are a number of ways."

"So, we're really not safe wherever we go."

"More space between us and them shall make it more difficult for them to find us." Callan cleared his throat. "However, there is a strong chance that they shall track us."

Hannah wished Nathaniel would stay dead, and the thought disturbed her. Maybe the reason why Mara's grimoire was so difficult for her to resist was because she harbored darkness within her. Hannah always considered herself a good person, but maybe she wasn't. Maybe the Convergence blackened her soul. She was the one responsible for killing her parents and she had already done Mara's bidding by reawakening magic. Even now, she felt drawn to the magetism of the grimoire in her bag.

"How do you kill a Vampire?" Hannah asked, nearly wanting to laugh at how ridiculous she sounded. Thankfully, the shuttle was empty of any other students. She still kept her voice low, however, so the driver couldn't hear her.

"Decapitation, wooden stake to the heart, or removing the heart entirely."

"Well, that one survived the test of time."

"Nathaniel shan't be the only creature Mara sends after us. Once she learns you are living, her will shall be strong."

Hannah's throat went dry, and her chest fluttered with

nerves. She braced herself to learn more about these other creatures, but the shuttle pulled into a commuter parking lot near the Cape Cove marina. One of the wheels dipped into a pothole, causing Callan to grab onto Hannah's wrist. His jaw clenched.

"You weren't afraid to bury yourself for eternity, but a bumpy ride makes you jumpy?" Hannah said.

Callan released her arm and sighed. "Just as magic is new to you, this contraption is new to me." The shuttle parked, and the driver opened the door. Callan remained still in the seat next to Hannah.

"We're here now," she said. "It's safe to get up."

Callan cleared his throat and unclenched his grip from the seat. "Of course." He stood up and let Hannah out in front of him. They got off the bus with only Hannah's bag in tow.

"We must get out of sight," Callan said.

"I don't have enough money for a hotel."

Before Hannah could formulate a plan, Callan took her hand and guided her to the marina. They walked along the long wooden dock that housed a number of small boats, only a couple tall lamps providing light against the darkening night sky. The marina was empty. Toward the end of the dock, Callan looked around before motioning for Hannah to get into one of the boats.

"Seriously?" she asked. "We can't go onto someone else's boat. That's trespassing."

"Might you have something else in mind?"

Hannah thought for a moment, but came up empty. She was too exhausted to think of a creative solution, and the thought of laying her head down was too tempting to ignore. She took Callan's hand and let him help her down into the boat. They went below deck and fastened the door closed behind them. The space was small. It had a couch, table, and a few chairs.

"Boats have certainly changed since the 1690s," Callan said. Hannah sat on the couch. Callan closed the curtains to the small windows that provided a view of the harbor. She took a deep breath and reveled in the silence. Water lapped against the side of the boat. The sail's metal clasps clanged against the mast. The gentle sway of the boat soothed her.

"Is Bryce going to die?" Hannah asked.

Callan sat at the table and looked straight at Hannah. "Yes," he said without hesitation. "Without feeding, he shan't survive."

"So, I guess there is a fourth way to kill a Vampire."

"Had I a wooden stake or such strength to rip his head from his body, I would have. 'Twould have been hastier than sentencing him to starve to death." Hannah could feel him observing her defeated demeanor. "Had I not, he would have killed many people, Hannah. I pray you understand that."

"I do," she whispered.

"Condemning the boy to death was not something I took joy in."

"I know." A heavy silence grew between them. Callan appeared on-edge, waiting for Hannah to say something. When Hannah finally opened her mouth, he sat up straight, ready to listen.

"How did I knock him off the cliff?" she asked. "I've felt that kind of spark before, but nothing like that."

"You may never have been in such danger before. Your magic is loyal to you. You do not yet know how to wield it, therefore it instinctively protected you."

"I was in danger like that before. I was supposed to

drown with my parents the night of my sixteenth birthday. I'm guessing I survived because of my magic?"

Callan nodded.

She stood up and paced through the enclosed space below deck. "If I had it my way, I would have died with them that night."

"Do not speak such things," Callan interjected.

Hannah raised her hand for him to stop. "Obviously, that wasn't what was meant to be," she said.

Despite Hannah's previous exploration into the supernatural, she had never been one to believe in destiny or fate. Now that she knew what she knew, however, who was she to claim that it didn't exist? "Even though this magic is a part of me, it's still a complete stranger. I'm a part of an entire story that I haven't read." She bit down on her lip and continued pacing as she gathered her thoughts.

Callan watched her pace back and forth with concern, anxiously tapping his foot. "Maybe I should not have dragged you into this endeavor," he said.

Hannah stopped and looked at him with disbelief.

"You released me from the cave, I know," he said, "but that should have been the end of it. I was treating you as I would have treated Raven. I was simply happy to have you —her—back. She was raised to understand magic—had knowledge of this world."

Callan shook his head back and forth before rising to his feet. He stood only inches from Hannah. "Even then, I failed to protect her. In truth, she protected me." He paused and looked as though he was reminiscing on a fond memory that turned sour. "You cannot be here with me, Hannah." His brows furrowed and his eyes filled with anguish. He turned away. "I shall destroy the grimoire. I beg you to flee far away from here—from me."

"Don't do that," Hannah said. She put her hand against his firm jaw and gently guided his face back toward hers. "You made me a promise," she said.

"That was before I knew the danger I had put you in."

"I've made my choice," Hannah said and kept her gaze tight on Callan's bright green eyes. "I'm not going anywhere. And it's time you follow through with your promise to answer my questions."

Callan hesitated. "Fine. However, you must make me a promise in turn." Hannah waited, considering his proposal, then nodded for him to continue. "If anything should go awry, you must promise that you shan't try and save me."

Hannah knew that she couldn't make that promise. Everything about Callan was comforting and alarming and soothing and invigorating. He was not compelling her to feel this way. She was choosing to be here with him, and that included sticking together if anything went wrong. So, if making a false promise got her closer to the truth, then so be it.

"Fine," she said, crossing her arms, never pulling her eyes away from his.

"Say the words."

"I promise."

Callan took a deep breath and then sighed with relief. He sat back down and weakly smiled at Hannah. "Prithee," he said. "Ask your questions."

"I think there is a better way to get my answers than simply asking," she said.

Hannah unzipped her bag and pulled out Mara's grimoire. She placed it on the table in front of Callan, careful to not leave her hands connected with it for too long.

"I want to use the memory spell."

CHAPTER NINE

"I is far too great a risk." Callan said. He pushed his back against the seat.

"It's dangerous for me to not know what we're up against. I still really have no idea what is going on."

"All you must know is if Mara retrieves her book, she shall track down the reawakened witches, manifest them into her creatures, and spread her evil across the world. The more darkness she unfurls, the more powerful she shall become."

Hannah nodded her head. Only ultimate doom laid before them if they failed to stop Mara. No big deal. She gulped. "What's her end goal? Why does she need more power?"

"There is no end. That is the crux about dark magic. It is seductive, addictive, and one can never quite get enough. Advancing darkness simply feeds her black magic. Thereby, it rewards her by making her more powerful, unstoppable." Callan stood up and stepped away from the grimoire.

Hannah furrowed her brow. *Seductive. Addictive.* Words

that exactly described how Hannah felt when under the influence of Mara's spell book. What worried her the most was that she liked how it felt; she reveled in it. It erased any sense of right versus wrong.

"So, where did Raven come into all of this?" Hannah wondered if Raven had been tempted by Mara's sorcery too.

"Raven was an opposing force to Mara. She was good and selfless and cared deeply for others. 'Twas why Mara desired her dead." Sorrow draped over Callan, as if he was remembering a saint.

Well, that answers that, Hannah thought. How could she ever compare to Raven, the good—the perfect?

"She cared deeply for you," Hannah said, watching as Callan nervously tapped his hands on his jeans. His desire to be reunited with his Raven was palpable. While Hannah may never live up to her memory, perhaps she could provide Callan with some solace—potentially the only contribution she'd be able to make on this insane quest.

"Why might you know that?"

"I've seen it."

Callan jolted toward Hannah. "How? You cannot access your magic."

"Ever since the accident, I've received glimpses of images that feel like memories. Everyone told me they were symptoms of my PTSD..."

"Pardon?" Callan was unfamiliar with the acronym—and probably acronyms in general.

"Post-Traumatic Stress Disorder. When you have nightmares, flashbacks, anxiety after some terrifying event." Callan nodded and looked to the floor, his eyes heavy with sorrow. "I had one earlier of you and me, well, Raven, and I could feel her affection for you."

Callan smiled. "Your magic desires you to remember."

"See?" Hannah stepped closer to Callan, grasping this opportunity. "The spell could help me put the pieces together."

Callan bit down on his lip.

"Would you trust Raven to do it? Nathaniel seemed to remember her being very powerful." Hannah placed her hands on her hips.

"Indeed, she was. However, Raven was raised and trained in the ways of magic since she was a child…"

"Her magic is in me. It's one and the same. Isn't that right?"

Callan didn't answer. He rubbed the back of his neck.

"I am able to resist your Siren influence and the commands of Mara's grimoire, just like she was able to. If I can do that, then what's one spell?" Hannah knew she wasn't as powerful as Raven, but she'd say what was necessary in order to convince Callan.

"Fine," he said, and Hannah was surprised that he conceded so quickly. "We shall do it in the morning. You need your sleep."

"What about you?"

"I have been slumbering for over three hundred years. I am not ready to close my eyes just yet." Hannah released a huff of laughter. "I shall keep watch."

Hannah rested her weary body on the couch, and Callan draped a knit blanket over her. No matter how hard the cushions were, it felt incredible for Hannah to lay her head down.

"Good night," she said.

Callan sat on a lounge chair across from her beneath a round window. "The sweetest of dreams to you," he said, gazing outside. The dock lights blinked, and the wood creaked as the boat rocked against it.

Hannah closed her eyes, and despite the comfort she felt with Callan sitting nearby, the silence brought her mind back to the burdensome realization that she was responsible for her parents' death. A couple tears slid out from under her closed eyelids, but she didn't have the strength to wipe them away. She was finally getting the answers she had been waiting for, but she'd carry the revelation with her for the rest of her life. And if the magic within Hannah was the cause of something so tragic, then she would now use it for good.

Drifting off to sleep, she was both nervous and excited to learn even more about her past and the world of magic first thing in the morning.

IN THE DEAD OF NIGHT, HANNAH WAS REMOVED FROM HER BED BY *Mara's intruders. She wasn't Hannah, however, and this wasn't her world. She was Raven with hair that reached down to her waist, dressed in a simple white sleeping gown. She didn't resist her captors' force and went with them willingly.*

She was brought to a clearing in the middle of the woods where a wooden post stood tall in front of a clan of darkly dressed men and women—witches. Callan stood next to a tall woman with black hair that blended into the night. He was statuesque and alert, like a soldier standing next to his queen.

Once Raven was bound to the post, the tall woman slowly walked toward her, her red eyes glowing through the darkness.

"I expected more fight coming from a witch such as you," the woman said. Her voice was deep and powerful, coated in malice.

"There is more than one way to fight back, Mara," Raven said.

Her voice sounded exactly like Hannah's, but smoother and more composed.

Mara laughed and looked down at Raven as though her words were nonsense and her presence was insignificant. "He is mine now. For good."

"We shall see," Raven said, looking past Mara at Callan. Her eyes were sorrowful as she gazed at him, hoping it could break through his impenetrable exterior.

"Indeed, take a long look at your beloved," Mara said. "For it shall be your last." She flipped her cloak and returned to Callan's side among the circle of her creatures and followers. "The life I take in the name of darkness, is that of Raven Harlowe." Mara began her chant, her voice loud as an announcement to her servants. "May her defiance cause her death, one that is grim and slow." As Mara proclaimed her spell, Raven muttered something inaudible beneath her breath. "May these eighteen years be her last—in no future lives, shall she grow. Now let the fire blaze and burn, condemning her to eternal woe!"

As soon as Mara's last word left her mouth, fire erupted around the wooden post and crawled over Raven's body. She quickly finished whatever she was saying beneath her breath—a prayer, perhaps—then screamed from the heat of the flames. The fire engulfed her until the crackling and hissing blaze drowned out her cries.

HANNAH LURCHED AWAKE, GASPING FOR BREATH and shrieking at the heat on her skin.

Callan was immediately at her side. "Shhhh," he said. "It is all right. 'Twas only a dream." He placed a palm to her cheek, brushing her skin with him thumb.

She bristled and sat up.

He pulled his hand back, balling it in a fist in his lap. "Your skin is burning. I'll get a cool rag."

He stood and went to the small bathroom, returning with a wet hand towel. He placed it across her forehead and Hannah reveled in the cool it provided.

"You just stood there!" Hannah clung to the damp towel and pressed it against her forehead. A single tear rolled down her chin.

"What? Stood where?" He shook his head, placing a hand on her shoulder. "'Twas only a dream."

Hannah peeled the cloth from her head and dabbed it at the base of her neck. "It was a memory. I could feel the flames burning my skin."

Callan's face fell.

"I thought you loved her." She shifted her shoulder from beneath his touch.

His hand hovered for a moment, but he soon brought it to his lap, folding his fingers together. "I was under Mara's compulsion. Her grasp was too tight."

"Why didn't you resist? Raven clearly could." She swung her legs over the side of the couch and pressed the towel to the back of her neck.

"I was too weak to resist. Raven was special. Her magic was stronger than most."

"So special that you let her burn alive?" Hannah shrugged off her blanket and rolled up her sleeves.

"I've admitted to my weakness." Callan stood and walked to the window. "Why do you believe I did what I did? Only Raven's death was able to break the compulsion. Once Mara's intentions were clear, and I had realized my own wicked acts, I sacrificed myself and all of magic to put an end to it," he said, running his fist against the windowsill.

Callan's words snapped Hannah out of her burning rage. Who was she to judge him when she too had been manipulated by Mara's magic? Granted, she never intentionally killed anyone, but if she allowed dark magic to consumer her, she could see how killing someone would be easy—effortless.

She stood up from the couch and walked over to him. "I'm sorry. I shouldn't have said those things."

"All your words are ones I have labored upon." He set his jaw, focused on the lapping waves outside.

"I was there, living through Raven. I felt everything she felt."

"'Twas the worst day of my life. I relive it each and every day." Hannah put her hand on Callan's shoulder, and he shrugged it off. "Stop. I do not deserve your comfort."

"She didn't blame you," Hannah said.

"What?" His voice cracked in desperation.

"Right before she died, she still loved you. She was fighting for you."

Callan's eyes welled with tears. "You are trying to appease my guilt." he said. "No matter which way you paint the portrait, I was the reason she was killed." Hannah couldn't help but empathize with him. The hurt he carried for Raven's death was the same she held deep within herself.

Dull light peered through the cracks of the boat's curtains and shone on the leather book. The sun sat low on the horizon.

Hannah moved to the table and placed a hand on Mara's grimoire. "The quicker I can remember, the faster we can get rid of this thing and stop Mara once and for all."

"I failed to put an end to her a time already," Callan

said, his voice low. "To lock magic away was my only recourse."

If she was going to convince Callan that he was not alone in this, to put his mind at ease, then she needed to portray resilience and strength. Despite knowing that she was no Raven, she had become quite good at pretending.

"And if that's what we have to do again, then we will. But last time, you didn't have me." She fiddled with the pewter clasp. She had her magic, and that counted for something. Perhaps if Raven didn't die in the past, she would have been able to help Callan destroy Mara without having to imprison magic.

"The sooner I have the whole picture, the closer we will get to figuring this out." Hannah could feel the grimoire's tug. She channeled Raven's strength and pushed away the spell book's temptation.

"Shall we begin?"

CHAPTER TEN

"$\mathcal{F}$ind the page that reads *To Remember a Past Life*," Callan said, keeping his distance from Mara's grimoire. He paced as much as he could in the small living area of the boat, peering at the book over Hannah's shoulder.

Hannah sat at the table and flipped through the crinkled pages until she found the spell.

"Why can't you touch it?" she asked.

"I have fallen to dark magic before. I would rather keep my distance than take a chance." Though she felt sympathy for Callan's guilt and his strict resistance, it actually made her feel better about herself. She could sense the temptation of the grimoire pulsing beneath her fingertips, and it would be so easy to submit to its will. Hannah did well to withstand its invitation.

"Should I be the one to read the spell, then?" Hannah asked.

"If you had access to your magic, your spell would have

worked against Nathaniel. It is clear that you have yet to connect with it," Callan said.

Hannah couldn't help but take offense. She crossed her arms and hunched over the table. "Well, I did only *just* learn about magic, so..."

"There is no need to fret, Hannah. Like I said, Raven was practiced in the ways of magic years before her Convergence. All witches were. It is not a fault of your own. Accessing your magic will come with time."

"But all the other spells—"

"Were the grimoire's doing. It was accessing your magic for its own bidding."

"Oh...right." She sighed through pouted lips, overwhelmed at how much had yet to grasp surrounding magic. "Well, if you read the spell, are you going to go all...evil again?"

Callan's face twinged. Hannah didn't want to hurt his feelings, but she needed to know.

"The memory spell, though included in Mara's grimoire, does not have a dark inclination. I should be fine." He grabbed the pillow from the couch and tossed it onto the floor. "You should lie down. Your conscious mind will be elsewhere, so you should make yourself comfortable."

Hannah laid on the floor, her head propped up by the pillow. She folded her hands over her chest and took a deep breath.

"You must focus on Raven," Callan instructed. "You may have many past lives by now, therefore, the more you concentrate on Raven, the greater chance you shall have to observe her life."

Hannah hadn't even considered the fact that she had

more than one past life. The emphasis had been on Raven this whole time. Who else could she have been?

"Are you prepared?"

Hannah took another deep breath and allowed the motion of the swaying boat to relax her. She nodded. Callan hovered over the spell, but was careful not to touch the book. He cleared his throat and read:

"I send the witch, one Hannah Fenwick, back to an older mind.

Let her see her distant self, unshackled, no longer blind.

To remember every sight, whatever she may find.

To discover her past beyond this time, their souls now intertwined."

Hannah's eyes shot wide open, but all she saw was a pearly white color, like liquid clouds swirling into a storm. She then fell deep into her dark subconscious, nothing but black silence surrounding her, ignorant to when she would land. Fear plagued her mind as the infinite darkness overwhelmed her senses. She was blind as she continued to fall, not knowing if she would soon crash or plummet aimlessly forever. Light flooded her mind, then faded into day. She found herself in an old marketplace, bustling with people dressed in period outfits—women in corseted dresses, aprons, and bonnets, and the men in long-buttoned coats, high socks, and puffy sleeves.

Raven stood at a cart with herbs and root vegetables. She was identical to Hannah in every way, except her curls were tamed into a long braid that nearly reached her waist.

"Raven?" Hannah called, though it didn't seem Raven

could hear her. She ran to Raven's side. "Can you see me?" Hannah asked.

Raven ignored her once again. Unlike the memories she had had where her and Raven were one, she was a simple observer in this spell.

This new world was so foreign, yet there was a sense of familiarity. The way the cobbles felt beneath her feet, the scent of musk on the breeze, the sound of creaking cart wheels, it was like déjà vu. Similar to the comfort she felt around Callan.

She followed Raven into a small wooden home. A simple stone and fireplace warmed the dwelling.

"Hello, my darling," her father said. He was probably in his fifties and wore simple cloth pants with an oversized beige shirt. His hair was gray, and his skin was leathered from years under the sun.

"The market provided a wealth of fresh vegetables, Father," Raven said, tossing her load onto a table by the stove. Turnips, cabbage, carrots, and parsnips spilled from a beige satchel. "I could cook a stew for supper?"

"Perchance enough for three?" her father asked. "Isabella may join our table."

"Isabella has joined our table on many occasions as of late." Raven smirked.

"I suppose she has. Does that upset you?"

Raven placed her hands on his hunched shoulder. "It pleases me if it pleases you. I am sure Mother would smile upon you both."

"I miss her still." He reached up and set his wrinkled hand upon hers.

"I know," Raven said, squeezing his hand. "As do I. But we shall meet again in our next life."

Hannah watched this interaction between Raven and

her father and wondered if she was destined to lose at least one parent in every life she lived. A knock on the door interrupted her thought.

Raven returned to her vegetables, and her father opened the door.

"Mr. Harlowe," a beautiful, deep male voice called from the entrance. "I have come to call upon your daughter. Is Raven at hand for a stroll?" Callan, as handsome as ever, stood in the doorway. Even though Hannah only saw him moments ago in the boat, her chest still fluttered.

Raven smiled at his appearance but maintained composure, organizing the vegetables.

"Nay. She is not available," Raven's father said firmly. "And even if she was, I should not want her spending time with a fellow such as you. I am aware of what you and Mara Eden's coven do in the woods at night."

Callan huffed. "I would not be so quick to judge what thee could not possibly understand."

"I understand what is evil, Mr. Delmonte." Raven's father stood straighter.

"Not evil, Mr. Harlowe"—Callan smirked—"simply more powerful. The kind of power that can protect your daughter."

"My daughter does not need protection."

"From anyone but you, I see." Callan took a step forward and put a hand on Mr. Harlowe's arm.

Raven rushed to her father's side. "It is all right, Father." She pulled him into the house, out of Callan's reach. "Mr. Callan Delmonte, I would be delighted to walk with you."

Callan clasped his hands together and gleamed.

"But the stew," her father protested.

"I shall finish it upon my return." She hugged him.

He gripped her wrist, pulling her closer and whispered, "Be careful of him. I shan't lose you too."

"Not to worry, Father. You know that light surrounds me." She kissed her father's cheek and left the house. Hannah followed.

This Callan was smug and arrogant, unlike the boy Hannah had left back in the boat. *Her* Callan was protective and caring; he was able to own up to his mistakes. She found it difficult to believe that they were one in the same.

Callan and Raven walked side by side. Hannah kept pace beside them.

"I am pleased you decided to walk with me, despite your father's protestations."

"When else might I see you? I have missed you at our Friday gatherings." Raven swiped her long braid over her shoulder.

"I have been quite engaged lately." Callan skipped ahead and plucked a wildflower from an overgrown hedge along the path. He returned to Raven and gently tucked it behind her ear. Raven blushed.

"No need to explain," Raven said.

Hannah found herself feeling irrationally jealous, but was quick to snap herself out of it. Not only was this a different time—a memory from her past life—but she couldn't even understand why she felt drawn to Callan in the first place. She barely knew him.

"People change," Raven continued, walking forward. "You are no longer the young boy who used to pull my pigtails at our lessons."

"No," he simpered. "I suppose I am not." He stood tall, running his hand through his hair. "And you are no longer the little girl who used to tell the preceptor when I was misbehaving."

"Are you misbehaving now?" Raven asked. She poked his shoulder, smiling, though her tone was serious.

"I am simply expanding my horizons."

Raven abruptly moved in front of Callan and placed a hand to his chest, stopping him. Her blue eyes vigorously concentrated on him. "You have changed, Callan. And not simply from a boy to a man. What has Mara Eden done to you?"

Hannah admired Raven in this moment. She had such conviction and exhibited steadfast strength with her every word.

"She has shown me that we are capable of more than what we were taught at our lessons growing up—greater things than what is preached at the Friday gatherings." Excitement filled Callan's voice. He outstretched his arms as if to make his claims seem grander.

"Our lessons and gatherings teach us to treat our magic with reverence and to identify the difference between the light and darkness." Raven kept her words hushed as she looked around them.

"Not everything is black and white," Callan responded.

"Perhaps. However, what Mara fosters is objectively dark. Practicing that kind of magic comes at a price. It does not only thrive on harming others, but comes at great personal sacrifice. Just look at Mara's physical transformation. Her hair used to be a breathtaking red and now is as black as night. Her eyes glow with a fiery hatred that brews in her soul."

"A small price to pay for unyielding power, no?" Callan paced around Raven. "And 'tis not harming people if they join upon their own volition. Might have you considered that there are those who find interest in tasting other magic?"

Raven turned with Callan, keeping her gaze steady upon him. "Is that what she promised you? Unyielding power?" Raven asked. "I have seen you with her. 'Tis as though she controls your every move. She may gain power by the darkness she spreads, but you shall never receive what she has promised you."

Callan stopped and took a step closer to Raven. "I hold more power now than ever before. Her promise has already been granted." Callan took Raven's hand, and his eyes looked as though they were glowing greener than before. "Join us. Come with me and be part of our coven. You shall understand soon."

Even though Raven was the focus of Callan's compulsion, Hannah could feel his influence. It was intoxicating. Raven, on the other hand, never even batted an eye. She looked from Callan's hands to his gaze. She pulled her hand away, remaining composed.

"Is that what you were going to do to my father? Force him to let you see me?" Disgust emerged on Raven's face.

Callan took a step back, shocked.

"She turned you into a Siren." She shook her head, disappointed.

"How do you know of that?"

"Simply because I do not practice dark magic, does not mean I do not keep myself apprised on it. Especially with all the trials happening in Salem. There are entire sections on dark sorcery in the town's library that sit on the cliffs. And if you are not careful, that witch hunt shall come to Cape Cove," Raven said. Her voice rose, and her calm demeanor faltered.

Callan looked bewildered at her resistance. He glanced between his hands and the steadfast Raven who stood before him. He mustn't have known yet that Raven could resist his compulsion.

She stomped away, a look of anger on her face, then turned on her heel. "Those people you are recruiting to join Mara's coven, they are not doing so by choice. You are compelling them. Do you not see that you are destroying lives?"

"W-Well," Callan stuttered, "some witches, perhaps, need simply be shown the way."

"A moment ago, you argued they were joining voluntarily. What is it you truly believe? How many of your coven resisted before you *convinced* them otherwise?" Raven marched back to Callan and stood at eyelevel in front of him. She held his gaze, her fists balled at her sides.

Hannah could see Callan struggling. He cowered a few steps away from Raven, and his posture sunk.

"You are conflicted," Raven continued. "As you do not know which thoughts are yours, and which were forced upon you by your master."

"She is not my master," he replied through gritted teeth.

"Mara created you. And within dark enchantments, the created is sired to their creator. The evil that has corrupted your magic instills you with a sense of gratitude and devotion toward her. But that is not truly you, Callan, is it?" Raven took a step toward him.

"I pray you to stop. I do not wish to hear it," Callan said, shutting his eyes.

"You *must* hear it. You must face what you have done and what has been done to you. Do you ever remember desiring to explore the darkness before Mara came upon you? Can you even remember your true self? Before you were enchanted to become a Siren?"

Callan's upper lip twitched in frustration. He grabbed Raven's forearm. "You shall not resist me."

She winced.

"You shall join us." Callan's concentration was so severe, it was frightening.

Raven struggled under his grasp.

"And you shall no longer ask questions." His fist tightened around her wrist.

Hannah lunged forward. "Callan, stop," she yelled, forgetting that they couldn't hear her.

"You are strong," Raven said, grinding her teeth.

Callan smiled, reveling in his power.

"But as am I," she continued. "Let my skin be fire and resist your desire."

A white spark illuminated beneath Callan's hand and shocked him backward. Hannah gasped. She committed Raven's spell to memory. Perhaps, one day, she too would be able to command the surging energy within her.

Callan held his hand and looked at Raven in disbelief. "How did you..."

"Great power may also come from the light." Her fingers twinkled with glistening orbs.

Callan rubbed his hand, glaring at Raven. "I should go," he said, his voice low and cross.

"Think about what I have said. If you desire to be free from the dangerous path you have chosen, I may help you." Though Raven exuded a tough exterior, there was a sadness behind her eyes.

Callan shook his head and walked away. No wonder Callan didn't want her to perform the memory spell. He didn't want her to see what he used to be.

HANNAH PROPELLED THROUGH HER subconscious to another time in Raven's life. Darkness swirled around her until her feet were steady on the ground. She blinked to clear her vision.

It was dusk now. Oil lamps lit the street. Raven, her father, and twenty-or-so other men and women left a gentleman's house, filing out, hugging goodbye, and exchanging pleasantries. He waved them farewell from the porch. Hannah assumed this was the Friday gathering of witches Raven mentioned.

Raven walked arm in arm with her father, and something caught her eye. Callan skulked beneath a large oak tree across the street, at the edge of the woods. Raven dropped her father's arm and walked toward Callan.

"Raven?" her father called after her.

"One moment, Father." She quickened her stride.

Her father watched after her warily, crossing his arms. Hannah followed Raven across the street.

"What have I done?" Callan's head hung in shame.

Raven sighed. "Let us take a walk." She held out her hand.

Callan blinked, his eyes glassy, and took her hand. Their fingers interlaced.

She led him a few feet into the woods, and Hannah followed. Raven put her arms around Callan and held him close. He hugged her back, anguish simmering in his eyes.

"It may take some time," she said, "but I promise to free you."

Callan took a step back and shook his head. "She is too powerful. Whatever she commands, I must obey." His hands trembled, but Raven clasped hers over them.

"Realizing this, Callan, is the first step of breaking the bond. We shall find a way."

"I am so sorry," Callan said. A few tears escaped his eyes. "I should never have attempted to make you…"

"You were doing as you were told." She gently wiped a tear from his cheek.

Callan covered her hand with his own upon his face and leaned into her touch. "I hope you understand how much I care for you, despite my poor behavior the other day."

Raven smiled. "I have known you since we were both small children, Callan Delmonte. You care for me just as I care for you."

Hannah watched their interaction and marveled at how simple and true their declarations of affection were for each other.

Callan placed a hand on her waist, pulled her hip against his. She tucked her chin. With a single finger, he raised her gaze to meet his. "I may be confused at which thoughts are my own, but I know for certain that I would like to kiss you."

Raven stood on her tiptoes and pressed her lips to his. She caressed her hands behind his neck. Callan ran his fingers into her hair and held her head as he slightly dipped her back. He kissed Raven with the same passion he kissed Hannah the moment she released him from the cave.

A sense of sadness washed over Hannah. Callan cared for Raven. And though they were identical in appearance, they were not the same person. Raven was strong, powerful, poised, and always seemed to know the right thing to say. Hannah thought of herself as the complete opposite. While Raven may have been surrounded in light, Hannah felt muddled in the fog.

"Mr. Delmonte," a deep and sultry voice called from deeper within the woods. Raven and Callan separated as

Mara emerged from behind the trees. Her red eyes sent a chill up Hannah's spine.

"I was looking to retrieve you for an evening wander, and Nathaniel told me you might be here." She scrutinized Raven. "Miss Harlowe."

"Mistress Eden. You have been greatly missed at our Friday gatherings." While Raven was the picture of composure, Hannah noticed her nostrils flare in Mara's presence.

"I doubt anyone has missed me, my dear. I have since found a greater use of my time rather than prattling along about the old ways of magic." Even though Mara only looked to be about five or six years older than both Callan and Raven, she spoke to them as if they were young children. Naïve and impressionable.

"I would not consider them old ways when their values and standards are still upheld to this day...by most, that is."

"I suppose we shall see how long that lasts, young Miss Harlowe."

"I suppose we shall." Raven and Mara stared at each other with pleasant smiles that masked their true feelings.

Mara caressed her hand against Callan's cheek. The slightest wisp of what looked like black smoke hovered between her palm and his face. Faint cries poured from the smoke. Hannah straightened.

"Shall we?" Mara gestured into the deep of the woods.

Callan nodded. "Indeed. Let us go. Have a pleasant evening, Miss Harlowe," he said, his voice stilted.

Raven held his gaze as long as she could as Mara led him farther into the woods. She glanced over her shoulder and offered Raven one last sadistic smile. Hannah's blood chilled. As soon as they were out of sight, Raven stormed in the opposite direction.

Hannah's head spun. She found herself in Raven's father's house, a fire crackling in the background. Raven anxiously paced back and forth.

A knock rapped at the door. She answered it and seemed relieved to find Callan there. She ushered him in as he looked over his shoulder, then shut the door.

"Did you bring it?" Raven asked. Callan nodded and pulled a folded handkerchief from his pocket. He unwrapped it and revealed a few strands of black hair.

"'Twas all I could get without her noticing," Callan said. "I gathered it from the ground after our last coven gathering."

"You are sure they are hers?" Raven asked, inspecting the hair. "We do not need much, but the strands must belong to Mara."

"Yes, I am certain."

Raven cupped the handkerchief and placed it on the stone floor in front of the fireplace. "The more we understand about Mara, the better chance we shall have of freeing you from her grasp."

"I am amenable for any option. She is becoming more arduous to resist," Callan said. "My mind only clears of her fog when I am a great distance from her. And even then, her influence lingers. It is then, however, that I think of you." He looked to the floor.

Raven smiled and opened a spell book beside her knee. Hannah felt her own cheeks flush.

Raven took a deep breath and hovered her hands over Mara's strands. Her palms glowed white as she spoke,

"Take me to whence her heart turned cold,

A story that has yet to be told.

Reveal Mara Eden's past to me,

When her light within was forced to flee.

The moment when darkness swallowed her whole,

And black magic infiltrated her soul."

Raven's eyes illuminated white. Hannah felt herself being thrust to wherever the spell was taking her. Within a matter of seconds, Hannah stood beside Raven. A girl with flaming red hair sat on a bed and stared aimlessly at a candle that burned on her nightstand. Her knee shook, causing the bed to squeak.

A light knock sounded at the door. The teenager startled and steadied her shaking knee. Her parents cautiously walked into her bedroom and offered weary smiles.

"'Tis nearly midnight, Mara. Are you ready?" her mother asked.

"I think so," Mara answered.

Her mother and father eyed each other. Her father sat at the end of his daughter's bed.

"You know that receiving this magic is a gift that comes with great responsibility. You must remember your teachings and the ways of our coven," he said.

"I know," Mara snapped, but caught herself, covering her face with her hands. "I'm sorry. You have told me this many a time." She looked between her mother and father. "Why are you so afraid?" Mara asked. Though Hannah could discern a hard edge in young Mara, there was also a softness she didn't expect.

Mara's father gulped and exchanged another glance with his wife. "We are not afraid, darling. It is simply that, with your occasional outbursts…"

"I have been working on my temper," Mara interrupted. "I have been better."

"We know you have, darling," Mara's mother said. "We only hope your magic does not aggravate the issue."

"I guess you simply must trust me, then." Mara stared them down, then exhaled through her nostrils. "I shall try to be good. Promise."

Her parents smiled and scooted closer to their daughter. "We know you shall," her father said. Trepidation still lingered in his tone. Her mother took her hand and gave it a light squeeze, but Mara snatched it away.

"'Tis going to happen soon," she said. "You do not have to wait and watch if you do not desire to."

"We would not dare miss such an exciting moment in a witch's life," Mara's mother said, feigning enthusiasm to mask her fear. Since learning about the Convergence, Hannah never thought of it as a positive experience. But from Mara's mother's comment, it was clearly supposed to be celebrated.

A surge of what resembled forked lightning, silver and dark, blasted through the bedroom ceiling. It struck Mara's chest.

Hannah lurched backward and gasped at the strike. Raven didn't even flinch. Fighting through her flaring nerves, Hannah made her way back to Raven's side and watched young Mara seize beneath the electrifying force that pierced through her body. Her parents watched, their eyes bewildered at the dark color of the magic surging through their daughter. After about a minute, the current dissolved into smoke. Mara rolled lifeless to the floor.

When she rose, her parents gasped. Her eyes glowed an unnatural amber.

"Are you all right?" her father asked.

Mara's mother clutched her husband's hand.

Mara looked from side to side. "I may do that?" she asked quietly, looking over her shoulder.

"Who are you speaking with, darling?" her mother asked.

"Always asking so many questions. I wish you would leave me be," she responded, a gritty tone in her voice.

"Please do not speak to your mother this way," her father interjected.

"I shall speak however I desire, and no soul shall possess the ability to do anything about it." An orb of black smoke formed in Mara's palm.

Her parents looked nervously at each other and nodded as if in agreement. "Your mother and I shan't hesitate to bind your magic, if you do not practice it properly. We have already spoken to the high priestess about it."

"Enough!" Mara screamed. The smoke rippled in her palm, and she breathed it in as if its scent were intoxicating. The smoke expanded and wrapped around Mara, like a soft blanket, luxurious against her skin.

> "You have had your time to meld my mind,
>> But now my magic, you shall not bind.
>> Take my parents from this life,
>> Steal their breath, this man and his wife.
>> Lead them away, like lambs to the slaughter,
>> For I am no longer their magicless daughter.
>> I accept the task of devotion to the night,
>> And spread its will, no matter the fight!"

Mara sang her spell as if it had been living within her the entirety of her life. Her black magic swirled around her body, then thrust toward her parents.

They cried out and choked on the smoke that swam into their lungs. Their bodies writhed, collapsing to the floor, and dissolving completely into the air like ash. Even after they were gone, their cries echoed in the air.

Hannah's jaw dropped, and air escaped her. She stumbled slightly, feeling lightheaded at the image that transpired before her. Even Raven's mouth was agape at Mara's first spell. But accompanying Hannah's shock was something else—determination. She forced herself to breath as her hands curled into fists.

Mara was ruthless. Witnessing her cruelty sparked a fire in Hannah. She was more determined than ever to stop Mara.

The smoldering black magic, laced with her parents' screams, returned to Mara's palms. Hannah expected her to look devastated or disturbed at the power she wielded, but that was not the case. Though Mara's hair dulled, her eyes glowed with a frightening intensity. She exhaled a loud sigh, filled with satisfaction. Her lips widened into a bestial smile.

"More," she said to the empty room.

In the next moment, Hannah and Raven were back with Callan in front of the fireplace. Hannah regained her footing on the splintering wooden floor and adjusted her mind. Raven took the handkerchief with Mara's strands of hair and threw them into the blaze.

"It was nearly immediate," she said. "There was light in her, but from the moment she converged, her sole purpose was to serve her dark magic. She is fueled by the spread of dark magic. Mara does not care about you or the witches she turns. Dispersing darkness intoxicates her and makes her more powerful. 'Tis as simple as that. If I could find a way to bring you into the spell with me, you could see for yourself. I am certain it would help you resist…"

"Slow yourself," Callan urged as he placed his hands on Raven's shoulders.

"She collected the fear of her parents, Callan. Fed off it. Their cries returned to her through that hideous black smog she exudes." Raven's gaze burned with such intensity, it sent a shiver up Hannah's spine.

Callan's jaw tensed. "That spell was powerful. You need to rest."

Hannah watched as Raven melted into Callan's arms. He rested his chin against her hair. Hannah saw a flash of this image when she first heard Nathaniel's name.

Nathaniel burst through the dwelling door, thrusting it against the wall. A canvas oil painting clattered to the floor.

Callan abruptly stood up. "What do you want, Nathaniel?"

"Mara seeks you. She told me I could find you here." Nathaniel had a look of disgust as his gaze switched between Callan and Raven.

A look of terror played on Callan's face. He untangled himself from Raven and was on his feet in seconds. "Tell her I shall be there momentarily," he said.

Raven stood and brought her face close to Callan's. She wrapped her fingers around his and held tight. "You do not have to go," she pleaded in a hushed tone. "Stay with me. We can face her together."

"It is too soon," he whispered. He removed his hand from Raven's and gave her one last gaze. Callan hurried out, his head hanging low. Nathaniel slammed the door shut behind them.

Raven dropped to her knees before the fire. The smell of

ash coated the air. She placed her face in her palms. Mara's hair popped in the flames.

The memory spell propelled Hannah to a different time within Raven's home. The house was silent. Raven wrote with irritated vigor in a journal under dim candlelight. Hannah peered over Raven's shoulder. She wrote, *If the balance between light and darkness is corrupted, then the world may never recover. The balance must be restored. It is the responsibility of those who have been chosen by the light—bestowed with benevolence and virtue—to fight against the harmful darkness. Though a witch may not have chosen the power granted to her by light magic, she must ignite that spark within herself and let it burn for the good of the world and the safety of those she loves.*

Hannah couldn't help but think she was speaking directly to her. Her mind buzzed with the memory of the manuscript she found in the library: *There is some magic that prefers a certain extreme. That magic searches for those who are most susceptible to channeling either light or dark and settles within them, creating magical prodigies.* Hannah's eyes widened as she pieced everything together.

Raven could resist compulsion. She possessed amazing strength from light magic—good magic. Though Hannah believed Raven to be incredibly different from her, their magic was supposedly the same. *Maybe I'm not doomed for darkness after all,* Hannah thought.

Raven put down her quill and left the journal open for the ink to dry. She stood from her chair and paced a few times, back and forth, back and forth. She then took a deep breath and swung her cloak around her.

She walked toward the front door, stopped, and turned

on her heels. She scribbled one more line in the journal, then blew out the candle. Smoke curled above the parchment.

While black magic may stop at nothing for power, white magic offers hope, even in the darkest of times.

HANNAH FOLLOWED RAVEN THROUGH THE WOODS. Up ahead, Hannah spotted a clearing illuminated by torches. The flames blazed over many faces, some of which she remembered from her previous dream of burning at the stake. Although Hannah knew that Raven's actions were leading to her demise, she couldn't do anything to stop her. If she could warn Raven—tell her that Callan would soon betray her, and to run for her life—she would. After reading what Raven wrote in her journal, Hannah knew that Raven was far too honorable and committed to the duties entrusted to her by light magic to ever abandon Callan.

They stopped behind a tree. Tall, Eastern White Pine trees circled a clearing of fallen needles and dried leaves. Light from the moon beamed through the hovering branches. There must have been fifteen or so people, all dressed in black cloaks, standing in a circle. Hannah spotted Mara's glowing red eyes. She stood inside the circle, Callan by her side. Two male witches dragged a young girl, no more than sixteen-years-old, through the dirt.

"Prithee, no!" she cried. "I want to go home." Tears streamed down her face, too small to fight against the two cloaked witches who held her in place.

Mara nodded to Callan. He placed his hand on the girl's

shoulder and looked directly into her eyes. "Be calm. You desire to be here. You choose to join our coven."

The young girl stopped crying and her body stilled. "The honor is mine," she said. She kneeled down and bowed her head to Mara.

Mara offered Callan a smug smile. "Rise, my dear. You have made a wise choice and shall be rewarded for your pledge of loyalty."

Without warning, Raven stormed into the circle. Hannah raced after her, terrified of what they were running into, even though this was only a memory.

"That is enough," she screamed, making her presence known.

Callan's eyes widened with dread.

"You cannot force people to join your coven, only then to convince yourself that they are here upon their own free-will."

Mara took a moment to look Raven up and down. She was stoic and never flinched at Raven's protestations. "You are brave to come and stand against what you do not understand. Perhaps you came upon us this night because you truly wish to belong with us."

"I completely understand what you are doing here." Raven's nostrils flared, and her lips trembled. She was unable to remain as calm and collected as Mara. "And I would never succumb to such darkness."

"You say that now. Why don't we enlighten you?" Mara signaled to Callan with a slow nod. He hesitated. "Callan," she said, her voice firm. "Do you not want your friend to see the truth in our ways?"

Callan's gaze shifted between Mara and Raven. Hannah's stomach twisted at the conflicted expression on his face.

"Go ahead." Raven offered Callan her hand. "Do your worst."

Callan took Raven's hand. She nodded and gave him a gentle squeeze.

"You desire to join our coven." He traced a finger over the lines on her palm.

Raven's lip quivered.

"You do not desire to resist us. Experience what the darkness has in store for you," he continued. Raven's eyes filled with tears, and she grit her jaw. She shook her head back and forth, and Callan dropped her hand.

"You see?" she said. "Your tricks do not work on me."

Murmurs spread throughout the circle of witches. Mara's eyes widened, and her wispy shadows manifested in the palms of her hands.

Raven turned to Callan and took his hands in hers. "Come with me. I shan't let her harm you."

"He cannot leave," Mara said.

"Because you do not let him. Would you not rather he stand by your side because he truly desires to?"

"He chooses to be here. Do you not, Mr. Delmonte?" Mara placed her hand on Callan's cheek. Tendrils of black smoke emitted from her fingers along with the faded sobs and shrieks of her past victims. Hazy coils crawled around his neck, toward his nose and mouth.

Raven's fingertips sparkled white. She wrapped her hand around Callan's arm, trickling a current of bright light over his skin. His hairs rose, and goosebumps tingled his flesh. The glowing light gathered beneath Mara's touch, and zapped her smoke away from Callan.

Mara backpedaled and gaped at the shock in her hand. She rubbed it and snarled.

"You are not the only soul who is gifted, Mistress

Eden," Raven said. She turned and faced the rest of the witches. "Though Mara may have made you promises, or compelled you with her darkness, it is never too late to walk away. Though it may not seem so, you do have a choice."

Whispers slithered through the circle. Hannah stood in awe at how Raven's declaration caused such a stir.

Mara stepped forward in desperation. "They are all here because they know that the old ways of magic only limit us from our full potential. Here, with me, they may experience power they have never before imagined."

"At what cost?" Raven's voice was sharp and cut across the cold night air. "They have sold their souls for a taste of your black magic in exchange for their undying servitude. You are not trying to enlighten them or help them find power. You are creating an army to serve at your hand."

"At the hand of darkness," Mara retorted, a conniving smile creeping up her face. "I myself am only a humble servant to that of black magic."

"The magic that made you kill your own parents?"

Mara's face tightened.

"You promised them that you would try to be good, remember?" Raven continued. "But your magic corrupted that promise, just as you are corrupting these people now."

Mara's jaw clenched, and her eyes darted back and forth.

"Look at you," Raven said, staring at Mara with a pitying gaze. "Look at what you have become. You too have a choice, Mara. You do not have to live like this."

Mara's upper lip quivered with utter disdain. "Senties dolorum," she muttered.

Raven fell to the ground and thrashed in pain. Hannah rushed to her side, but was useless. Callan lunged toward

Raven, but Mara quickly outstretched her hands and impaled every crevice of his body with wisps of black smoke. The more magic Mara emitted, the louder the cries and fear of her past victims.

"She is your enemy," Mara said. She turned to the other witches and declared, "She shall try and poison you against me, derail you from the greatness you are destined for."

Callan's eyes glowed green. The crowd stilled. Mara returned her hand to her side, and her tendrils of darkness seeped back into her fingertips.

Raven writhed against the dehydrated pine needles, but managed to utter a short spell. "Though this darkness causes pain, from my body let it drain."

After a moment, Mara's spell diminished. Raven lifted herself off the ground. She staggered to Callan and took his hands once more. "You see what she has done to me? She spreads pain and takes pleasure in it."

Mara grinned at the desperation in Raven's voice.

Callan's facial expression remained steady—vacant. "Mara warned that you might try and sway me."

Raven's eyes gushed with hopelessness, but only for a moment. She pursed her lips and gulped. "She is controlling you. You are under her command. Do you really want to be doing this? Helping her change these innocent witches into creatures of the night?"

Callan looked to Mara, who offered him an encouraging nod. He tore his hands from Raven's and stepped back. "Who are you to say what is right and what is wrong? What is good and what is bad?"

"Callan, fight against her. Do not let her do this." Raven's voice cracked.

Hannah ran her hands through her hair and bit down on her lip in frustration. She circled them, wracking her brain for ways to warn Raven. If Hannah could only be seen and heard, she would tell Raven of the fate she was soon to face. But the leaves and twigs didn't even crunch beneath Hannah's feet as she paced. It was no use.

"Mara Eden has not only given me great power, but she has shown us a new manner of magic. If you resist, you shall be left behind to fend for yourself when day permanently becomes night." The way Callan spoke reminded Hannah of modern-day cults, where members were brainwashed beyond recovery. And then a terrifying thought took over Hannah's mind: What if this happened again? What if Mara got hold of his mind? Raven was no longer here to bring him back. Hannah needed to keep her from him, no matter what.

"If you do not leave with me now," Raven said, "your soul shall be lost forever. I do not know if I will be able to help you." Raven's eyes searched Callan's face, as if searching for any sign of humanity or hope. Hannah's heart ached at Callan's indifference. Raven placed her hand against his chest, her expression pleading with him through her swelling sorrow. "If you stay, you are going to hurt people."

Callan lowered his lips to Raven's ear. "So be it," he whispered.

Raven stumbled back. She stared at him and tears welled in her eyes. Hannah realized there was nothing else she could do. Callan was lost. Raven ran into the woods, disappearing into the night.

Hannah wanted to follow her, but she learned all she needed to from the memory. She had to ensure Callan never fell victim to Mara's enchantment again.

Wake up, Hannah.

Hannah spun around and tried to locate the voice. It

sounded like Callan, but he stood emotionless by Mara's side.

You must wake. The voice was urgent, frightened even.

Mara turned and looked directly at Hannah. Her piercing red eyes sent a shock up Hannah's spine.

Mara smiled insidiously. "I shall be seeing you soon, Ms. Fenwick."

CHAPTER ELEVEN

*H*annah jolted awake. The room below-deck was empty. She stood up. No sign of Callan. Hannah's breathing accelerated when she noticed the mayhem around her. The cabin was scattered with broken chairs, smashed dishes, the capsized table, and large gashes in the couch. A loud *thud* sounded from above-deck, and Hannah's heart skipped a beat. *Callan.*

She raced up the small staircase. The door was already ajar. She pushed it open just enough to peek out.

Callan lay unconscious against the stern. She ran to him and checked his pulse. A massive sense of relief washed over her when she realized that he was still breathing.

The marina was empty. Though the sun had risen, the silence surrounding the dock indicated early morning.

Hannah had no idea how long she was under the memory spell. Her head spun, and part of her feared that when Callan came to, he might be the same Callan she left behind in her memory—dark and cold. Clearly something attacked him while she was exploring her past life, so the present was what she needed to focus on.

Trying to remain as quiet as possible, she hoisted Callan to a seated position. She cupped his face. "It's your turn to wake up now," she whispered. The side of his forehead was red from some kind of impact. She shook him gently, but he was out cold. Suddenly, Hannah felt a warm breath on the back of her neck. She paused and fought the urge to whip herself around. A low and crescendoing growl emitted from behind her. She turned, shielding Callan with her body.

Though it took all of Hannah's strength not to scream in terror, she felt her intestines flip and twist up into her chest. A massive black wolf with bright yellow eyes stared her down. Its lips curled over its sharp teeth and drool dripped down its fangs. Hannah held her breath, afraid that the tiniest flinch would set the beast off.

The wolf stepped closer, and its growl grew louder and more threatening. Hannah knew that staying still wouldn't work for long. *What would Raven do?*

The wolf pounced. Instinctively, Hannah rammed her fist into the wolf's nose, and it stumbled back. She held her hand in her lap, knuckles throbbing, but knew she had to move. Hannah rushed past the wolf and retreated below deck. She hoped it would follow her away from Callan.

She hunted through the rubble of the cabin and located Mara's grimoire beside the overturned table. She picked it up and held it to her chest as she crouched against the table.

"Use my power," she chanted under her breath. "Come on, come on." Hannah could hear the wolf's paws pound the stairs. The wood creaking beneath its weight. Thankfully, however, her fingertips pulsed upon the spell book's leather. It took hold of her, just as she had hoped. She breathed in a cool, electric breath, allowing the book's power to fill her.

Suddenly, she was overcome by the urge to reveal herself to the massive, black wolf. She scooted an inch to the edge of the table.

Beatrice will take good care of me, the book whispered in Hannah's mind. *Hand me over and you will be spared.*

Hannah allowed the liquid warmth of the book to course through her veins. She stepped out from behind the table and felt blissful at the idea of giving the book to Beatrice. The wolf crept closer and closer, her shoulder blades rotating beneath her black coat.

Hannah paused. The book wouldn't wield her. She was the witch. She would wield it. "Senties dolorum," she commanded.

Beatrice yelped in pain and fell on her side. She flinched, her joints popping. Her snout shortened into a human nose as her fur peeled back to reveal smooth, creamy skin.

Hannah recognized the young girl howling at her feet. It was the girl from the memory spell who was compelled to join Mara's coven before Raven tried to intervene. This was what Mara had turned her into? A shapeshifting wolf?

Hannah's heart pounded against her chest, and her hands trembled upon the grimoire. Fear prickled at the back of her neck. But almost immediately, her grip tightened around the spell book, its influence soothing her nerves. Her hands steadied and the fluttering in her chest eased. The grimoire took advantage of Hannah's surprised state and reigned her back in under its influence. *Remedium,* the book chanted to Hannah, and she had no choice but to repeat the grimoire's spell. "Remedium," she repeated through gritted teeth. Despite the comfort it provided her, she needed to resist its pull.

Beatrice's naked body relaxed. She sucked in deep breaths and lifted herself to her feet. Even in her human form, she bared her teeth and snarled at Hannah.

"Hand over the book."

Hannah held out the book, then gripped it to her chest. "Do you remember me?" Hannah winced, clutching the book. "I tried to stop Mara and Callan from turning you into this. It's me, Beatrice. I'm Raven Harlowe."

Hannah didn't know whether Beatrice would remember Raven's efforts to save her, but it was the only trick she had left. And when she declared herself to be Raven, she somehow felt stronger against the grimoire's compulsion. In the game of tug-of-war they were playing, Hannah was winning.

Beatrice, however, seemed too fixated on the book to listen to Hannah's words. She burst forward to grab it. Hannah swung it away and smacked it against Beatrice's face. The pewter lock cut her cheek. She stumbled back, pressing a finger to her temple.

Beatrice snarled, and black fur rippled up her arms. As Beatrice transformed, Hannah felt the grimoire's magic leave her body. It was as if it didn't want to chance being used again; the book only wanted Hannah to do its bidding, not the other way around.

She knew she couldn't outrun Beatrice. She'd be torn to shreds before she reached the dock. She didn't want to die, but maybe she could see her parents again. Would it be quick? Slow and agonizing? Would Callan miss her? Would Mara plague the world with darkness? Would Callan succumb to evil? Was this all real?

Beatrice's last claw punctured out of her paw, and she

ferociously snapped at Hannah, drool sliding off her fangs. Hannah managed one last terrified breath before Beatrice propelled toward her.

Hannah crashed to the ground. Her head banged against a table leg. The weight of Beatrice on her chest made it difficult to breathe. Her snout was so close that she could smell Beatrice's metallic breath. The wolf's growl vibrated through Hannah's entire body, causing her to tremble. Beatrice widened her mouth before rearing her head back.

Hannah closed her eyes and reconciled herself with death. She'd be with her parents soon.

Before any teeth sank into her skin, Beatrice yelped in pain and her entire bodyweight slumped on top of Hannah. She felt something warm spread across her stomach and seep onto the floor beside her. Blood pooled in the carpet.

Callan pulled the dead wolf off Hannah and helped her to her feet. Her entire body quivered at the sight of her blood-soaked shirt. Thankfully, none of the blood belonged to her. She looked down at Beatrice and saw the fishing spear Callan pierced through her hide.

"Are you all right?" he asked, except Hannah was too distracted to answer. She watched as the dead wolf shrank into a dead young girl.

Callan followed her gaze to Beatrice and recoiled. "I did this," he said quietly.

"She was going to kill me," Hannah said, still stunned by how young Beatrice looked.

"She would not be here, following Mara's commands, if it was not for me." He wrapped his hands over his head and winced at the swollen lump forming on the side of his face.

Hannah remembered the memory: Callan didn't want to

do Mara's bidding, but she was simply too powerful to deny. Callan punched the wall so hard that it cracked. He screamed—filled with anger and pain. He slumped onto the floor and held his face in his hands. When he removed them, they were soaked with tears.

Hannah grabbed a blanket from the floor by the couch and draped it over Beatrice's dead body. She crouched next to Callan and gently cupped her hands around his face, gazing into his vibrant green eyes.

"You didn't do this," she said. "Mara did this. She is to blame."

Callan brushed Hannah's hands away and stood up. He paced away from her, his hands stiffened into fists. "Do not absolve me of this. I knew of what Mara was doing. I could feel her control over me. I was simply not strong enough."

"Callan..."

"'Twas easier to follow her. And because I could not fight it, people died. I helped Mara curse their souls to darkness without blinking an eye."

"I was there, Callan." Hannah stood in front of him. "I know exactly what happened. Raven, the only one in Mara's magical league, couldn't even do it. You tried. And she knew that. *I* know that. Mara was just too strong—too dark."

Callan looked Hannah over, seemingly unburdened by her words.

Hannah couldn't help but feel protective over him. She couldn't stand that he blamed himself for all that had happened. A massive sense of guilt for ever doubting him snuck up on her. Her heart was filled with an overwhelming desire to hold and care for Callan. She couldn't tell, however, if those were her feelings or Raven's. Was there any difference? Hannah took Callan's hand and interlaced their fingers. "Which is why we have to stop her."

Callan nodded, unable—or unwilling—to break his gaze away from Hannah. "The spell worked? You remember?"

"Yes." Hannah's heartbeat accelerated as Callan moved himself closer to her. "I saw the hold Mara had over you." Callan brushed one of Hannah's rogue curls behind her ear. "I also saw how drawn you were to Raven, and she to you." He tilted his gaze, seeming solely focused on Hannah's blue eyes. "You truly loved her." Callan barely let Hannah finish her sentence before he kissed her.

The press of his lips on hers was exhilarating. The adrenaline that had been fighting to escape her for years pumped through her veins. It felt like many small electrical currents were hovering over her skin and zooming out of control, but in a good way—a passionate way. Hannah wrapped her arms behind Callan's back and grasped at the defined muscles beneath his shirt. He ran his fingers through her hair and pressed her body to his.

Hannah felt his Siren influence tug at the back of her mind, but ignored it. This wasn't because of what Mara turned him into. This was Hannah's own attraction and feelings for the man she was so cosmically entwined with.

Callan sweetly kissed Hannah's neck. Between a breath, he whispered, "How I have missed you."

Hannah paused and took a step back.

"What is wrong?" Callan asked.

Hannah looked at him and tried to ignore how handsome he was—how drawn to him she felt. Though she wasn't ignorant to the fact that the familiarity she felt for him was a result of having known him—having loved him —in a past life, she was certain that the emotions growing within her for Callan were her own. He had opened her up to an entirely new and impossible world where she had discovered more about herself than she ever had before. He brought her answers. And though they may not have been answers Hannah wanted, they were honest and exactly what she needed. He had helped her understand the mysterious energy, adrenaline, anxiety that had been brewing within her over the last two years. While Callan had been explaining magic to Hannah, she felt that he *was* her magic. He was unlike anyone she had ever met, already unable to stand the thought of life without him. But he didn't feel those things for her. He felt them for someone else.

"I am not Raven," she said.

"I know that."

"Do you? Because you haven't known me long enough to miss me."

"That was not my intention. It simply pleases me that you remember. You know what we experienced together." He reached for Hannah's hand, but she pulled back.

"That spell connected me to Raven's memory. And even though I saw what happened between the two of you, I didn't experience it. It was like watching a play or a movie."

"I am sorry," Callan said. "But even if you do not feel it, you *are* Raven. You used to be, at the very least. You appear the same, you possess her magic…"

"I'm nothing like her," Hannah shouted. Tears burned behind her eyes. "She was strong and powerful and determined. She was brave."

"You are brave."

"I'm scared shitless! I was nearly killed by a wolf who was also a young girl. There's a Vampire on the loose, and the Devil *herself* is looking for us." The Hannah who was comforting Callan moments ago had completely disappeared. Too many emotions whirled within her that she didn't know how to feel. The confusion resulted in panic.

"I know 'tis much to handle." He took a cautious step forward.

"Midterms are a lot to handle. Supernatural creatures and learning I have magic are unthinkable." Tears slipped down Hannah's cheeks and their presence only frustrated her further. She released an embittered huff. "And now I'm crying. Great."

"You should be crying." Callan's words surprised Hannah. "I would be concerned if you were unaffected by all of this. It is still baffling to me, and I have been living with it for over three hundred years. Granted, I have been frozen in stone for most of that..." Callan grinned. "And I know you are not Raven. It is an adjustment, but I do feel the difference."

Though Hannah appreciated Callan's ability to differentiate between herself and Raven, it deflated her. While the memory spell provided her insight to her past life, it also created a massive inferiority complex within Hannah. She could never be as good as Raven, and maybe Callan saw that too.

"You are in error, however," Callan continued. "Despite your differences, I see her within you. You are strong and brave and forgiving and smart." He inched closer to Hannah as he spoke. "You know how I know this?"

Hannah tilted her eyes up toward his, waiting for his answer.

"Because you are here with me now, desiring to defeat Mara. Raven did not have to fight against her, but she did. In that way, you are exactly the same."

Hannah looked upon Callan's tender face and allowed his soothing voice to brush against her skin. Her tears subsided. He skimmed the few remaining droplets away from her freckled cheeks.

"Thank you," she said. "Still, I think we should avoid... kissing and stuff..." Hannah cringed at her awkwardness and attempted to push away the intense attraction she felt for him. "...until we figure some things out."

"What things?"

"Until you get to know me—Hannah. And then you can decide whether you actually have..."

"Feelings?"

"Yes." Though Hannah knew this was the best course of action, she hoped he would reassure her that he already shared how she felt now.

"All right," he said. Callan stepped away and shook his head.

Hannah's heart dropped. "Okay then," she said. They stood with a few feet of space between them. The grimoire rested, tempting, on the floor.

"So, how do we destroy this thing?"

CHAPTER TWELVE

*A*fter sending Beatrice into the water, Callan and Hannah arrived at *Cape Cove Campgrounds: Untouched by Time*. She was able to replace her bloodied sweater with a long-sleeved polo shirt she found on the boat. It was oversized, a men's size, but it was better than walking around damp with the irony scent of a young girl's blood across her stomach.

Without any money for a bus or taxi, they walked along the New England backroads for about an hour, barely speaking the whole way there. Hannah could tell that Callan was wracked by guilt. Not only had he helped turn Beatrice into a dark creature, but he also killed her in order to save Hannah's life. No amount of reassurance could ease the anguish he felt.

"The rest of the town appears entirely different. These woods, however, have not changed in the slightest," he said. Hannah felt relief at the broken silence.

The leaves of the trees bristled with vibrant shades of yellow, orange, and red. As the sun broke through the branches, the varying colors created a warm glow to the woods.

"Why these woods? Don't you think Mara and Nathaniel will know to look for us here?" Hannah asked.

"Perhaps, eventually. For now, they provide us distance from your school and the town. Journeying deep into the woods will bestow us privacy to destroy the grimoire once and for all."

Hannah's bag was slug across her chest, the spell book safely inside. Though it still attempted to lure her to its pages, it was easier for Hannah to resist since the memory spell. Destroying it would weaken Mara. After experiencing what the she-Devil was capable of, Hannah knew they needed every advantage against her.

"What was the spell I said that caused you pain?" Hannah could remember the terrifying words but was afraid to say them out loud in case her magic followed her command. "The one that Mara's grimoire told me to say?"

"Senties dolorum. 'Tis a Latin command to feel pain."

"Pretty on-the-nose..."

"Latin is the old tongue used to access magic. Just as any speech progresses throughout time, the way witches communicate to magic changed as well. Those old spells take great power to access, which is why the language faded within spells among witches. Only those granted with extreme tilted magic have the power to cast those spells."

"Tilted magic?" Gravel crunched beneath Hannah's feet.

"Do not pretend as though you do not already understand," Callan said. "While Mara was granted with magic that slanted toward darkness, Raven converged with a power that favored the light. Magic that is now within you."

Hannah lowered her head, feeling guilty for possessing power she didn't even know how to use. "How did you know I knew?"

"The memory spell worked," he said. "And though your words often sound foreign to me, I understood your meaning when you stated that Raven was in *Mara's magical league*." Birds flitted from branch to branch above. Chipmunks skittered through the brown and orange leaves that coated the path.

"I'd actually read about it before even meeting you. As if fate was trying to prepare me for my destiny...or some crap like that." Hannah cringed. Though she felt it more and more with everything she learned, it still felt unnatural to surrender to such an unknown force. "Why didn't you tell me?"

"I did not believe Raven could be reincarnated—no spell of Mara's has ever failed. Therefore, I could not be certain if that kind of prodigy magic could be reincarnated. 'Twasn't until you resisted my compulsion that I knew."

"You could have told me then." What other useful information could Callan have been holding back from Hannah?

"I sensed you were already overwhelmed with the discovery of magic. You had only learned about the Convergence..." He breathed a long pause. "I did not think it wise to tell you that you are one of the most powerful witches the world has ever known."

Callan's words hit Hannah like a cannon ball. She stopped walking and felt as though she might be sick. She wasn't powerful. She killed her parents with this unknown magic. She was sad—tragic even—but certainly not formidable in any way. She was chasing a new life, but it felt like running away.

"I'm not powerful. I may have some sort of magic within me, but it's useless." She ground her shoes against the pebbles and dirt.

Callan stopped alongside Hannah and faced her. "Your magic saved your life. It protects you whenever it senses danger. And it has done this without you even knowing it existed. I would not call that useless." Callan continued walking, but Hannah remained in place.

"If I'm so powerful, then why haven't I cast any spells? I've had magic for nearly two years, and I've never even accidentally said a spell."

"That is why spells rhyme and sound different from our everyday speech. Your magic must be able to differentiate and feel the intention behind your spell. Otherwise, any moment a witch wished ill feelings upon another, their magic could make it so."

"That's good, I suppose," Hannah said, following Callan through the woods. They weaved through tall conifers and oak hickories off the beaten path, wrens chirping above. The scent of pine and rich soil emanated from every crunchy step they took.

"'Tis good until one's brain goes blank and cannot think of a proper rhyme to fit the spell."

Hannah gulped. "Maybe it's a good thing that I don't have access to Raven's magic, then."

"It is your magic, Hannah. And you do have access to it. It simply takes time to connect to it properly—to learn how to wield it."

Hannah nodded, still doubting whether she would ever fully comprehend or connect to the unknown force that whirled within her. And why would she? It invaded her body and caused the death of her parents. What if connecting to her magic caused more harm than good?

Could she really bring herself to wield the weapon that murdered her mom and dad?

"In the meantime, your magic is protective of you. You can feel it communicating with you, and in time, you shall be able to communicate back."

"If Raven had all this power, then why did she die?"

Callan paused, but kept looking ahead, deep into the forest. Sunlight peered through yellow and orange leaves. His skin shone golden brown. "I ask myself that question every day."

THEY ARRIVED AT A CLEARING IN THE WOODS, and it was exactly the same as Hannah remembered from the memory spell and her vivid dream of burning at the stake. The tall post even remained in the center of the open space, decaying and shaded by overhanging branches. A tension hung between them as they both stared at the stake—Callan with a look of shame, and Hannah fighting off the lingering heat she felt and the phantom scent of seared flesh from the memory of Raven's execution.

Hannah pulled the grimoire from her bag. She threw it on the ground and paced around it. "What now? How do we destroy it?" she asked.

"Burning it shall be a good start."

Hannah nodded.

Callan leaned over the book. Hatred filled his face as he hovered his hands over its leather binding. "Be rid of these pages, this book of malice and dread. Burn its binding, never again to be read."

The grimoire erupted in flames, but the fire didn't curl the binding or burn the brittle pages. Callan continued,

"Fight through its magic with lightning's flash, dissolve its evil to eternal ash!"

A bright stream of lighting shot down from the sky and struck Mara's grimoire with a relentless roar. Hannah shrieked and fell backward. She was overcome by the memory of the white light that pierced through her parents' car and the look of terror on her mother's face.

The same look appeared on Hannah's; blood drained from her cheeks, and pressure rose in her chest. Callan broke his focus and glanced at Hannah over his shoulder. The lightning ceased, and he dashed to her side.

Despite clutching onto the red and yellow leaves against the earth, Hannah could feel the cold water rise higher and higher, drowning the car. Her breath was fast and erratic. "I'm sorry," she cried. "I'm sorry. I'm sorry."

"It is all right. I should have remembered," Callan said. He reached his hand under her thick hair and caressed her neck.

But Hannah wasn't apologizing to Callan for freaking out. She was apologizing to her parents. She saw them struggle as they inhaled the unrelenting water, eventually fading to stillness—their expressions transitioning from panic and fear to absolute nothingness. She tried to ground herself from the flashback by holding onto Callan's side, bunching his sweatshirt in her hand, but was overcome by a new vision she had never seen before.

Hannah choked back water as she watched life fade from her parents. Her eyes soon matched their vacancy, her body having submitted to drowning. In the next second, however, a flash of white light darted from Hannah's chest and snapped her seatbelt. Another vast strike of light burst the car door open. It pushed Hannah out of the sunken car. Enveloped in glowing orbs, she was brought to the surface. It ushered her ashore, Hannah lying unconscious against the muddy embankment. The glimmering light settled above her chest and dissolved inside of her.

Hannah gasped for air as she broke out of the memory. But this wasn't a memory of hers, as she never knew how she made it to the bank of the lake. This must have been her magic showing her what *it* remembered from that night. It rescued her, truly protecting her from death. While her first instinct was to be angry that it hadn't saved her parents, she also came to the realization that her magic was simply trying to survive—and that meant keeping Hannah safe.

"What just happened?" Callan stared at Hannah with both shock and concern. "Your eyes went white, and you were in some kind of trance. Did the grimoire take hold of you?" Callan cradled her as if she were dying in his arms.

"No," Hannah said, still catching her breath. She sat up and held steady in Callan's arms. "It was my magic... talking to me." Hannah's eyes filled with veneration.

Callan relaxed.

"You were right," she said. "It does protect me."

THEY MADE ZERO PROGRESS ON DESTROYING Mara's grimoire despite being there for hours. It was clearly protected, which meant they had to find another way to destroy Mara.

"Is there a magic binding spell? In the memory spell, Mara's parents mentioned binding her magic..."

"You require an entire coven to perform that spell. And only high priestesses are taught how to bind magic. 'Tis not an option." Callan paced back and forth. Every so often, he'd pause and look up at the warm-colored trees.

"Should we keep moving, then? The longer we stay here, the faster she could track us, right?"

"In order to destroy her, we may need her to find us." Callan turned to Hannah, and she could see that he was deep in thought, eyes creased and nodding to himself.

"Destroy her?" Hannah asked. She gulped. "You mean kill her." Though Hannah had considered this, she didn't want to say it out loud. Not only was the thought terrifying, but it also seemed impossible.

"'Tis the only way," Callan said.

"Right now? Shouldn't we keep moving until we figure out a plan?"

"She shall defeat us every time when it comes to magic."

Hannah's face soured. She knew he wasn't doing it intentionally, but it was as if Callan was reminding Hannah of how ineffectual her magic was. Though she was supposedly the most powerful witch the world had ever known, her magic was smothered within her useless shell of a body.

"You defeated her before."

Callan looked at Hannah as if he were missing something.

"Imprisoning her in stone for all those years."

"And all other magic, including myself. That spell nearly killed me, Hannah. I was not strong enough for it." He paced, his knuckles whitening against his fists.

"Then how did you pull it off?"

"I was empowered by rage and so overburdened by guilt that I did not care if the spell *did* kill me. I had nothing to lose." He raised his chin.

"I think you're more powerful than you know." Hannah smirked at Callan, who shook his head in denial.

"The only way I foresee us defeating her," he continued, "is by tricking her. Getting her alone. Earning her trust. And when she lowers her guard, I strike."

"Strike? Like what? Hit her over the head with a tree branch? Stab her with the scissors in my bag?"

"Scissors would not be sufficient."

"You don't think she'd see an attack like that coming? If she casted a protection spell on her grimoire, I'm sure she would cast one on herself."

"Well, I cannot come up with superior options." His voice raised in frustration. "Can you?"

The grimoire nestled against the forest floor, unscathed by their attempts to destroy it. "Maybe there is something in there that can help me access my magic. You said it yourself. Raven was a magical prodigy, which means her magic—my magic—might be the best option we have at defeating her."

"'Tis too risky," Callan said. "Raven studied how to use magic for the entirety of her life. She then had two years more of practicing her magic once she converged. Even then, she could not defeat Mara."

Hannah felt unsettled by Callan's words—his confirmation that she would never be as good as Raven. He was right. Raven was much more skilled than she would ever be. But in her dream of burning at the stake, Raven never put up a fight. If she had such strong magic within her, why didn't she use it?

"Furthermore," Callan continued, "the only spells you shall find in that book, which would connect you to your magic, are ones that do not end well."

"What do you mean?"

"You may end up like me, or some other creature destined for darkness."

"You're not destined for darkness." Hannah placed one hand on the side of his face. Although she knew she shouldn't, not comforting him at all felt cold. "Look at all you've done. If anything, you bring hope to every one of Mara's victims." She found herself getting lost in Callan's green eyes. She stepped away. "The fact that you broke out from under her control proves that you are strong, and you are good." Hannah's gaze shifted. Brown and white mushrooms clustered around a fallen tree, bland in comparison to Callan's enchanting green eyes.

He, however, looked straight at her. "Thank you," he said.

Hannah cleared her throat. "So you think the best way to beat her is to regain her trust?"

"I do have two things that would make my story plausible."

Hannah already knew the two things he was referring to. He had the grimoire and he had her.

"I shall claim that the grimoire brought me back to darkness—that if I desired to regain favor with her, I would have to bring her something special. Who better than Raven reincarnate?"

"And what if she tries to compel you again? I won't be able to snap you out of it."

"I broke that bond. Unless I voluntarily submit to it, she shan't have that power over me."

"How do you know?"

"Because I know the consequences of yielding to her power. I shan't allow myself to do that again."

Hannah searched for another option, but they'd already been at this for hours. "And what if she kills me?" Mara hadn't hesitated to kill Raven. What was to stop her from murdering Hannah the moment Callan offered her up?

Callan arrived at her side and went to take her hand. When Hannah rolled her fingers into a fist, he simply offered her a gentle touch on the shoulder. "I shan't let that happen. I promise you."

Hannah took a deep breath and made the active decision to trust Callan. She hoped to God, or whatever supernatural forces out there, that he was strong enough to pull this off—because she was not.

CHAPTER THIRTEEN

*C*allan tied Hannah's hands behind the charred post in the middle of the clearing. "How does that feel?" he asked. "You should be able to slip out of them if you must."

"Good," Hannah said. Her voice was dry, and she desperately tried to keep her memories of Raven burning at bay. She was just a college freshman focused on normal college things, and now, somehow, she was bait in a plot to kill an evil witch.

How had this happened? Hannah took a few deep breaths to calm herself. However, the dark clouds rolling over the forest didn't help her anxiety. The clearing's warm glow dissipated into a cool and eerie atmosphere. The rotting wood smelled of ash and mildew. As shadows occupied the air, Hannah felt a sinister shiver roll up her spine.

Two figures glided toward them. One was Nathaniel, his grey eyes glowing through the gloomy air. The other donned a long, black cloak with a hood that arched over most of her face. When she looked up, the hood revealed her blood-red eyes. Every muscle in Hannah's body tensed, her nerves on fire. This wasn't a dream or a memory spell. Hannah was face to face with Mara Eden, the Devil herself.

Callan walked away from Hannah. He rolled his shoulder back, standing straight, the grimoire at his feet.

"We meet again after all these years," he said, conjuring a look of wonder and admiration.

Before he could continue, Mara flung out her hand and commanded, "Volant." A gust of black wind plumed from her palm.

Callan flew through the air and hit a tree with a *thud*.

Hannah knew that she couldn't call out in concern. She was supposed to be his captive. Therefore, she only let a whimper escape her.

Mara held Callan against the tree, a few feet above the ground. "Suffocant." A ring of black smoke tightened around his neck. His face twisted at the terrifying wails sounding from Mara's magic.

"Mara," he pleaded, scratching at his neck. "I am sorry. Prithee...stop..."

Mara held both her hands in the air toward Callan. Her expression was one of hatred and vengeance. "You cursed me to stone," she shouted. "For over 300 years." She closed her hands into fists. The black smoke constricted tighter around Callan's throat.

His words came out as rasps. His face darkened to purple.

"You betrayed me," Mara's voice cracked. Maybe Callan was more to her than a simple puppet. Maybe she actually cared for him. But was someone so consumed by darkness capable of such emotion?

When Callan's eyes rolled back, Mara dropped her hands. The smoke rushed back to her palms as Callan crashed to the forest floor. He coughed, over and over, unable to catch a breath.

Nathaniel stood a few paces behind Mara and laughed—probably happy to see him suffer after snapping his neck on the campus cliffs. Hannah wanted to release herself from the post and help Callan, but doing so would ruin their charade. At least the panic she felt aligned with being held captive.

"I have seen the error of my ways," Callan said, rubbing the ashen marks against his neck. He crawled against the brush and kept his head bowed. "If I could go back in time and undo the spell I cast, I would."

"You seem to be singing a different tune, brother." Nathaniel marched to Mara's side. Not only did Callan have to convince Mara of his loyalty, but he would have to persuade Nathaniel that he had changed his mind overnight. Hannah hoped that Callan could lie convincingly.

He struggled to his feet and gaped at Nathaniel, an ache in his eyes. "I apologize for resisting you, Nathaniel. I had not yet remembered the magnetism of the dark—the potential for power in submitting oneself to black magic."

"And how did you arrive at that conclusion, my young Siren?" Mara asked, her eyes burning bright.

"Your grimoire must have sensed my inner turmoil." Callan motioned to the spell book that sat on the ground beside him. "It connected with me. Reminded me of how I was once liberated from conventional magic by your teachings. Raven never cared for me," he said, a bitter sorrow in his voice. "She only cared about defeating you. I was weak. I fell for her lies."

Mara's face softened, her lips showing the vaguest hint of satisfaction. Callan took another prudent step forward.

Hannah was pleased that he was so persuasive, but she was also nervous that perhaps there was some truth to his speech. After all, she knew that he was capable of turning to the dark.

"And so, you betrayed your beloved and tied her to the very post where she burned all those years ago." Mara puckered her lips and peered at Hannah as if she were a snack to devour at any moment.

Hannah squirmed at the ants she felt crawling up her arms, but that was nothing compared to Mara's piercing glare.

Callan showed the slightest hint of concern. "She is not my beloved," he said. "Hannah, unlearned in the ways of magic, is Raven reincarnate. She is my offering to you. A symbol of my remorse. To prove that I am your loyal servant once more."

Mara took slow steps toward Hannah. Beneath her dark cloak, she wore a crimson corset and black skirt, smudged with dirt. Her frame was slight—definitely not a reflection of the power she possessed. Despite the crow's feet etched into the corners of her eyes, the rest of her skin was smooth, unburdened by the darkness she cast. "When Nathaniel informed me that he saw Miss Raven Harlowe reborn, I did not believe him. How could one of my spells, revered by darkness, possibly have failed? But here you are, as Miss Hannah Fenwick. Offered up on a silver platter for the taking." Mara stepped closer. Hannah could feel her own magic surging through her. It could sense Mara's presence, and it either wanted to flee or attack. "This is not the first time we have crossed paths, though, is it?" While keeping her eyes glued to Hannah, Mara flung her hand back toward Callan and chanted, "Vinculum!"

The black smoke whipped out of Mara's hand and

wrapped Callan like a lasso. It forced him back against the tree and restrained him upon it. Piercing shrieks swallowed Callan whole. His face contorted in anguish. Even Hannah wished she could block the fearful squeals from her ears.

Nathaniel blurred to Callan's side and dragged a rusted dagger against his throat. If Callan continued to squirm, the blade would surely slit his flesh. "You should have come with me when you had the chance," he whispered.

"You did not think I would have sensed the memory spell?" Spit sprayed onto Hannah's face as Mara screamed. It smelled of rot, and Hannah itched to wipe it away. "I am surprised wee Hannah here did not disclose of our encounter."

Hannah's heart raced at the memory.

"And where is Beatrice, might I add? I guess you did not have the warm and fuzzy reunion I had hoped for?" Mara didn't display any signs of grief or heartbreak when she mentioned Beatrice. She was simply a soldier to her—a casualty in her war of darkness.

Hannah's skin heated to the point where she could feel perspiration hovering on her brow. Her face turned a feverish red as Mara circled her, sniffing the air.

Mara drew in a sharp breath, then exhaled slowly, exuberantly satisfied. Her vermilion eyes smoldered. "I can smell your fear, my dear." She licked her lips. "How luscious."

"Mara, prithee, do not—" Callan called from the tree, but Mara abruptly cut him off with a blow of her hand.

"You think me that foolish, Mr. Delmonte?"

Hannah knew that the charade was up, and when she looked at Callan, she could tell that he knew as well. Fear crawled over her skin, like frost invading the shadows on a cold wintery night.

They had failed.

"I had hoped." Callan's facade dropped, and he looked at Mara with distain.

"You know me better than that." Mara smirked at Callan and released a brief cackle. Mara refocused on Hannah, looking over her with sour curiosity. "Now," she said, rubbing her hands together. "I think 'tis time I see where my spell went wrong." She raised her hands toward Hannah's head.

Hannah felt panic in every crevice of her body. She was tempted to surrender to the hopelessness that grew with every step Mara took toward her. But she wouldn't let her fear feed her. She needed to be brave. This couldn't be the end of their story.

In one swift motion, Hannah tore her hands from the binding. She could feel her magic surge within her. She swung her hands at Mara, and a spark of white light burst from her fingertips.

Mara stumbled backward but used her shadows to keep her from falling. The screeching tendrils rebounded against the dry forest floor and propelled Mara back on her feet.

The white magic radiated around Hannah's hand. She was mesmerized by its pearly sheen. It disappeared back into her body, but its energy coursed through her blood. It was a shield, protecting Hannah while she was vulnerable. Hopefully someday soon, she'd forge her magic into a sword.

Hannah snapped out of her daze. She stretched her hands in front of her, palms outward, sparked with shards of light. She hoped that Mara was ignorant to the fact that she had no idea how to truly use her magic.

Mara laughed, turning to face Hannah. A raw, pink burn bubbled upon her ashen skin. "You silly girl." The burn peeled away. Fresh, smooth skin replaced it as ruinous clouds rolled above the trees. "Impediendum," she hissed.

Black smoke sprouted from Mara's back like reptilian wings. It came down upon Hannah like a dragon's fiery breath. She was deafened by the petrified screams, paralyzed with fear. Hopelessness engulfed her. She would do anything to be free of this terror.

"Hannah!" Callan screamed.

Hannah was blind against the thick smog and could barely hear him over the mass of cries that smothered her. She remembered the freezing spell Callan put on her when they were in the cave and thought that this might be similar. But when Hannah felt her magic freeze inside herself, she knew this was so much worse. She felt as though she had been solidified—her organs were rocks beneath sheets of dry, cracking skin. She tried to move, but it was impossible; even breathing proved difficult.

The smoke cleared, and with it, the terrified screams. Mara was only inches away, her eyes burning into Hannah's gaze. Hannah was frozen, stunned by the overwhelming fear Mara instilled within her. While she could hear Callan struggling against Nathaniel, she couldn't move, couldn't see him. She was trapped beneath Mara's red glare.

"Let us see where I went wrong, shall we?" Mara burrowed her sharp fingernails into Hannah's skull. Her magic seared into her mind, blazing the meninges of her brain. She gasped and tried to scream, but like a nightmare, no sound came out.

This wasn't like the memory spell. Hannah felt as though she had been pushed off a cliff, plummeting into the memory of Raven's death. Hannah was not a spectator here. She was Raven, tied to the post as Mara taunted her with her smugness.

"*Take one long look at your beloved,*" Mara said. "*For it shall be your last.*" Mara flicked her cloak and returned to Callan's side, among the circle of her creatures and followers.

Before Mara started her spell, Raven summoned her magic. She called upon as much power as it could offer, mustering all her strength and courage. She knew that in the next few minutes, she would be dead. But she also knew that this was necessary. Pure sacrifice in the name of white magic will tip the scales away from evil, Raven thought, reassuring herself of what she must do. She pushed away any ounce of fear within herself and put complete faith in her magic. As **Mara** cast her spell, <u>Raven</u> quietly chanted along with her, line by line.

"The life I take in the name of darkness, is that of Raven Harlowe." | <u>"The life I save in the name of light, is Callan Delmonte, my love."</u>

"May her defiance cause her death, one that is grim and slow." | <u>"May the sacrifice of my death, give him the strength to rise above."</u>

"May these eighteen years be her last—in no future lives, shall she grow." | <u>"Fight against this evil chant, that prohibits my rebirth…"</u>

"Now let the fire blaze and burn, condemning her to eternal woe!"

As soon as Mara's last word left her mouth, fire erupted around the wooden post and crawled over Raven's body. Despite her burning flesh, Raven knew she had to finish her spell to successfully bargain with the pulsing magic in the clearing, both white and black fighting against each other.

<u>"Make it so, every eighteenth year, that I'm returned to the earth."</u>

Raven felt the flames against her flesh and screamed louder than the high-pitched whistle of the cracking wood.

Hannah was pulled from Raven's burning body to the sound of Mara's minacious laughter. She plummeted back into her own body in the clearing with Mara, Nathaniel, and Callan.

"Absolvo," Mara said between her cackles.

Hannah gasped for air as elasticity returned to her body. It was as if the cement shell plastered on her skin was cracked and brushed away, allowing her magic to awaken. She frantically pieced together Raven's spell and recited it in her mind.

The life I save in the name of light, is Callan Delmonte, my love.

May the sacrifice of my death, give him the strength to rise above.

Fight against this evil chant, that prohibits my rebirth.

Make it so, every eighteenth year, that I'm returned to the earth.

It took Hannah a few seconds to decipher and absorb Raven's spell. Once she did, she understood why Mara was so pleased.

Mara had found the answer she was looking for—how Hannah, the image of Raven Harlowe, could possibly be standing in front of her. Raven had sacrificed herself so that white magic would set Callan free.

Callan stood, bound by Mara's shadows. He looked at Hannah with concern, clearly not understanding what had just transpired. Despite being released from Mara's spell, Hannah couldn't bring herself to move or speak.

Callan struggled against the tree, but Nathaniel pressed the blade to his neck. "Listen to my voice, Nathaniel,"

Callan said. Hannah could hear his Siren tone coming through, and she knew it wouldn't work. "Release me and impale yourself with that blade."

Nathaniel winced and shook his head, resisting Callan's charm. "I already told you, brother. Mara's commands trump your trickery."

"You may release him, Nathaniel. Let him run into the arms of his beloved," Mara said. Nathaniel freed Callan, allowing him to rush to Hannah's side. "For he may not have long left to be with his Raven," Mara whispered.

"What happened?" he asked. "What has she done to you?" Callan ran his hand over Hannah's hair and gazed into her disturbed eyes. Hannah was too stunned to answer.

"Sly Miss Raven Harlowe made a deal with the Devil," Mara said with a smug grin.

"What is she talking about?" Callan shook Hannah. Tears rolled down her cheeks.

"And not a very good one, might I add," Mara said.

Callan turned to Mara. "Spit it out, you miserable crone. What did you do?"

"Raven cast a spell within mine. She would be reborn, but not for very long." Mara looked down at Hannah. "I wonder if this version of Raven is as selfless or devout as the Raven I knew three hundred years ago."

Desperate, Callan turned to Hannah and placed his hands on her shoulders. "Hannah, prithee. What does she speak of?"

Hannah swallowed a dry knot in her throat and took a deep breath. "Raven made it so that she could be reincarnated, but only until she turned eighteen in each life." Having been inside Raven's mind, Hannah knew that it was not only a compromise to not being reborn at all, but also an offering she made in order to set Callan free.

Though Callan's face dropped, he didn't let go of Hannah. She could tell that he was trying to be strong for her sake. She knew that she couldn't tell him that Raven's sacrifice was partially a bargaining chip for his freedom. It would destroy him. She only hoped that Mara didn't divulge this information.

"How long?" he asked, his voice quiet and controlled.

Hannah's entire body shuddered just as a car would before breaking down. "I turn eighteen in one week."

CHAPTER FOURTEEN

*N*umbness glazed over every inch of Hannah's body. She embraced it. Tall trees loomed above, the sunlight making their bark appear red. She breathed in the cool air and basked in its fresh, earthy scent. She wondered what this place would look like once winter hit. Glistening white snow would erase all the dead leaves. She was looking forward to experiencing a New England winter for the first time, but now, that wasn't going to happen.

Hannah shuddered to erase the thought. If she were to truly process the fact that she only had one week left to live, she would crumble to the forest ground and disintegrate into the earth.

"Undo this now!" Callan was on his feet in seconds, charging toward Mara.

"That is far enough," she said, threatening him with her shadows swirling in the palm of her hand.

"There must be something you can do," Callan pleaded.

"And why would you think that?"

"You do not need me to tell you how powerful you are,

Mara. She is harmless to you now. Prithee, undo this curse."

Mara stepped closer to Callan, bringing her face in front of his. She sniffed in his scent and exhaled in satisfaction. Enthralled by him, she hovered her lips close to his, almost as a test to see what he was willing to stand for Hannah's benefit. Callan didn't move. Mara giggled behind pursed lips. It echoed in her throat. "You know I do not do anything for free," she said. She licked her lips and moved away from Callan. She picked up her grimoire and caressed it as if she had been reunited with a long-lost child. She pulled her hood over her jet-black hair and prompted her shadows to dance up her arms. She smiled, invigorated by their cries, and sauntered away. "Come, Nathaniel. Let us leave these two to say their goodbyes." Nathaniel followed Mara as she glided out of the forest.

"Prithee, wait," Callan pleaded.

Mara turned. Her red eyes shone from beneath her cloak. "You know what I desire, Mr. Delmonte. Come find me when you are ready to give it to me." Callan stared after them even once they disappeared into the trees. When he finally turned around, Hannah stared at him. She couldn't bear the panic on his face. She was hanging by a thread trying to deny her own dread. She couldn't possibly deal with his.

Callan rushed toward her. "I do not understand. Why would Raven do such a thing?"

Raven cursed herself to die over and over again in order to save Callan. Hannah had never known such love. Perhaps, with time, she could grow to love the beautiful young man standing before her. Time, however, was something she didn't have.

"She, uh..." Hannah's voice cracked, and she gulped

back another irritating knot. "She had to match Mara's spell in order to counteract it. So instead of *this eighteenth year* being her last, she made sure that magic understood that *each* eighteenth year would be her...my last." Hannah knew that she was bending the truth, but it was better than Callan blaming himself more than he already did. Though she could feel her numbness fading, she fought as hard as possible to keep it in place—tight fists, tensed stomach, fixating on the trees, the leaves, the sun, the air.

"Raven was more powerful than that. She could have done something differently," Callan shouted. He stalked back and forth, then paused to look at Hannah. Her body trembled, no matter how much she fought against it.

Callan stopped. He tucked her hair behind her ear and caressed her cheek with his thumb. "I am sorry. I am not ready to lose you again."

She didn't want to lose him either. She had learned more about herself in the past two days than she had in her entire life, and that was because of him. It was also because of him, however, that she was fated to die in one week's time. Her heart accelerated, causing her chest to heave. The shock was wearing off, and it felt as if her emotions had broken through the dam holding them back. Tears flooded her face and her knees buckled beneath her. She crumbled to the ground despite Callan catching her. He lowered her down and held her tight.

Hannah could feel her magic going wild, as if it was rupturing inside her. Little white bursts of light skipped all over her body. Callan jolted at the shock of her magic, but still he held her close, embracing the sting.

Hannah hyperventilated just as she did on top of the cliff after discovering the truth behind her parents' death. She should have just killed herself then—beaten her fate to the punch. Her magic may have saved her life, but it killed her parents. This was her punishment.

Her thoughts raced faster than the air trying to get into her lungs. A succession of memories plunged her below the surface of dark waters.

Drowning in the ocean. Salt water filled her lungs. She choked, coughed, bubbles exploded from her lips.

Lying in bed with a high fever, her entire body aching.

Falling off a horse and snapping her neck. Hannah grasped at her neck as if the pain were real and very present.

"Make it stop," she cried.

"What is happening? What can I do?" Callan asked, his voice trembling.

Choking to death on a piece of food.

Crashing into another car while driving and flying through the windshield.

"Siren me," she pleaded.

Callan's brow furrowed, and he shook his head. "I promised you I would never..."

"Do it," Hannah cried. She tapped her fingertips to her thumbs, over and over, but the coping strategy did nothing for her.

Crushed beneath rocks in an earthquake.

Freezing to death in the dark woods.

Hannah's teeth chattered, and her skin turned cold. He cupped her face in his hands and sweetened the quality of his voice. "Relax. Be at peace. You are safe. You do not feel any pain. There is nothing amiss."

She allowed his voice to wash over her, and the memories ceased to stab her mind. Her body stilled. Though her magic tried to fight against Callan's charm, Hannah ignored it. Hopefully, it would soon realize that Callan shared its overarching goal—to protect her.

She felt mesmerized by his green eyes and gazed at his soft lips. Without reservation, she kissed him. What had she been waiting for? She inhaled his satisfying scent and ran her finger along his neck. Her chest fluttered at how his smooth lips felt against hers. Maybe this moment could last forever.

He pulled away. "This is not you," he said.

Hannah had one week left to live, and she was going to give into her urges. "Compel me not to kiss you," she said, her daring blue eyes tilting up toward his gaze.

"You do not want to kiss me. You do not desire me at all."

Hannah identified his command and ignored it. She wrapped her arms around his neck, drew him close, and kissed him again. This time, he didn't pull away. It felt different from before. He was gentle and cautious, as if kissing someone for the first time.

Hannah dwelled in his embrace, only to feel her chest tighten and nerves prickle. When she resisted his command not to kiss him, she must have also pushed away his compulsion to feel no pain. Hannah stumbled out of Callan's embrace and kneeled in front of him. Sorrow, fear, and anger whirled through her all at once. She held her fists to her chest as if this would ease her distress. "I'm sorry," she said.

"You mustn't be sorry." He hugged Hannah tight, and she rested her head against his chest. He kissed her forehead. "We shall find a solution," he said. "I am not going to let you die."

"It's inevitable, Callan. I've died in every single one of my past lives on my eighteenth birthday. This time won't be any different." Hannah pried herself out of his arms, stood up, and stepped away. She ran her fingers through her curly chestnut hair.

Callan stood and brushed the dirt from his pants. "It is different. Magic has been reawakened in this life." He stepped toward her and offered her his hand. "And I am here with you now." Hannah looked at his hand as if taking it was an agreement to fight for her life. At first, she didn't know if she had the strength. Perhaps she should take her punishment in stride and accept her cosmic fate.

After a moment, however, she felt her magic swirl within her. She had come this far and learned so much about herself. Did she really want to start over? Or was this the life she was willing to fight for? It was far from perfect, but if she ever wanted to grow old in a world that wasn't overcome by darkness, this was all she had. She took a deep breath and put her hand in Callan's.

"I guess fighting against evil is as good a way as any to spend my last few days." Hannah forced a smirk, thinking it might distract her from the ticking clock that echoed in her head.

"We shan't fail, Hannah. I promise you." Callan kissed her hand.

She smiled, wishing he wouldn't make promises he couldn't keep. Then again, she promised that she wouldn't try to save him. If she was destined to die anyway, then keeping him from falling under Mara's spell wouldn't be much of a sacrifice. Maybe she was more like Raven than she thought.

"We must find Mara and take back her grimoire. I am certain there shall be a spell within those pages that can fix this," he said.

Hannah pursed her lips. "Before, you didn't even want to touch that book. Now you're ready to read from it?"

"I do not see any other option. No spell I conjure will be strong enough. The spells in that grimoire strike greater force than improvised spells."

Hannah took a deep breath. "Okay. How do we find her?"

"There is a tracking spell..."

"Great."

"But 'tis in her grimoire." Callan looked down at his shoes.

Frustration filled Hannah's chest. Time was moving faster than before, and for someone who was supposed to have prodigy magic within her, she felt helpless. And then, an idea dawned on her. Hannah's eyes widened, and she felt the tiniest glimmer of hope. "I know where we have to go."

CHAPTER FIFTEEN

The Cape Cove shuttle bus dropped Hannah and Callan outside the Harbor House Cafeteria on the Bellcliff campus. Callan followed Hannah's determined march. With only one week left to live, there was no time to waste.

"I don't know why I didn't realize it before," she said. "I recognized Raven's handwriting in the memory spell. I didn't connect the two before, but now...I think I know where it is."

Callan's face lit up. "Where?"

"Her writing is the same as an old manuscript I was reading for a class, at least...I think it is. It's in the Bellcliff Library."

They ran across campus.

"It's naïve to think that Mara is the only one who created a spell book," Hannah said. "Raven is her counterpart. She was just as powerful as Mara, but white magic acts different than black magic. It's not as...ostentatious or immediate, I guess."

"Someone is a quick study," Callan said, a lightness in his tone.

"I think Raven was creating her own book."

When they reached the library, Hannah wasn't surprised to find it empty. The sun was setting, and it was still only the first week of classes. The air smelled stale as Hannah led Callan up the spiral staircases to the third floor. Lamps provided dim light between the stacks. Hannah hesitated at the doorway of the Occult and Mysticism room. Goosebumps rose along her forearms. It felt like a lifetime ago that the grimoire whispered her name. Now, she stood there with only days left to live. She was no longer chasing some new, fresh start; she was trying to keep the life she already had. She thrust open the door, consequences be damned, and crossed the threshold.

It seemed smaller to her now, perhaps because her world view was so much larger than before. And just where she left it, the soft-bound, handwritten manuscript sat on the old table.

Callan and Hannah looked down at the piece of Raven that had lived on. Callan pointed to the sigils marked on the cover. "Raven would always sketch this."

"What does it mean?"

"'Tis a balance between light and darkness. She enjoyed drawing the sigil for light a little lower than the sigil for darkness."

"Having it outweigh the darkness," Hannah said. She gently picked up Raven's book and felt the softness of its pages on her fingertips. As she looked down at the work of her past life, she saw the sigil for light glow white, and the sigil for darkness float upon shadows. Hannah had seen this before, but she'd chalked it up to a symptom of her PTSD. Now, however, she knew that she wasn't imagining it. "Did you see that?" Hannah asked, unable to pull her eyes away from the animated sigils on the page.

"It recognizes your magic," he said.

The manuscript pages flipped on their own. They settled open on a spell with the heading, *To Discover What You Seek.* Below the heading read a small passage before the spell: *If your intentions are pure and in the name of light, then this magic may help you.*

"This is exactly what we need. It reads like an instruction manual," Hannah said.

"She wanted to become a High Priestess when she grew older—someone who teaches magic the *right* way," Callan said, imitating how Raven may have said it. "It does not surprise me that she was writing this to aid others."

Hannah and Callan shared a smile.

She handed the book to him. "I'll let you do the honors, since my magic is useless."

He held it open in his palms. "Your magic is not useless," he said. "You simply do not yet know how to access it."

With only a week to live, Hannah doubted she'd ever know what it truly felt like to connect with the magic inside herself.

"Here it goes," Callan said. He took a deep breath and read the words Raven crafted over three hundred years ago.

"Whether 'tis by heart or by mind, the desire that I need to find;
   Show me the way to what I need, ignore me or assist my plead.
   I shall speak it now, for what I desire,"

Callan broke from the chant.

"Mara Eden—and discover whence I follow the fire."

Callan's eyes lit up as if he were watching something

mystical transpire before his eyes. "Do you see that?" he asked.

"I don't see anything." Hannah searched the room for anything out of the ordinary, but nothing seemed different.

"'Tis a path of fire," he said. "Only the spell caster must be able to see it. We have to follow it before the spell wears off." He placed the spell book on the table and moved to the door.

"You don't know where it leads?" Hannah asked. "We have no idea how far away Mara may be. We could be walking all night." Her jaw tightened, and her entire posture stiffened in an attempt to control her vexation. She didn't have time to waste.

"Raven's book opened on this spell for a reason. Come, 'tis moving fast." Callan left the room.

Hannah followed, leaving Raven's manuscript behind.

She chased Callan down the spiraled staircases to the main floor. His eyes remained glued to the hardwood as he tracked the invisible trail of flames. He turned the corner and traveled down the corridor between two tall bookshelves. Fading streams of light highlighted the dust disrupted by their movement. When they got to the end of the aisle, Callan paused.

"What? What happened?" Hannah asked.

"It went through the floor," he said, tapping his foot back and forth over the hardwood.

"Maybe there is a staircase to the basement?"

"No, the flame knew to bring us down the staircases before. This must be the way."

Hannah waited a moment, then felt her blood boiling with frustration again. She stomped her feet against the floor. "There's nothing here." She prodded the solid wall, then slapped her hands at her side. "Why would Mara be in the library? The spell didn't work."

Callan's face twitched with worry, but instead of responding to Hannah, he hovered his hands over the floor.

"Let me find my lost desire, the one where flames did sway.
Show me now, the proper path, reveal the truest way."

A square outline illuminated on the floor and a metal handle appeared at its edge.

"It's a door?" Hannah asked.

"A hidden door. Mara must have enchanted it." Callan reached for the handle, but Hannah clutched his arm.

"Wait. What are we going to do? We don't have a plan."

"The plan is to steal back the grimoire and end your curse."

"That's not a plan."

Callan placed a hand on Hannah's freckled cheek. "You do not have to worry," he said. "I have a plan."

He kissed her. There was an urgency in his kiss that worried her. What was Callan about to do? He pulled away and yanked open the door.

Beneath lay a winding stone staircase. Callan lowered himself inside. "Come on," he whispered.

Hannah was careful to close the trap door above her quietly. They descended into an underground cave.

"I do not care how you get them here, just do it!" Mara shouted.

"Apologies, Mistress," Nathaniel's voice echoed. "But how do you propose I find them? Without a Siren…"

"They are witches from the sixteen-hundreds. They shan't be too difficult to differentiate."

Hannah and Callan paused on the last step. Hannah

peeked from behind the pillar. Mara and Nathaniel stood in the open, cold space before a fire that burned in the middle of the slate floor. Candles illuminated the otherwise dark and damp cave.

How did Mara discover such a cave beneath the library? Did she create it? Had it always been here? Had *she* always been here?

Mara flipped through her grimoire. "If I am to tip the scales from good to evil," Mara continued, "then now is the time to strike. This world does not yet know of magic. They would not know what was happening to them. I can already taste their fear. It would be seamless. Easy. Like a blank canvas asking to be painted black."

Callan rolled back his shoulders and, without warning, stepped off the last ledge.

"Callan, what are you doing?" Hannah whisper-yelled after him. He ignored her. Despite being uncertain whether Callan wanted her to stay hidden or not, she was not about to let him face the Devil alone. She took a breath and followed him, trusting he had a plan.

Mara perked up at the sight of Hannah and Callan. Her surprise switched to a delighted smirk. "Those must have been some swift farewells," she said, her voice taunt and smug.

"There shan't be any farewells," Callan said. The candlelight illuminated his warm skin.

"Is that so?" Mara asked.

"I have come to give you what you desire," he said.

"Callan, what are you doing?" Hannah asked under her breath.

"I will serve you—allow you to compel me once again— in exchange for breaking Hannah's curse. Allow Hannah to live past her eighteenth birthday, only to be reborn when she dies naturally, years from now, as an old woman, ready to pass on."

Hannah's mind reeled. If only he knew the sacrifice Raven made so that he could be free of Mara. While compromising Mara's spell allowed Raven to be reincarnated, she willingly died and entered into this curse so that Callan would no longer be shackled by darkness. It was her bargain with the black magic being cast upon her. By surrendering himself to Mara, he was undoing what Raven wanted.

"No," Hannah screamed. She grabbed his hand. "I won't let you do this."

"This is my penance," he said, a certainty in his eyes. "This shall make up for all the horrible things I have done. This shall make things right."

"And what about all the horrible things you've yet to do? If you do this, you will hurt so many more people, and unlike Raven, I won't be able to stop you!" Hannah's veins pulsed within her forehead. Her magic raced through her, which only angered her further. What was the point of having this power if she couldn't use it?

"But you shall be saved. You shall get the chance to live that Raven never had."

Hannah lowered her voice and brought her lips close to Callan's. "What makes you think Mara will actually let me live? Say she does agree to end my curse. That doesn't mean she won't kill me here and now. You do this, and you only help her turn the world to darkness."

"Right now, I do not care about the world," he said. "I only care about you." While Hannah should have been overwhelmed by his devotion, she was only irate at the sentiment.

Callan stepped toward Mara.

"Raven wouldn't have wanted this," Hannah said.

He looked back at her and smiled, having surrendered to his decision. "You are not Raven."

Hannah's heart thudded against her chest, and she found it difficult to find the right words to say next. She still wanted to yell at Callan—tell him what he was doing was reckless and stupid—but she also felt as though he couldn't have said anything more perfect.

"Do we have a deal?" he asked Mara.

"I am a woman of my word," Mara said. She moved toward him, her body slithering like a snake. She put her hand out for Callan to take, but he hesitated. "Is there a problem?"

"Break the curse first. Only then shall you have me." At this moment, Hannah thought that maybe that was his plan. Mara would break her curse, and then they would make a break for it before Callan could once again be trapped by her influence. If this was his plan, it was not a good one. Mara was too powerful for both of them. Trying to outrun her was the definition of futile.

"And how am I to trust you? You have betrayed me before." Mara snarled at Callan.

"If I do not follow through with my promise, you may kill me."

Hannah's heart beat against her chest so hard, she wondered if anyone else could hear it. How could he be so reckless with his own life? Especially after everything he had been through. This wasn't happening. This *couldn't* be happening.

Mara pursed her lips and released a long hum. "Not good enough." Relief flooded Hannah's heart, but the sensation was fleeting.

Callan took a deep breath. He darted a sorrowful look at

Hannah. "If I do not surrender myself to you after freeing Hannah from her curse, then you shall kill her."

If there was one thing that Hannah was certain of, it was that Callan would never risk her life. This was how she knew that he truly intended to allow himself to be controlled by Mara once again.

"Now that shall do nicely." Mara licked her lips.

Hannah couldn't let this happen. She had to do something. If she could access her magic, she *would* do something. She would combat Mara and hope that Raven's sacrifice and white magic would prevail over darkness. She would keep Callan from having to turn himself back into someone he loathed.

"Wait!" she shouted. "I have a better offer to propose."

"Hannah, what are you..."

"Be quiet, Callan," Hannah said, not surprised at her sharp tongue. While she may have had strong feelings for Callan, his white knight mentality wasn't helping her anxiety.

"I am listening." Mara brushed back her long black hair and crossed her arms.

Despite her tall and intimidating posture, Hannah made sure to look straight into her glowing, red eyes. "If you break my curse, I will eventually learn how to use my magic. It may take some time, but I will come for you, and I will destroy you."

Mara and Nathaniel laughed at the prospect.

"Laugh all you want, but you killed Raven because you were afraid of her. She was a threat to you." Hannah's legs trembled, nevertheless she maintained a stoic expression. She had to make Mara believe that she was strong—that she was fearless.

Mara's laughter subsided, and Nathaniel followed suit.

Hannah took a step toward Mara in order to solidify her appearance of bravery. "You want all the witches who were recently awakened brought to you, so they can become your creatures, correct?"

Mara swept a finger to her chin. "Go on."

"Do you want to be looking over your shoulder for the rest of your lives—just waiting until I prove exactly how powerful I am? Or would you rather use me, my magic—Raven's magic—to do your bidding?"

"Hannah, stop," Callan urged.

She ignored him just as he ignored her. "I may only have one week to live, but if you agree to spare Callan—to never go after him again—then you can turn me into a Siren."

"That is enough." Callan ran at Mara. He clenched a fist and leapt toward her.

In a blur, Nathaniel caught him and twisted his arms behind his back.

Callan struggled against the Vampire, tears glistening in his eyes. "You made me a promise," he yelled, his voice harsh.

Hannah promised never to save him, but she couldn't keep that promise now. She offered him a sorrowful glance.

"I lied."

CHAPTER SIXTEEN

*C*allan's face fell. Hannah looked away, holding back tears. She cleared her throat and redirected her attention to Mara. "While Callan would have to track down each witch individually and compel them to go with him, my magic would dramatically speed up that process." Hannah gulped, her throat dry, not knowing if this was actually true. While Mara could probably smell her fear, Hannah only hoped that she couldn't sense her uncertainty.

"An interesting proposition," Mara said.

Hannah knew that Mara could never give up the chance to control Raven's white magic. "And then, once my time is up, you'll never have to worry about me again."

"She shall break her curse after you are under her control," Callan yelled. "She would not dare let you perish if she possesses your magic. You shall be her prisoner for the rest of your life!"

Hannah didn't consider this. Though her expression froze, she resisted the urge to show any signs of panic. If she only had one week left to live, then she had nothing to lose. She couldn't back out now.

Raven's words scrawled across her mind: *Though a witch may not have chosen the power granted to her by light magic, she must ignite that spark within herself and let it burn for the good of the world and the safety of those she loves.* Hannah hoped that if Mara turned her into one of her creatures, her magic would be awakened and would somehow find a way to fight back. Hannah had learned that magic was an entity unto itself. It had its own desire and agenda. Even if Hannah was compelled by Mara, she hoped her magic would fight for light.

"I have had witches break my bond before," Mara said. "I would not want to risk keeping you around."

While she didn't trust her, Hannah felt a soothing relief at Mara's interest and reassurance in their proposed deal.

"I believe you," Hannah said, even though she assumed she was lying. The only reason Callan was able to break free of Mara all those years ago was because of Raven's counteractive spell. "I still need to hear you say it. Vow to leave Callan alone." Hannah felt a sense of pride surge within herself.

Before, she thought she was nothing like Raven. She considered herself a downgrade—not as strong, not as smart, not as brave, not as selfless. But there she was, confident in her actions, despite the fear that trembled beneath her skin. Maybe she was exhibiting such bravery because she only had days to live, or maybe she and Raven truly were one soul.

"I promise to never go after Callan," she said. "As long as he desires to be free of me, it shall be so."

Good. Hannah nodded and pushed aside her fear. If Mara was true to her word, then Hannah will have upheld

Raven's sacrifice. And in a matter of moments, she'd access her magic.

She held out a hand to Mara. "Do we have a deal?"

"Hannah, stop!" Callan shouted. "Don't do—" Nathaniel smothered his mouth with his hand.

Hannah avoided looking at Callan. She knew she was hurting him. History was repeating itself, and there was nothing he could do about it.

Mara took Hannah's hand and shook it tight. Hannah's magic writhed within her, and she could feel a sharp shock between their hands.

Mara winced, yet held her grip. Her lips curved into a venomous sneer. "Welcome to my coven."

HANNAH KNELT IN FRONT OF MARA'S ALTAR—A natural elevation in the cave with a boulder that acted as a podium for her grimoire—encircled by candles and raw crystals.

Mara took her time flipping through the pages of the book with a smug expression. "You know, this was where I was buried for all those years." Mara loured at Callan. He sat restrained and gagged on the other end of the cave. "I could sense my book in this godforsaken library. Before I could reach it, however, I was cast beneath the earth."

Hannah's hands trembled. She wished Mara would shut up and get on with it. "You can let Callan go. I'm not going anywhere."

"Once the deed is done, he shall be as free as a bird." She cleared her throat and returned to her insufferable diatribe. "As I was saying...because my magic is so powerful, despite Callan's spell, I was awake for three hundred and twenty-six years."

Shocked, Hannah saw the fury behind Mara's flaming eyes. These past few days had felt like a lifetime to Hannah. She couldn't imagine being trapped in stone, fully conscious, for over three hundred years. It was too devastating to fathom.

"I was paralyzed and embedded in stone, but my brain was very much awake. Sensing my book above was like a feather tickling the sole of my foot. I couldn't reach it to scratch. Torturous wouldn't even begin to describe it. I should never wish such a thing upon anyone—and I thrive on spreading evil." Mara cackled to herself. "After years of thinking spells that I could never say, I had resigned myself to die, hoping sheer will would make my mind go blank. But it was never so." Mara gazed down at Hannah. "So, let us say, I am grateful my spell did not work. If it were not for you, then I would still be trapped in these walls."

A massive wave of guilt crashed over Hannah. If it weren't for her magic, her parents would still be alive, and she never would have awakened the greatest evil there ever was. Then again, she never would have met Callan. And though she seemed to be causing him pain, she was selfishly happy that she was able to meet him before she possibly died in a matter of days.

Mara looked back at Callan and shot him a warning glare. "Know that if you ever cast that spell again, you are dooming your precious Hannah to an eternity of endless torture. A fate far worse than death." She settled on a page in her grimoire and ran her fingers over the crinkled sheet. "Ah, here it is." She took a deep breath in through her nose and released a long, satisfied exhale. "Shall we begin?"

Hannah's heart thudded against her chest so hard that

she feared it might leave a bruise. She took slow, deep breaths while touching each of her fingertips to her thumbs. She heard Callan's muffled cries behind her and did her best to ignore him. She hoped that his hurt would eventually turn to understanding. It was too late to turn back now.

Mara raised her arms as if she was a preacher.

"The witch before me hath come to surrender.
  What once was day, now yearns for night's splendor.
  She vows to serve black magic's will,
  In exchange for the gift of one dark skill.
  Let her words sing to her victim's soul,
  And their every move be under her control.
  Awaken her magic to the shadow's dark force,
  And through her veins, let power course.
  Her compass now points only toward sin,
  Re-born a Siren, let her service begin."

Mara's dark magic oozed from her body like black liquid vines crawling up her skin, sprouting in every direction. Mara seemed intoxicated—crazed—by spreading her black magic. Her hair floated in every direction as she inhaled the fear that roared from her magic. It was clear, however, that the difficult spell was taking a toll on Mara. Veins bulged from her neck and her limbs tensed as if she was carrying a heavy weight.

Mara took a deep breath and added one last Latin phrase: *"Vos malum."* The spell surged Mara's fluid black tendrils forward, and they pierced Hannah's body.

Hannah gasped in pain as the dark magic consumed her. Anxiety that didn't belong to her and the terror that wailed through Mara's smoke scraped against her skin. She couldn't focus on anything but her white magic being devoured by the dark force that impaled her. It washed over her organs and suffocated her pores. Her lungs were like cement, breathing impossible. She was drowning once again; this time by an evil force.

Her magic screamed for help. She felt as if she was being torn apart from the inside out. Tears filled her eyes. The skewering tendrils of smoke lifted her into the air. Hannah was dying. She was sure of it. Mara must have broken her promise. She screamed, barely any sound coming from her mouth.

Her chest tightened as if all her fear and pain had gathered there. But then, it released, floated out of her body, and dissolved into Mara's wisping smoke. Their cries softened, no longer grating against Hannah's ears.

A calming song echoed in her head, interrupting Hannah's torture, soothing her. It sounded like the purest, most beautiful note ever sung. Hannah felt as though she were in the ocean, floating through clear blue water, its tranquil touch alleviating her pain. She felt calm and empowered. Was this what the Siren gift felt like? Calming? Seductive? She embraced the stillness.

Hannah looked down at her body, still floating in the air, and rather than feeling her magic trapped in a cage deep within her, she felt it release and swim through every limb. A warm, white glow hovered over her skin, and finally, she felt whole. She sighed.

The white glow of Hannah's magic intertwined with the shadowy vines. It darkened to smoke.

She was overcome with a sense of guilt and regret. The black magic smothered all sense of hope and light. She did it for Callan and for Raven. If she could hold on to the reason for her sacrifice, perhaps that was all the hope she needed.

Hannah lowered to the ground as the spell's magic seeped from her body and flowed back into Mara's hands. She balanced herself, her shoes settling against the stone floor. She closed her eyes. Surprisingly, she was still the same old Hannah, but with one significant shift. She no longer felt as though the unknown magic within her was out of control. Now, it had completely dissolved into her blood, and they were one connected entity. The only question now, was how would it feel to use? Would she scourge the earth with evil? Or was Hannah's magic still innately good?

What was good?

She could no longer be sure.

CHAPTER SEVENTEEN

*H*annah opened her eyes. Mara stumbled as she re-accepted her black magic. She gasped but managed to straighten her posture in their presence.

"How do you feel?" Mara asked, and her voice swam into Hannah's ears like sweet nectar with a magnetic pull.

"Good," Hannah said.

Mara smiled and strode toward Hannah. The closer she got, the warmer she felt. She remembered her magic writhing whenever Mara came too close. She could no longer understand why that was. A magical glow surrounded Mara. Hannah gazed in awe.

"Turn around," Mara commanded, and Hannah obeyed.

Callan was tied up with a cloth knotted around his mouth. His face was soaked with tears. The sorrow she saw behind his expression caused an odd sensation to twinge at the back of her mind, but she was unsure what it meant.

"What do you feel for this boy?" Mara asked, scrutinizing Hannah's every move.

"He's upset with me for allowing you to change me. I'm sorry for that, but I don't regret it."

"Before I performed the spell, young Hannah, I agreed to release Callan. It was part of our deal. Do you still desire—"

"Yes," Hannah said.

Mara took a step forward and caressed Hannah's face with the back of her hand. "What if I do not desire his release?"

Hannah wanted to appease Mara's desire. She had allowed Hannah to become one with her magic, so she felt immense gratitude toward her. She would always be in Mara's debt, and that didn't bother her in the slightest. "Then you should keep him, if you like," Hannah said, a tranquility in her voice.

Callan furrowed his brow and moaned behind his gag. Alarm filled his gaze.

Mara cackled. "Oh, you mustn't worry, my dear Callan. As I said before, I am a woman of my word."

A small sense of relief panged in Hannah's gut.

Mara looked back to Hannah. "In fact, why not test your magic?"

Hannah wasn't sure what she meant.

"Release Callan with a spell. Go on." Mara motioned for her to step forward.

A mixture of nerves and excitement filled Hannah's body. An alluring sensation filled her. She took a deep breath, exhaled, and raised her hands toward Callan.

"Release one Callan Delmonte from being bound.
    Allow him to walk freely upon this ground."

The words were clunky and rusty, but she still felt her

palms tingle. When she noticed his ties loosening, joy replaced Hannah's embarrassment for her first spell. She smiled and looked at her hands in wonder. Her magic was doing as she wished, and she felt empowered at the potential she sensed within herself. She knew she owed this all to Mara.

"Very good," Mara said. "I see young Mr. Delmonte here has taught you a thing or two."

Callan shimmied his hands from the loosened constraints and pulled the rag off his mouth. He raced toward Hannah and placed his hands on the sides of her face. "Do not listen to her, Hannah. Whatever you do. Resist her."

"Arcum," Mara said.

Callan was forced to his knees. His head bowed as if someone was holding him down. Hannah winced. Feeling his hands upon her face stirred something within her. She shook her head and blinked hard, brushing the twinge away. She had more important things to focus on—her magic.

"What else can I do?" Hannah asked Mara, as if she was the gateway to unlocking her full magical potential. She ignored Callan's groans as he fought against Mara's enchantment.

"Why not test your Siren's song? Nathaniel would be delighted to oblige." Mara waved Nathaniel forward, and he obeyed. "Just as you wish to appease your creator, so does Nathaniel," Mara said to Hannah. "So as long as your influence does not contradict any of my commands, he shan't have any other choice but to do as you say."

Nathaniel stood in front of Hannah. "Prithee be gentle," he said with a tiny smirk.

The memory of Nathaniel sinking his teeth into Bryce's

neck flashed in Hannah's mind. The memory felt as if it was from another life.

Hannah stared into Nathaniel's grey eyes and felt her soothing Siren's song in her mind. Not only did it provide her with a sense of calm, seductive power, but she already knew Nathaniel would feel relaxed and eager to comply. She took Nathaniel's hand and said, "Bite yourself. Draw blood. You want to."

Hannah could see the haze of her voice draping over Nathaniel's body. His eyes glazed over. She released his hand and watched her magic at work.

Nathaniel exposed his fangs and pierced them into his forearm. He groaned in pain as blood dripped down his skin. Hannah felt completely invigorated. She was powerful—in control. She decided, in this moment, that this was how she wanted to spend the rest of her life—even if that was only one week.

When Nathaniel retracted his teeth, he snapped out of his trance and growled. "Very funny." He held his other hand against the wound. The skin mended itself, and Nathaniel wiped the blood away.

Hannah pressed her palm against Nathaniel's chest. "Again." Her voice was breathy and captivating.

Nathaniel returned to his trance and punctured his skin in the exact same place. She stared at him with awe. He couldn't resist her. Hannah's lips drew into a grin at the thought.

"Stop it, Hannah," Callan yelled from the ground. "This is not you!"

Hannah felt an instinctual sense of rage toward Callan. She desperately wanted him to be silent and to let her enjoy the new sense of freedom she had. At her internal desire for Callan to be quiet, a single word rose to the surface of her brain.

"Silentium," she said. Her magic jolted within her, causing her body to jerk forward. The feeling startled Hannah and caused her body to ache. But as soon as she saw Callan's lips fuse together, rendering him silent, she knew it was worth it.

Mara's eyes widened. "I did not realize you had knowledge of the old language," she said.

"It just came to me."

Mara's lips twitched.

Nathaniel pulled his teeth from his arm and glared at Hannah. "Stupid wench. I should rip off your head."

In one swift, beautiful motion, Hannah turned to Nathaniel and placed her hand on his cheek. "You'll never do such a thing. You will never hurt me." Nathaniel's eyes glazed over before returning to their natural state.

"I am sorry," Nathaniel said. He took a step backward and lowered his chin.

Hannah had never been able to command such respect in her life. After her parents died, she never thought she deserved it. But now, she knew that no one would ever cross her. And if they did, they'd regret it.

Mara stepped between Hannah and Nathaniel, looking slightly agitated. "I think that is enough for today," she said.

Hannah deflated at Mara's comment and less-than-enthusiastic demeanor. "Did I do something wrong?" she asked.

Mara was quick to plaster a smile on her face. "Not at all, my dear girl. You simply do not require as much practice as I thought."

"It feels as if I've been waiting for this my entire life. I finally feel whole." Hannah couldn't remember why she was so afraid of Mara—why she and Callan were trying to resist her. She had awakened Hannah to who she was always meant to be. The best part of Hannah's transformation was that she no longer felt weighed down by the heavy guilt she had been carrying with her for the past two years. If her parents had to die in order for her to be converged with this incredible magic, then it was simply meant to be. She was no longer responsible for their death. If only they could see her now, she was sure that they would be proud of her. "Thank you," she said sincerely to Mara.

Mara shifted. "No need to thank me, Miss Fenwick. You shall repay me soon enough."

Hannah nodded and turned to Callan, whose lips were stitched shut. His eyes looked heavy and his body defeated. She remembered the Latin word Mara used when they were in the forest to release Callan from his binds. "Absolvo," she said.

Her organs lurched against her abdomen and her intestines twisted upon themselves. She dropped to her knees and curled over, clenching her teeth in order to keep from screaming.

Callan's lips separated.

He ran to Hannah's side and cradled her to her feet. She leaned against his steady frame until the lurching pain subsided.

Mara smiled and sauntered toward Hannah. "You are still new to magic, dear. I would council you to not indulge so thoroughly in your confidence. The old language may be too arduous for you just yet."

"It didn't hurt before," Hannah said. She remembered when Mara's grimoire took hold of her magic, the Latin spells didn't affect her this way.

"That is because you had the help of my precious grimoire. Performing the old spells by yourself, without assistance, is another story."

Hannah didn't mind Mara's condescension. She realized that Mara knew better than she did. She would listen to her.

"Now, what are we going to do with this one?" Mara said, pointing a bony finger at Callan.

"He is free to leave," Hannah said. It was difficult for her to care about the deal she made with Mara while she had this new command over her magic. All she wanted to do was use it.

"I am not going anywhere," Callan said. "I shan't let you use her like you used me."

Hannah felt frustrated at Callan's unnecessary chivalry. "You don't need to feel guilty, Callan," she said. "Truly. I feel amazing, and you don't have to feel indebted to anyone here."

"The thrill you are experiencing," Callan said, "shan't last. Once you realize that Mara is using you to do her bidding—to spread evil—the gratification shall fade, and you shall violently crash to reality with only guilt and regret to comfort you."

Hannah's magic lurched within her. She didn't care for the discomfort his words were causing. "Don't worry about me. What's done is done. Just leave."

"I am not giving up on you." Callan took Hannah's hand in his and held it tight. "Just like Raven never gave up on me."

His touch tingled, and goosebumps traveled up her arm. She was reminded of the comfort and familiarity he had provided her even when they first met. His bright green eyes glowed against his dark skin, and Hannah felt a pang of affection when he gazed in her eyes. His touch was cracking away the hard shell this new magic provided—an impenetrable skin that had rid her of her guilt and given her free reign to use her magic as she desired. She was not ready for that exterior to be shattered.

Hannah pulled her hand away, convinced that how he was making her feel was some sort of trick.

"Raven should have given up on you," she said. "If she just left you alone, she never would have died for you."

Callan looked at Hannah with confusion.

She reveled in the fact that she was about to invert his world. "The spell Raven cast to counteract Mara's was only partially to ensure her rebirth. The other half was sacrificing herself so that you could break out from under Mara's command." Hannah watched with delight as this news punched Callan in the chest. She could almost see him remembering his devotion to Mara melting off of him as soon as Raven's body crumbled to ash.

Mara smiled at Hannah, and it gave her the validation she was looking for. She was right to tell Callan the truth. Perhaps if he understood what really happened, he would leave Hannah to explore her magic in peace.

Callan didn't move. He looked like a ghost who was only now realizing he was dead. His eyes glossed over with water and his chin trembled.

Hannah knew he already carried the burden of Raven's death. But the knowledge that Raven purposely sacrificed herself to save Callan, probably doubled his guilt.

A small spasm of sympathy stabbed at the back of Hannah's mind. Her mouth went dry, and she swallowed a hard knot down her throat. Discomfort itched her skin when Callan didn't say anything.

"I think it's time for you to go," she said. It was easier

for her to act like she felt nothing than give into those pesky pangs of guilt and compassion that scratched at the back of her neck.

"No, I shan't." Callan nodded to himself. "I think it time for me to return the favor."

Hannah had no idea what this meant, but she felt a sense of panic rise in her stomach.

Callan looked to Mara and took a deep breath. "Go on," he said. "Sire me. I shan't betray you this time—I shan't be able."

"No," Hannah yelled, though she was not too sure where her urgency came from. She grabbed Callan's arm and projected her Siren's song over him. "You do not want to do this. You want to leave. You will forget about me and this place." Though Hannah could feel the soothing lull of her words, Callan's demeanor didn't falter.

"A Siren cannot compel another Siren," he said.

Hannah whipped her head to Mara. "We made a deal."

"Indeed," Mara said. "The deal stated that as long as Callan wished to be free of me, then he would be. However, he seems to be volunteering his loyalty to me."

Hannah realized that Mara was right. Her chest felt heavy and swollen, as if her heart were being torn in two directions. She wanted Mara to get all that she desired. Mara gave Hannah the world. But not at the expense of Callan's freedom. Her body heated and a sheen of sweat lined her brow. Without realizing it, Hannah tapped her fingertips to her thumbs and tried to pay attention to her breathing.

"Shall the spell be prepared?" Callan asked.

"My pleasure." Mara licked her pale lips as she returned to her altar, caressing her grimoire.

Callan approached Hannah. He brought his lips to her

ear and whispered, "Perhaps my sacrifice will aid you in finding yourself again." Hannah looked at Callan with an alarming expression. "Only then shall Mara be stopped." He turned his back on Hannah and knelt in front of Mara's altar.

She didn't want to stop Mara. Find herself again? Hannah had never felt more herself than she did now. She screamed these words in her mind. If he desired to rejoin Mara's cause, then so be it. It didn't affect her in the slightest. She walked to the altar and feigned indifference despite the raging battle in her mind and body.

"Suit yourself," she said. She stood behind Mara, Nathaniel, and the grimoire.

"Ignis," Mara said, and the candles surrounding Callan ignited. She cleared her throat and raised her hands in his direction.

"Who once was loyal and served the dark,
    Has agreed to reignite his undying spark.
    Let him devote himself once again to me,
    And promise that he shall never flee.
    Allow his Siren's song to be under my command.
    Let him revel in power, and his darkness expand."

Mara took a deep breath and concluded her incantation with an old-language chant: "Servus ad tenebras."

Her black smoke plumed over Callan. He gasped for air. Hannah looked away and focused on the cracks in the stone wall.

When Mara's black haze cleared, and Callan fell silent, Hannah returned her gaze to him. His eyes were closed, and he swayed as if he had fallen asleep.

His eyes darted open. If at all possible, his eyes were an

even brighter green than before. He rose to his feet and stood tall, resembling a soldier reporting for duty.

Mara stepped down from her altar and circled Callan. "How do you feel, Mr. Delmonte?"

Callan inhaled through his nose and released a satisfied sigh. He cracked his neck in a circular motion, relaxed his shoulders, and, for the first time, looked truly at ease. He took Mara's hand and kissed the back of it before smiling larger than Hannah had ever seen before.

"I am home."

CHAPTER EIGHTEEN

*a*s soon as Callan opened his eyes, Hannah knew he had reverted back to the Callan she experienced in the memory spell. She remembered how devoted Raven was to freeing him of the dark magic Mara seduced him with. Callan tried to entice her to join Mara's coven, but she was stronger than that. Her strength was what helped Callan realize that the dark magic he was practicing wasn't right. It was his cry for help that pushed Raven to sacrifice herself to save him from darkness. Now, it was all for nothing.

Hannah's mind flooded with a sense of failure. At first, she couldn't discern why she felt this way. Then she remembered. It was as if Mara's spell erased parts of her mind—the parts that were connected to her white magic and the goodness that came with that. She failed because she allowed herself to be swayed by darkness. She made the deal with Mara in order to spare Callan of the fate he was imprisoned by for so long—the fate that Raven freed him from. All these puzzle pieces came together. She failed Callan. She failed Raven. She failed herself.

Hannah identified the reality of her situation, and she could feel Mara's darkness tug at the back of her brain. *Ignore it. None of it matters now that you have this power,* it whispered. *You can do whatever you desire—feel however you desire. Do not be weighed down by your past. This is your future.*

The voice was tempting. It would be so much easier to enjoy the new magic that shadowed her perception of the world. But that was all it was: a shadow. And shadows disappear when the light breaks through.

She visualized the white magic inside her surging against the black smoke that clouded its vision. She hadn't failed yet. Just as Hannah was able to resist Callan's Siren ability and the lure of Mara's grimoire, she desperately combated the darkness that coursed through her veins and plagued her mind.

As she battled against the seductive pull of Mara's black magic—and the undying devotion she felt toward her—she grasped onto Raven's strength and the memory of Callan's lips upon hers. She remembered how her magic was prodigy magic—just like Mara's.

Raven's written words echoed in her mind. *It is the responsibility of those who have been chosen by the light—bestowed with benevolence and virtue—to fight against the harmful darkness.* That was what Hannah had to do now. She had to fight.

Her face scrunched with pain as she felt closer and closer to banishing the darkness from her body and mind. Her skin was on fire, and her head throbbed as though it was being stabbed over and over. It was as if a layer of flesh was being peeled from her body. Hannah couldn't take it anymore and released a piercing scream which reverberated throughout the cave.

Her knees fell hard against the ground, and she suddenly felt lighter. It was as though her body had been dipped into cool, refreshing water after being set on fire. Tears of relief seeped out of the sides of her eyes. White orbs hovered in her palms. She clasped her hands shut before anyone could see.

Mara, Nathaniel, and Callan turned toward Hannah, alarmed. Callan stood by Mara and stared at her with confusion. She hoped that Mara hadn't seen her white magic glow upon her skin. Hannah wondered, however, whether Mara could feel that she had broken free.

Mara took a few paces toward Hannah, suspicion painted on her face. "What was that?"

"I don't know," Hannah lied. Without Callan on her side, Hannah was a mouse trapped in a lion's den. "I just felt a sharp pain. I'm not used to feeling this kind of power."

Mara stepped closer and closer to Hannah, an eyebrow raised. Hannah could feel her white magic sparking in her blood, warning her of approaching evil.

She couldn't believe she ever felt gratitude toward the woman who lived and breathed such darkness. The worst part was that it took Callan submitting himself to her for Hannah to break free of her delusion. She was more susceptible to darkness than she thought possible.

"Stand up, dear," Mara commanded. Hannah obeyed. Mara circled her like a vulture. "Now that young Mr. Delmonte has rejoined our ranks, how do you feel? I understand you would have preferred his freedom. That was our deal, after all."

Hannah gulped. "I can't quite remember why I cared at all. It makes no difference to me." Hannah fixated on Raven's strength as to not let her body fall to fear.

"You are not pleased that your beloved stayed for you?" Mara's words prodded Hannah, but she maintained composure.

"I am only pleased that you have one more witch following your command."

Mara smiled. "Kiss him," she commanded.

Hannah's stomach churned. She knew she had to obey. She walked toward Callan.

"Not him, dear."

Hannah halted.

"Kiss Nathaniel."

Hannah didn't let any emotion play on her face. She simply changed direction and stopped in front of Nathaniel. She'd rather have swallowed soap than be forced to kiss the vile Vampire who changed Bryce and attempted to kill both her and Callan. Disgust tickled the back of her throat.

She pecked her lips to his then took a step back. Nathaniel smiled, and Hannah tried not to gag.

"I think you can do better than that," Mara said. "Go on. Really kiss him."

Hannah took a deep breath. Callan didn't seem to care in the slightest. If anything, he looked amused.

Hannah rested her hand on the back of Nathaniel's neck and reminded herself that she needed to be convincing. She moved her head closer to his and closed her eyes. She kissed him and forced her lips to linger.

Nathaniel parted his lips against hers. Hannah sucked on his bottom lip and did her best to control her gag reflex. She could tell that Nathaniel would have kept going, but she had had enough.

She pulled away and swallowed her revulsion. Her eyes glazed over Callan. He didn't seem fazed. Sadness filled

Hannah's heart, knowing that she was that cold to him before he submitted himself to Mara.

Nathaniel gazed down at Hannah, his eyes fixated on hers, his mouth agape. Hannah wanted to slap the drool off his face and remind him that she was ordered to kiss him. She looked to Mara, and she appeared unsatisfied.

"Nathaniel," Mara called as she sauntered toward them. "I think it is your turn to return the favor."

Nathaniel's eyes lit up. Hannah wanted to curse whatever sick game Mara was playing, but all she could do was stand there, neutral, and happy to play out Mara's deranged fantasies. Nathaniel puckered his lips and leaned in toward Hannah.

"Do not *kiss* her," Mara interrupted. "Bite her."

Hannah froze.

"You are certain?" Nathaniel asked.

While Hannah had no idea what his bite would do to her magic, she was certain that it would turn her into a Vampire. She felt the instinct to flee, but she knew that she could never outrun Mara's quick tongue. If she tried to escape, Mara would know that Hannah was no longer under her compulsion.

"I am." Mara folded her hands and let them rest against her stomach.

Nathaniel ran his tongue over his fangs. Hannah trembled. She was desperate for Callan to intervene, but he didn't. He simply stood there and watched.

"I thought you wanted me to be a Siren? Help bring all the awakened witches to your side," Hannah said, fighting the nerves that shook her voice.

Mara took a taunting stride forward. "You are a powerful witch. Maybe you could be both. A Siren and a

Vampire. Would that not be incredible?" Her tone was fiendish.

Hannah wouldn't give Mara the satisfaction of finding her out. She was already destined to die in a number of days. Perhaps a set of fangs was all she needed to defeat Mara. Hannah nodded. "It would."

She took a breath and offered Nathaniel her wrist.

In a blur, he leaned Hannah back in his arms and revealed his fangs. His teeth skimmed her flesh and he hesitated.

"Nathaniel?" Mara asked, her voice threatening. "I thought I gave you an order."

Nathaniel nodded, but he looked conflicted. He squinted and pushed his teeth closer and closer to Hannah's jugular, each inch looking like an effort. Hannah wondered if her previous compulsion for Nathaniel never to harm her had anything to do with his hesitation. But when he re-opened his eyes and released a menacing growl, the suggestion fled her mind.

Hannah closed her eyes and hoped he'd make it quick. Just as the tips of Nathaniel's fangs scratched her skin, Mara sprung forward.

"Stop," Mara shouted. "I have changed my mind," she said, a quiver in her voice.

Nathaniel retracted his fangs and placed Hannah on her feet. Hannah studied the relief on his face, but knew that she couldn't show her own. Hannah had called Mara's bluff. She wouldn't dare lose her precious new tool. Hopefully now, she would no longer be suspicious of Hannah.

"Bringing the witches here should be our priority." Mara clutched at her cape, and her right eye twitched.

Tiny beads of sweat gathered on Hannah's forehead.

She was grateful that she wouldn't have to feed on humans to survive, but she wasn't free and clear just yet.

"Are you certain?" Hannah asked. If Mara truly believed that Hannah was compelled to her, then it wouldn't have sounded like a subversion at all.

Mara brushed a strand of black hair from her forehead then calmly folded her hands. "You shall learn that I am always certain. Best not to question me."

"Of course." Hannah bowed. This must have been enough for Mara, because she turned her attention to Callan.

"You have been awfully quiet, Mr. Delmonte."

"Simply awaiting your command." Callan looked at Mara as if he would do anything for her. Hannah recognized the gaze, and her heart ached.

"I have a command for you." Mara tapped a finger against her chin. "Nathaniel took far too long to obey an order. Kill him. I shall make it so that he is susceptible to your command."

"What?" Nathaniel released a nervous laugh. "Do you jest, my mistress?"

"Are you questioning me?"

"Of course not. I trust you completely." Nathaniel's lips parted.

"Then keep silent."

Hannah's eyes darted between Callan and Nathaniel. Could he be pretending just like her? Hannah knew that Callan would only kill a fellow witch if he was truly compelled to do so. Then she remembered Beatrice. Callan didn't hesitate to kill her. However, she was only seconds away from ripping Hannah's head off, and Callan was overcome by a massive sense of guilt afterward. Would he really kill Nathaniel only to keep up a charade with Mara?

Callan didn't blink an eye. He nodded and marched to Nathaniel. He placed his hand on his shoulder and looked into his eyes. "You desire to rip out your own heart. You may not think you are capable, but prove yourself wrong. As a Vampire, you have the strength to do so." Callan stepped back.

Nathaniel cracked his neck and shook out his arms, preparing himself for the task. "Prove myself wrong."

Hannah looked to Mara to see if she was going to intervene like she did before. She expected her to make him stop—to award his loyalty with the dignity of not dying a gruesome death at his own hand—but no such thing happened.

Nathaniel reached his fist out and plunged it into his chest. It made a hollow popping noise.

Hannah held her breath and averted her gaze. Water dripped from the high ceiling, echoing with every drop. Hannah didn't know how much more pretending she could take.

Nathaniel gasped, and his pale eyes filled with blood. His mouth twisted as he released a grisly cry. His hand moved back and forth inside his chest, bone snapping.

Hannah flinched. She fought the urge to throw up as the contents of her stomach boiled.

Nathaniel tore his hand from his chest and hoisted his own heart into the air like a trophy. His delight didn't last long. The veins beneath his pale skin turned black and spindled over his body. A metallic liquid seeped from his eyes and nostrils, and his lips cracked. Nathaniel collapsed against the cold, hard ground.

Hannah balled her hands into fists to hide how much they were shaking. She had never seen anything so gruesome or horrifying in her life. Her intestines swarmed in on themselves, burrowing as far as they could into her spine. She felt lightheaded at the smell of the fleshy heart that tumbled out of Nathaniel's palm. Her eyes rolled into the back of her head. Everything went black and she fell to the ground.

Even while she laid there and fought the impending darkness, she ached for Callan's embrace. She remained alone, slipping into night.

CHAPTER NINETEEN

*W*hen Hannah came to, she had no idea how long she had been unconscious. Mara's cave was only lit by scattered candles. She had no clue what time of day it was. Sadness tugged at the back of her mind as she realized she laid exactly where she collapsed. While she was thankful that Nathaniel's body had been disposed of—despite the lingering blood stain from where he ripped his own heart out—the Callan she had come to know would have taken care of her. He would have picked her up, covered her with a blanket, and soothed her aching head. That Callan was gone. The thought of never seeing *her* Callan again forced tears to her eyes.

She stood up, her body aching. Conspiring whispers came from the altar where Mara and Callan flipped through the grimoire. Her hand waved over the cave wall, and a beautiful white rose bloomed from the stone. Mara closed her fingers into a fist, and the pedals turned black. They deteriorated to the floor. Callan looked amazed by Mara's spell. They returned to the grimoire for more. Hannah couldn't tell whether he was smiling at his reunion with the book or whether he was never allowed the privilege to peruse her spells before. She blinked back her tears and wiped away the few that escaped. She walked towards the altar and straightened her posture.

"She has risen," Mara said, an attempt to mock Hannah.

"How are you feeling?" Callan asked, his face stone cold.

Hannah opened her mouth, but before she could get a word in, Mara answered for her. "Quite rested, I would imagine." She came to the edge of the altar and looked down at Hannah. "You slumbered through the night."

Hannah felt an immediate sense of relief and gratitude. She was unsure whether to attribute it to the fact that she had a full night's sleep or that she was still breathing after being defenseless in the company of two dark witches.

"I am not sure why you look so pleased," Mara continued. "You have delayed my plans half a day's time."

Hannah wished she knew a spell that would banish her from this earth for good. A spark ignited in Hannah's mind. She needed to get back to Raven's spell book. There had to be something in those pages that could help her. In order to get out of here alive, however, Hannah had to continue to play along. Mara was supposed to be her master, so Hannah was forced to act as though she was a willing and dutiful follower.

"I'm sorry," she said. "I'm so embarrassed. Guess my magic can't protect me from my aversion to blood."

Mara stepped off the altar and came close to Hannah. She caressed her face with her long, bony fingers. Hannah looked directly into her demonic red eyes.

"Do not fret, dear. I shan't have you draw any blood." Though this provided Hannah with a small sense of relief, it was short-lived. "You simply must bring the witches to me, and I shall do the rest."

Hannah's heart sunk, but she couldn't let it play on her face. She now had to perform the duties that drove Callan to so much guilt that he imprisoned himself and all witches into stone for hundreds of years. She wouldn't let that happen. Not only did she not want to betray the white magic that, as Raven put it, *chose her*, but she also knew that if Mara turned the awakened witches into her creatures, she would not stand a chance against them. If Hannah failed, then she would be happy to die on her eighteenth birthday. However, that meant she would be reborn into a world plagued by darkness. If Mara broke her curse and allowed Hannah to live, then she'd have to run for the rest of her life, always looking over her shoulder. Or she'd probably die trying to stop Mara. Hannah's mind raced with the endless possibilities of what could happen, but she needed to focus on one thing at a time. Step one: Escape. Step two: Protect the re-awakened witches. Step three: Defeat Mara and free Callan.

"Thank you." Hannah bowed her head. "I will do as you please."

Mara grinned and puffed her chest.

"Mr. Delmonte," Mara called. "You shall take our sweet Hannah to the highest point in the cliffs, and you are to show her how it is done."

"Right away," he said.

"Will you not be joining us?" Hannah asked. Her absence would make it easier for Hannah to escape to the Occult and Mysticism room. She would also be better able to gage how lost Callan truly was.

"I must conserve my strength and prepare. The outside world shall know me soon enough."

Hannah nodded, feigning disappointment.

"Not to worry, dear," Mara continued. "We shall be reunited soon enough. Tonight, with your help, our long-lost brothers and sisters shall join our cause."

Callan smiled with pride and exhilaration. She swallowed her disgust.

———

WHEN HANNAH AND CALLAN LEFT THE LIBRARY, she squinted her eyes against the daylight. She considered trying to convince Callan to go back up the stairs to the Occult and Mysticism room, but she didn't want to risk him seizing Raven's book and bringing it back to Mara.

She sucked in the cool air and felt as if she was emerging from the underground cave as a new person. She could feel her light magic filling every crevice of her body with strength and hope. And despite the discouragement Hannah felt at not having Callan on her side and going up against the Devil herself, she took solace in the fact that she was able to resist the most powerful compulsion the world had ever known.

"This way," Callan said, pointing up the edge of the cliffs.

A few students walked along the cobblestone paths. The rest of the campus looked empty—quiet and desolate. She imagined that most students were sitting in classrooms, learning the information that was supposed to prepare them for the rest of their lives. That was her only days ago. She imagined her professors scoffing at her lackluster attendance so early on in the semester, but none of it mattered now. Unlike Hannah, her peers had lives left to live.

"How are you feeling?" she asked, trudging beside Callan up a narrow path along the cliff's edge. "What is it like for you, being back under Mara's command?"

Callan looked straight ahead and kept pace. "I feel valorous. Lighter."

"What do you mean, lighter?"

"All the guilt I carried with me 'twas akin to having a massive boulder glued to my back. I was miserable and moaning and...I cannot quite understand why I ever desired to leave Mara in the first place."

"You told Raven you thought Mara's actions were wrong." Hannah snorted a laugh.

Callan halted his feet against the gravel and dirt and looked down upon Hannah. She worried that maybe she pushed too far.

"Is that what you believe? That all of this is wrong?" He stepped closer to her. "Embracing the potential of our magic and doing whatever we desire without consequence?"

Hurting people.

Hannah knew she couldn't say that to Callan. "Of course not. I'm just making sure you're truly on our side." Hannah winced.

"If anyone should be wary, 'tis me of you. You are Raven Harlowe reborn, after all. Pious witch." He spat out these last words with disdain.

"Mara sent me here with you," Hannah said. "She trusts me. Does that mean you're questioning her judgement?" This shut Callan up. She tensed her jaw and focused on the gravel—one foot in front of the other. One step at a time.

Callan was gone. Until she could find a way to free him from Mara's chains, he was her enemy.

"Let us get to the highest peak and be done with it," he

said.

"Why must it be the highest point of the cliffs?"

"The hope is that your song will blanket over as much of Cape Cove as possible from there. Should Mara desire to expand her hunt, we may eventually travel farther afield."

"You won't be...helping?"

"You are the one with prodigy magic," Callan said. "And you did tell Mara you could reach all the awakened witches with your almighty power."

"I said I *think* I'd be able to do it. It's not like I've done this before. What if it doesn't work?" Hannah felt her magic within her. It was intense and a force to be reckoned with. That, along with her new Siren ability, she did believe she could gather all the witches under her influence. If she did this, then they would all be at Mara's mercy. She couldn't let that happen.

"Then you shall have to answer to a disappointed Mara Eden."

Hannah would be dead in a few days, anyway. What was the worst she could do?

They walked farther along the cliff's edge than Hannah had before. The campus was merely a backdrop to the wild cliffs. The ocean was so far below that the crashing waves only hummed in comparison to the whistling wind. Her stomach growled, and she realized that she hadn't eaten anything since yesterday.

"Just up here." Callan pointed to an elevation in the cliff that hung out beyond its surroundings over the ocean.

Hannah considered jumping. It would keep her from having to call all the witches and absolve her from any responsibility before her expiration date. Six days. That was how much time she had left before she inevitably was killed off.

Hannah wanted to crumble and cry, but she knew she had to remain stoic if she planned to keep up her charade. While Hannah had broken down, she never fully absorbed the fact that she was going to die...and soon. She didn't want to. She didn't want to waste what little time she had left feeling devastated, lost, and hopeless. Instead, her and Callan threw themselves into finding a way to break Mara's curse. How arrogant. As if one impressionable witch susceptible to darkness and a newbie could outsmart the darkest, most powerful witch of all time. Somehow, that quest ended in both of them offering themselves up to save the other. It had clearly worked out well.

But flinging herself off the edge would be the easy way out. If she were to end it all now, Callan would still compel the re-awakened witches. It may take longer, but he and Mara wouldn't have anyone standing in their way. *If the balance between light and darkness is corrupted, then the world may never recover.* Hannah held Raven's words close to her heart. Though Callan had told her a hundred times that her and Raven were one and the same, it had taken Hannah a long time to warm to the idea. Now, she felt Raven within herself, weaving her knowledge and power through her magic. Raven's cause now consumed Hannah, and she would do whatever she could to fulfill it.

"You are quite silent," Callan said.

"Just focused on what needs to be done."

"Good," he said. Hannah eyed him and reminded herself that his distance and stony demeanor were only temporary.

They strayed off the dirt path as they reached the highest point in the cliffs. Hannah breathed heavily from the steep climb as she hiked through the yellowing grass to the stony overhang. Patches of drying moss were scattered within the dirt and rock. She and Callan stepped onto the ledge that jutted out over the ocean—like a plank leading to impending doom. Hannah's brain scrambled. She knew it was time for her to use her Siren song to call the witches to Mara. How was she going to get out of this?

"So, what do I do? Just yell for the witches to meet us all back at the library?" Hannah laughed, shifting her weight from foot to foot.

"You cannot be serious." Callan cocked his head to the side.

Below, waves crashed against the sharp rocks, frothing as they broke.

"I've never done anything like this before."

Callan sighed. "When you are compelling one-on-one, you must simply touch your target and they shall do as you say."

"Yeah...that's the part I do know."

"When your aim is to compel the masses, you must transmit your song from your head," he said.

When Hannah broke free of Mara's chains, she banished that song to the deepest depths of her brain, hoping she would never be able to reach it again. But now, Hannah could hear its enticing tone in the back of her mind. It was like the forbidden fruit in the Garden of Eden.

"Go on," Callan said, waving her to the edge of the cliff.

Hannah stepped toward him but pushed the tempting melody from her mind. She knew she had to act fast.

"Senties dolorum!" she screamed.

Both her and Callan fell to the ground. Callan's body seized dangerously close to the edge of the cliff. Hannah's magic raged within her, protesting against the old language spell. Sweat gathered on Hannah's forehead and back, and she felt as though she may erupt into flames any moment.

Because the Latin words caused Hannah to writhe in pain, its effects quickly wore off of Callan. He stood up tall, clenching his fists and grinding his teeth.

He wrapped his large hand around Hannah's neck and lifted her to her feet. "I knew it," he said. "You must be completely committed to dark magic for those spells to not eat you alive. You are pure light, aren't you?"

Hannah struggled to breathe, let alone speak, as his grip tightened around her throat. He lifted her higher. Hannah scrambled to find the ground. The tips of her shoes scraped against the gravel.

"Ca-Ca-llan." She coughed. "St-stop." Aura spots stormed her vision.

Callan threw her at the edge of the cliff. Hannah rolled toward the rocky rim. Her hands clutched at stone, dirt, moss, anything. But everything slipped through her fingers.

She tipped off the side of the cliff, and for a moment, her body felt weightless. She gasped in a shriek and swatted her hands through the air. Her fingers somehow curled around a jagged part of the peak, her nails splintering against the stone.

"Callan!" Panic charged through her. "I can't hold on." Her voice matched the high-pitch whistle of the wind.

Callan stood above her.

"Please, Callan. Don't do this." He was fully capable of compelling the witches without her. Now that she was not on his side, he had no use for her.

"Promise to call the witches, or you shall fall." His voice was unfeeling. All he cared about was following Mara's commands. He had no affection left for Hannah.

"Why? You don't need me." Hannah's fingers slid a centimeter.

"'Twould be a lie if I said I was not curious to see your

power at work. Such a shame 'tis back to being white."

Hannah retightened her grip. In doing so, her hands slipped even further, and her feet flailed.

"Furthermore, Mara has waited too long for this. I do not desire to keep her waiting much longer."

"Okay, fine, I promise!" She only had seconds left before she crashed to her death. She was committed to stopping Mara, and if that meant freeing more witches than simply Callan from her command, then so be it.

Callan crouched down so that his eyes were closer to Hannah's. "No trickery." He taunted her now.

"I promise!" she shouted. The strength it took for Hannah to proclaim this last exclamation subtracted from her hands. They slipped. She scratched at the stone as she fell. She needed a spell to make her fly, to land her softly on the ground, or to return her to the cliff. Her mind, however, couldn't focus as she was suspended in the open air.

Callan's hand wrapped around her wrist. Half of his body hung over the edge of the cliff as he held onto Hannah. Relief, surprise, and terror filled her all at once as she looked up at Callan. His face was red with veins protruding from his forehead. He was struggling to hold her weight and keep himself on the cliff at the same time. Hannah recognized Callan's expression as she hung suspended in the air: *concern*.

"Light as a feather, assistance from the weather." Despite Callan's strained voice, his spell took immediate effect. A gust of wind blew Hannah upward. Callan hefted her to safety.

She laid on the mossy ground and held onto it tightly. She couldn't believe she was alive. Her gaze found Callan, and his green eyes were tight and worried.

"Thank you," she said. She knew that he was the reason she was tossed over the side of the cliff in the first place, but if she noticed a glint of hope in him, she was going to take full advantage of it.

He shook his head. "'Tis not for me to decide your fate. I shall let Mara choose what to do with you."

"For a moment, it looked like you cared about me." Hannah reconnected her gaze to his, but he avoided any eye contact.

"I care only about what you can do for our coven." He stood up and brushed the dirt off his jeans.

"Do you remember why you surrendered yourself to Mara again?" Hannah rose to her feet and moved a safe distance away from the edge. Callan knew that Hannah was no longer compelled by Mara, so she was free to push him —to try and guide his mind back to the light.

"'Tis irrelevant."

"No, it's not!" Hannah stood in front of Callan, too close for him to avoid her gaze. "You did it for me. You thought sacrificing yourself would snap me out of my trance—pull me back to the light. And you were right. It did." Callan's brows furrowed.

She dug in deeper. "If you stay like this, you will hurt people. Remember Beatrice? Only sixteen years old and you took the rest of her life away from her. You helped Mara turn her into a beast whose only purpose was to kill on Mara's behalf."

"Stop it," he said.

"And then you killed her when she tried to hurt me. Do you remember the guilt you felt after doing so? Even though you did it to protect me, it still consumed you."

"I said *stop it*," he shouted.

"I'll only stop once you remember that this isn't you."

Hannah took another step closer. "Come back to me, Callan. Fight it." She placed her hands on the sides of his face. She believed she was getting through to him. "You're stronger than you think. And you care about people more than dark magic. You care about me." Without thinking, she pressed her lips against his. If she could make him feel again, then she knew he'd return to her.

Callan pushed her off. All hope disappeared. He gripped her upper arm and yanked her close to his face. "The Callan you knew is gone. I do not care for you at all. You are simply a means to an end." His words deflated her. "And thankfully, I shan't have to endure you much longer." His words were a knife in Hannah's heart—cold and sharp.

Callan released her arm, bruises forming where his fingers dug into her muscles. He shoved her toward the edge of the cliff. "Sing your song, or I shall push you over for good this time." His voice was low and threatening. Though she thought she caught a glimpse of the old, caring Callan, she realized that it would take more than some captivating words to free him from evil's seduction.

Hannah tried to think of a spell that would keep her from having to go through with this, but her mind was too frazzled to piece rhymes together. She knew that she was more powerful than Callan, and that she could defeat him if she really needed to. But she had to remember that Callan wasn't her enemy. He needed to be saved.

"Let us speed this along, shall we?"

Though Hannah tried to ignore Callan's impatience, soon it was impossible.

He hummed a low, sweet tone that soaked into her mind. It was similar to the song she heard when she was first turned into a Siren. It felt like soft silk against Hannah's skin and wrapped her in a warmth she never wanted to be without. Furthermore, it made her want to sing her own song—to create a duet of beauty and bliss.

Singing to each other felt wonderful. It was like an intimate dance that made her feel close to Callan. Hannah was powerful enough, however, to realize that Callan only wanted her to sing. Nothing else. And in this moment, Hannah really didn't see any other option. She had to call to the witches. She only hoped she could somehow intervene before Mara destroyed them with the evil she wielded.

Hannah allowed her melody to swarm her mind. It was so beautiful and enchanting, that tears brewed behind her eyes. She opened her mouth and allowed the song to slip through her parted lips. She never considered herself a great singer before, but the voice she heard emitting from herself now was far more appealing than she ever could have imagined. It was higher in tone than Callan's song, like a clear, sweet note that would mesmerize anyone who heard it. And Hannah knew how to use it.

"Think of all the awakened witches," Callan said. Hannah projected her voice across the ocean and surrounding lands. "Call them to Mara's location."

Hannah imagined the waves carrying her alluring melody far and wide. The expanse of her magic within her song was both amazing and troubling. She was filled with a confidence and certainty that witches would hear her and follow the song back to the cave beneath Bellcliff Library. But maybe, just maybe, she'd be able to save them.

After a few more long moments of singing her enchanting song, she felt Callan's touch on her shoulder. "That should do," he said.

Hannah swallowed her song and shoved it back to the depths of her mind. Tears fell from her eyes, and she couldn't hide the sadness on her face. She very well may have just destroyed the lives of witches who were reawakened from Callan's spell, taking away their second chance at living.

"What now?" Hannah asked. This wasn't the end. There was still a chance she could save them—save Callan. Therefore, Hannah tried to overwhelm her self-doubt and sorrow with determination and courage.

"We return to the library and wait. We shan't only be greeting our new recruits, but shall also be welcoming back our old coven members." Callan smirked as if he had pulled one over on Hannah.

Her entire body tensed. "More of Mara's creatures?"

"They are of the re-awakened witches, are they not?" Callan paced away from the ledge with a brash smile. "You have now given them the map back to their master."

Sparks sizzled over Hannah's palms.

"Do not look so cross, Hannah. You too are one of Mara's creatures. I promise you shall feel a sense of...camaraderie amongst them."

"She may have turned me into a Siren, but she is not my master." Her voice thundered from deep within her chest.

"Ah, yes. I wonder how Mara shall feel about that."

Hannah gulped. She knew that when she saw Mara again, she'd either have to submit to her punishment, or fight her to the death. A fight with Mara could only end with one of them breathing. "You don't need to threaten me, Callan. I know I can't defeat her," Hannah said, lulling him into a false sense of security. She had no other choice but to end Mara's reign of evil once and for all. Perhaps she could use her sense of defeat to her advantage. "I just called all the witches to her. Clearly, I am falling in line."

"So you desire that I do not tell her? Is that it?" He

spoke to Hannah as if she were a small child—slow and patronizing.

"Do whatever you want, Callan. It's not like I'm going to live long anyway." Hannah pushed past Callan and returned to the dirt path that lined the cliffs. While she hoped her performance convinced him that she would no longer resist, it wasn't difficult to portray. He didn't say anything as he followed after her. As she pounded her feet against the dusty gravel, she wracked her brain for ways to stall—ways to evade Callan and get to the Occult and Mysticism room in the library. As she walked, her stomach growled. She turned to Callan, keeping her failed demeanor intact.

"Can I at least change my clothes before we return? And maybe get some food. I stink and I'm starving."

Callan surveyed her with suspicion. "You do not stink," he said. "Sirens always smell incredible to others."

"Well, I can smell myself, and I can smell you. We've been in the same clothes for far too long. Trust me. It's not alluring at all."

Callan's glare pierced Hannah. Her stomach roared with hunger. Callan sighed and slapped his hands against his sides. He nodded. "Fine, but we are to move with haste. No trickery." Hannah knew that he too hadn't eaten in a long time. He must have been equally starved.

Though they walked down the cliff in silence, Hannah's thoughts were as loud as ever. Had she lost Callan for good? How was she going to ditch him? How was she possibly going to defeat Mara? Did it even matter? She was going to die in a few days anyway.

Then a different thought dawned on Hannah: It *did* matter. She didn't care what she had to do to succeed. She had nothing to lose.

CHAPTER TWENTY

*W*hen they arrived at Hannah's dorm, part of her longed for the normality she associated with it. Learning to live with a new roommate, getting ready for classes, focusing on her clean slate. But without everything that had happened, Hannah would have died without knowing who she truly was or the story of how she came to exist.

Entering her dorm room, Hannah hoped that Amelia wasn't there. When she opened the door, however, Amelia threw her arms around Hannah.

"Oh my god," she screamed. Hannah winced. "Where have you been? I thought you might have died!"

Not yet.

Hannah's side of the room was untouched, still plagued by unpacked boxes.

Amelia stepped back from her but kept her hands on Hannah's shoulders. "I left voicemails. Sent you about a hundred texts."

"I'm sorry," Hannah said. "My phone died."

Callan leaned in the doorway.

"Oh, I see." She offered Hannah a suggestive smile. "You've just been...occupied." She winked.

Hannah feigned a small laugh. "I guess I just lost track of time."

Amelia put her lips close to Hannah's ear and whispered, "He must have been good, because you are glowing. Your eyes even seem brighter." Amelia sniffed. "You even smell incredible. What perfume is that?"

Hannah glanced back at Callan, who gave her a *told you so* look. "I'll get you some," Hannah said.

"Amazing," Amelia said. Her eyes were glassy, and her smile seemed forced. Her demeanor was less effortless than usual.

"Is everything okay?" Hannah asked.

"Uhhh..." Amelia's voice cracked. "I was actually on my way out. Bryce is in the infirmary."

Hannah knew what was wrong with him. He was a Vampire who wasn't allowed to feed on blood. He was dying. But Amelia didn't know that. "What's wrong with him?"

Callan cleared his throat. "We should really be on our way," he said.

Hannah ignored him.

"They don't know." Tears glistened in Amelia's eyes. "He's just pale and can't keep any food down. He's trying to be brave, but I can tell that he's in a lot of pain."

"Amelia, I'm so sorry."

"Do you want to come with me? Landon is meeting me there."

"We do have a previous engagement," Callan interjected.

"I could really use my roommate right now," Amelia

said. Hannah knew that this was another chance to stall and possibly ditch Callan. Maybe she could even help Bryce.

She turned to Callan and gave him a daring stare. "Why don't you go, and I'll meet you there. I'd like to see Bryce. See if there is any way I can help."

"Just being there would help," Amelia said.

"I thought you said you were starving," Callan said, shifting on his feet. He was getting impatient, and Hannah feared that he might try and use his Siren's influence to get rid of Amelia. She wouldn't let that happen.

"There's a small café right next to the infirmary. We can grab food there before we leave." She turned back to Amelia and brought her in for another hug. She accessed her own Siren's voice and soothingly whispered into Amelia's ear, so that Callan couldn't hear. "You're not to listen to anything Callan says. If he gives you a command, you do not have to obey."

Amelia nodded in a daze. "I'm just going to change into some fresh clothes, and then we can go."

"Okay, I'll wait outside." Amelia walked past Callan and eyed him warily.

Callan closed the door behind her and lunged toward Hannah. "What did you say to her?"

"Relax. I just told her that everything would be okay. She doesn't need to worry." Callan crossed his arms and leaned back. He seemed to believe her. "Now, turn around. I need to change."

Callan turned, and Hannah felt in control. She changed into black leggings, a sports bra, sneakers, and soft, white Under Armour sweatshirt. She figured that she better wear something that allowed her to run if she needed to. She pulled her curly hair into a low, messy ponytail, and looked at herself in the mirror that hung on the back of her armoire. Amelia was right. Her eyes were brighter than before. She took a deep breath and looked at her reflection with determination.

"Okay, let's go."

Hannah headed for the door, but Callan stepped in front of her. "Heed my words, Hannah." He loomed over her. "I shan't tolerate any nonsense."

Though Hannah considered what approach to take with Callan, her instincts took over before any sense of strategy could intervene. "I've had about enough of you trying to intimidate me," she said, taking a step even closer to Callan, her eyes looking up to meet his. "I've already told you that I'm not going to resist, and it would be in your best interest to believe me." Hannah conjured a white orb of light in her hand.

Callan stepped back.

Hannah closed her fist, and the magical ball of energy dissipated. "If I wanted to escape you, I would have already."

"You may be more powerful than I, but Mara..."

"Which is why I'm still here." Hannah kept her voice firm. "Now, are you going to get out of my way?"

Callan stepped aside, and Hannah joined Amelia in the hallway.

———

AT THE CAMPUS INFIRMARY, AMELIA LED HANNAH and Callan to Bryce's stall—a hospital bed with only a curtain surrounding it for privacy. "Why haven't they sent him to the hospital?" Hannah asked.

Amelia kept her voice low and gentle. "They say he's

too sick for transport. One of the doctors from Cape Cove Memorial consulted with them and said that they'd be doing the same thing there as they would be here. Just fluids, pain management, and monitoring him. Hopefully he takes a turn for the better soon."

"Yeah, hopefully." Hannah knew that Bryce would die unless he was unleashed on the world and free to feed on human blood. Part of Hannah wanted to let him go—undo Callan's compulsion and give him a shot at a normal life. But she also knew that he could hurt a lot of people.

Amelia pulled back the curtain.

Hannah was taken aback by Bryce's ashen complexion. His skin was so pale that it looked like clear wax with brittle blue veins beneath it. Though he was asleep, each labored breath sounded like a raspy moan. A pang of pain stabbed Hannah's heart. Bryce was in the wrong place at the wrong time, and it was all Hannah and Callan's fault. Just as Callan didn't ask to be turned into a Siren and Hannah didn't ask to be converged with magic, Bryce never asked to be a Vampire. It was a cruel fate thrust upon him.

Landon slumped in a chair next to the bed. "H-Hannah. You're here." He stood and tried to rub the wrinkles from his shirt.

"I came as soon as Amelia told me." Hannah hugged him tighter than she intended. If things were different, he could have been the boy she cared for; the young man she brought back to Sonoma to meet her uncle; the boyfriend she brought to her parents' graves. But it wasn't meant to be.

Landon hesitated at first, but soon wrapped his arms around Hannah. She knew he probably thought she was a freak, but his embrace was warm and comforting none-theless.

"I called you a couple times," he said. He scratched the back of his head.

"She's been busy." Amelia smirked.

"My phone died," Hannah said. "Lost my charger." Hannah turned to Callan.

He was stiff, standing tall with his arms crossed. His eyes scanned the medical center. Hannah imagined it looked very different from medicine back in the 1600s. Machines, tubes, needles, wires.

Hannah took a step toward him and whispered, "Technology has upgraded since you were last in a hospital."

"Indeed," he said, stone cold.

Hannah missed the old Callan—the Callan who held her hand when the shuttle bus took a sharp turn, or the Callan that caressed her face when she was upset. She had to remind herself that this wasn't her Callan. She'd get him back. She had to.

Hannah turned her attention back to Bryce, whose eyes fluttered awake. He opened his mouth to speak, but his lips were dry and cracked. His fangs were dull and barely noticeable—probably from a lack of feeding.

Amelia was quick to take a mouth swab, dip it in water, and rub it over his lips. "Look who came to visit," she said, her voice high-pitched and animated.

Hannah stepped forward and looked down at him, trying to picture the fresh-faced, vibrant Bryce she met at her first college party. It was impossible to think that he had degraded in just a matter of days.

Bryce looked up at Hannah. His eyes widened and he shifted away from her in his cot.

Callan stepped forward.

Hannah took Bryce's hand. "Calm down. You're okay.

You're safe." Hannah could feel her glossy words flow into Bryce's ears. He relaxed into a trance.

"That was weird," Amelia said. "Are you in pain?" she asked Bryce.

"I'm okay," he croaked through an eased smile.

"It probably just took him a moment to recognize me," Hannah said. "He seems okay now." Her stomach growled, and Hannah realized that this was the perfect moment to make her escape.

"Jeez, get some food in your belly, Fenwick," Landon said, trying to lighten the mood.

"Callan, would you mind running to the cafe next door? Get some sandwiches and chips or something?" she asked.

He looked at her with suspicion. "You shall accompany me, yes?"

Landon and Amelia exchanged glances.

"I'd like to stay just a little longer," she said. "Maybe I'll be able to help Bryce."

"I do not have any coin," he said. Hannah realized that she didn't either. Any cash she had was in her bag, which was still in the cave with Mara.

Landon reached into his pocket and pulled out his wallet. "Here, man." He handed Callan his credit card. "It's on me."

Hannah smirked at Landon's power move, even though it was completely lost on Callan. Callan took the card and puzzled at it.

"You just give it to the person at the cafe. It has money on it," she whispered. "We did this to him. I just want to make sure he isn't in any pain."

"I did it," Callan whispered, looking to Bryce. "You had nothing to do with it." Hannah thought that some of Callan's humanity was showing, but that was simply wishful thinking. "If I had simply killed him, we would not be wasting our time here." His words dripped with frustration and an utter lack of remorse.

"By the time you return, I'll be ready to leave," Hannah said.

Callan formed a fist around the credit card and tilted his head. He turned to Amelia and placed his hand on her shoulder. "You should retrieve our food." His Siren's voice was clear and enticing. "You desire this." He handed her Landon's credit card.

Amelia looked at him like he had lost his mind. "No, I'm good. Thanks, though."

Hannah smiled to herself, knowing that her compulsion had trumped Callan's.

Callan eyed Hannah, probably piecing together that she told Amelia not to listen to him. He looked to Landon and must have realized that he was too far away to touch without being completely awkward.

"Fine. I shall go," he said. He moved his mouth close to Hannah's ear so that no one else could hear him. "You best be here when I return."

Hannah nodded with annoyance, conscious not to lose the assertion she exhibited against Callan back in her dorm room. He turned to leave and disappeared behind the infirmary doors.

"He's not as charming as I remember," Amelia commented, but Hannah didn't have time to entertain her gossip.

She took Amelia's hand and put her other hand on Landon's shoulder. She looked back and forth between them. "Go back to your dorms now." She felt the current of her song course on the sound waves that came from her mouth.

They nodded and walked away. Hannah placed her hand on the side of Bryce's cheek. "You don't feel any pain. That hunger you feel is no longer there. You can let go now. You're at peace." She noticed his eyes fill with tears, and he sighed with relief.

"Thank you." His eyes closed, pressing a couple tears down his face. His chest rose with a shallow breath and fell once more. One arm slid off the edge of the bed as his body went limp.

Hannah's eyes filled with water. Though she knew that without her compulsion, he would die a long, slow, and agonizing death, she still felt overwhelming torment at what she had done. But there was no time. She had to go before Callan returned.

FOG ROLLED OVER THE COBBLESTONES LEADING up to Bellcliff Library. Lightning cracked, followed by the humming grumble of thunder. A shiver crawled up Hannah's spine. And despite it only being the afternoon, the threatening weather turned the day into night. Perhaps the weather was lured by Mara's evil.

She tip-toed up the spiral staircase, trying to keep her feet light and silent. Though Mara was underground, Hannah didn't want to alert her to her betrayal. When she reached the Occult and Mysticism room, she sighed at the sight of Raven's wilting manuscript. She held the knob and inched the door shut.

Hannah picked up Raven's spell book, her legs shaking. Her hands glowed as she touched the enchanted pages. Goosebumps erupted on Hannah's skin.

"Come on, Raven," Hannah spoke to the book as she

flipped through the pages. "Give me something I can use." As her eyes scanned over the handwritten scrawl, she vaguely remembered something she read the first time she was in this room. *Magic can be gracious, vengeful, rewarding, punishing.* And just as the thought entered her head, the pages flipped toward the front binding, as if prompted by a gentle wind.

Hannah looked down at the page, her eyes quickly moving back and forth as she read the words in front of her. Her eyes filled with tears. Her legs stopped shaking, and her shoulders relaxed. She sat down at the aged, wooden table. A tear slipped down her cheek and onto the page, causing the old ink to bleed. She tapped her finger-tips to her thumb on her right hand. She paused, thumb pressed to pinky.

Hannah was not anxious. She was certain. This would work.

She wiped a tear from her cheek and inhaled the dry, stale air.

She stood up from the table and shut Raven's spell book.

She brushed her fingers over the sigils on the front cover—good outweighing evil. And she intended to keep it that way.

CHAPTER TWENTY-ONE

$\mathcal{H}$annah paused on the last step of the spiral staircase.

"Can I help you? Hello? Are you even a student here?" Edwin's haughty voice echoed upon the walls.

She crouched on the stairs and peered through the intricate iron railing. A middle-aged woman in a petticoat and coif walked right past the circulation desk. An older man followed, wearing breeches and stockings. A younger man and woman were close behind, dressed in mis-matched modern clothing. More followed. People, young and old, some dressed in Puritan garb, others in present-day fashion, walked past Edwin and headed toward the back of the library—toward the hidden entrance to Mara's lair. Their gazes were set straight ahead, and their steps were automatic. They all appeared to be under a trance—Hannah's Siren song.

Callan must have realized by now that Hannah had evaded him, so she expected him to barge into the library at any moment. Before he did, however, she realized that she had an opportunity to save the re-awakened witches.

She scurried across the marble floor and went straight to Edwin.

"Ah, a familiar face," he said, flustered by the unusual amount of people entering his empty library. "Do you know anything about this? Is there some kind of convention on campus? A parade? Some kind of protest?"

Hannah didn't answer. She reached across the circulation desk and took Edwin's hand. Though he looked overwhelmed, Hannah sung her words to him before he could resist. "Run. Don't come back until it's safe."

His eyes glazed over, and he nodded. He weaved between the witches.

Edwin opened the door to exit. Callan stood just outside. When he spotted Hannah, his expression turned red and irate.

Callan thrust Edwin aside and pushed his way through the witches.

Hannah raced back up the spiral steps. She was happy that she chose to wear sneakers.

She found a spot on the second floor where she could look out over the witches trailing into the library. She held onto the railing, took a deep breath, and called forth her buried Siren's song. It didn't take much before the melody filled her mind and seeped from her lips. She reveled in the sweet notes she projected.

The witches paused, and Hannah felt a momentous sense of accomplishment.

You're headed into a trap, Hannah thought as her harmony rang along the many shelves and marble floors. *Leave now and never yield to Mara's influence. Surround yourself in light and repel the darkness.* The longer she sang, the more the witches snapped out of their trances. It was as if they were being re-awakened for a second time. They stopped and looked around the library. Some gasped, others stumbled. They didn't seem to know how they got to this place and were only just noticing the others walking beside them. *Run! You're free.*

Hannah's song was abruptly interrupted. Callan grabbed her shoulders and pushed her to the floor. She slammed into a bookshelf. Callan breathed heavily and bared his teeth. He picked Hannah up, one hand grasping at her sweatshirt and the other around her neck. "I thought I said no trouble."

Beyond Callan's hostile expression, Hannah saw the witches below filing out of the library. She smiled. "When this is all over, you'll be glad I caused a little trouble." She remembered a spell Raven used and decided to tweak it for her own use. "Let my skin be fire, and your grip expire." Hannah felt her neck heat beneath Callan's hand.

"Ah!" Callan released a beastly snarl. He tossed Hannah aside and cradled his burnt hand.

She had little control over her limbs as they flailed onto the hard marble. She could try to run and escape Callan yet again, but that was not part of her plan. She needed to get back to Mara, so she had to allow him to take her to the she-Devil.

"Mara shan't be pleased," Callan said between clenched teeth, tending to his singed hand. He aimed to please Mara. His very existence depended on it—under Mara's compulsion, that was.

"She knows I'm powerful. She won't blame you for my actions." Hannah understood the desire and gratitude Mara's influence demanded. It was intoxicating and all-encompassing. The thought of disappointing her or failing a command was not only devastating, but painful. All that mattered was her happiness. And though Callan may have been her enemy in this moment, she cared for him. She would free him. Soon.

"I should not have left your side or agreed to go to the infirmary to see that stupid boy."

"Well, don't worry," Hannah said, achingly raising herself to her feet. "We won't have to go back there. That stupid boy is dead."

Callan's face froze, and for the tiniest moment, Hannah thought she spotted sorrow in his eyes. That moment passed, however, when his green eyes went dark. "Good."

Remaining sympathetic toward Callan was difficult for Hannah when he was such a heartless monster under Mara's command. She forced herself to think back to the Callan she first met—the Callan who was devastated to find out that she had reawakened magic and was ashamed at the weakness he portrayed when previously confronted with dark magic. That was the person she was fighting for. Hannah understood now. Callan wasn't weak; he just didn't have prodigy magic like she did. Other than Mara, no one did.

Callan gripped Hannah's upper arm and pulled her back toward the stairs. "Maybe Mara shall put us both out of our misery by killing you early," he said. Though Hannah knew that was the evil speaking, it still made her heart ache. Her magic simmered beneath her skin, ready to shock his hand off of her if she so commanded. But it was fine. It would all be over soon.

"I AM OF NIGHT. FORSAKEN THE LIGHT," CALLAN said, his hand hovering over the hardwood floor in the back corner of the library. The enchanted hatch to Mara's lair appeared. He opened it and shoved Hannah in. She stumbled down the underground stairs into the cave. Six witches knelt before the stone alter where Mara stood.

"I am grateful for your return, but where are the others?" Mara demanded from one of the women before her. The witch gazed up at Mara, awestricken—loyal to her —already under her command.

"Upon entering the library, we heard a compelling song telling us to leave. Telling us that we mustn't serve you." The woman folded her hands over and over. "But your pull was greater, Mistress Eden. I speak for us all when I say that we could not wait to be reunited with you again." The other witches nodded in agreement, eager to please their creator. It was clear to Hannah that these were the creatures Mara created before Callan imprisoned them all in stone.

Callan pushed Hannah off the last step. Her heels punched against the slate floor.

Mara looked past her creatures and stared at them. If her red eyes could burn holes into bodies, Hannah would have been incinerated by now. The other witches followed her gaze. Their admiration turned to wrath. They rose from their knees and seethed—ready to attack. But they weren't focused on Hannah. They fixated on Callan.

"At ease," Mara cooed to her creatures. "Mr. Delmonte here knows that his betrayal was wrong. He has come back home and has re-committed himself to our cause. To me." The witches calmed, their fury simmering to begrudged grimaces. "Miss Fenwick, on the other hand, has proven to be even more infuriating than her past self. At least Raven Harlowe knew when to surrender."

Callan pulled both of Hannah's arms behind her back and shoved her forward while holding her wrists together. Hannah winced at the discomfort of his grip, but was even more apprehensive at being pushed into a den of demons.

"She evaded me for mere moments. In that time, she did irreparable damage. For that, I am so sorry." Callan bowed his head with reverence to his master.

Mara looked down at him. Though she feigned pity, pouting her lips and blinking her eyes, Hannah could sense her satisfaction at his groveling.

She placed one of her pointy fingers on Callan's chin. "You returned her to me. That is all I care about." Hannah suspected that this was a lie. Mara couldn't risk losing another follower, especially a Siren like Callan. She must have feared that he would turn on her, just as he did before. How else would you explain her mercy? Hannah bet that if Mara had a massive new crop of witches, she would have punished Callan as an example of what happens to those who are incompetent under her command.

"You, on the other hand, disappoint me." Mara's red gaze settled on Hannah. "Here I thought, in exchange for activating your magic and providing you with the beauty of a Siren's song, you would be an asset to me—that you would be grateful and obedient."

"I guess my magic allows me to think for myself." Despite Hannah's quivering legs, she did well to hide her nerves. "Just because I'm no longer one of your mindless drones, doesn't mean I'm not grateful. If it wasn't for you, I may never have experienced my magic before I die."

Mara's nose twitched in vexation at Hannah's response.

Hannah needed Mara to realize that she was a threat.

"And it feels…" Hannah baited Mara. "Like I could do absolutely anything." She had nothing to lose. The thought helped keep Hannah's fear docile.

Mara forced a cackle. "Lucky for me, dear child, your life has an expiration date. You may thank your past self for that delightful twist." She stepped closer to Hannah and swiped her long black hair behind her shoulder. "Unfortunately, patience has never been a strength of mine. I think today is as good a day as any for you to perish."

Good.

Though her heart raced faster than her blood could pump, she was happy that Mara walked right into her plan. Hannah took controlled breaths through her nose and let them seep out her lips. "I suppose if I were you, I would do the same thing. Get rid of the threat before they impose any more risk."

"You are more of a nuisance than a risk," Mara said.

Hannah shrugged.

Mara raised an eyebrow. "You are quite calm for a girl about to die."

"I guess because I know I'll be reborn. I'll get a second…third…chance at stopping you."

Mara released a howl of laughter, mimicked by her small army of creatures. Even Callan chuckled at the suggestion. "I fear you overestimate your capabilities, young Hannah. You truly believe you shall be able to remember any of this by the time you are reincarnated?"

"Singing to the awakened witches wasn't the only thing I did after I eluded Callan. I cast a spell. I'll remember. Trust me," Hannah bluffed, but Mara didn't know that. Her smug tone scraped at Mara's ego, and it was written all over her face.

"I have had enough of this!" Mara screamed, no longer

trying to keep a cool head. "Even if you do remember, you shan't be converged until your sixteenth birthday. Perhaps you shall kill your new parents then as well." Mara's words cut deep. Hannah felt a sharp pang in her chest at the memory of her parents' fading into the water. "Kill her," Mara commanded to her minions, snapping her cloak as she turned on her heel.

Callan pushed Hannah forward and followed Mara.

Mara's servants surrounded Hannah. One witch with long, blinding white hair, and skin so thin it appeared colorless, fixated on her and released a blood-curdling screech that felt as if it could shatter glass.

"Oh, good," Mara called from her altar. "Gwendolyn here is a Banshee. Her cries are a herald of an impending death." Callan stood by Mara's side like a loyal pet.

Her words didn't concern Hannah. She knew her death was right around the corner, but it needed to be at Mara's hand. That wouldn't happen, however, if she let Mara's creatures rip her to shreds. One of the witches slithered forward. His skin glistened with scales. His eyes were yellow, and he heaved forward heavy breaths, as if there was something stuck in his throat. He opened his mouth, revealing a forked tongue. Hannah recoiled. Red and orange sparks flickered inside his mouth. The witch spat out a long stream of fire.

Hannah threw up her hands, and a shield of light deflected his flames.

His blaze fizzled out. Tendrils of smoke curled from his lips and glided up his scaled face.

Hannah braced herself, hands radiating with light. A young girl, sixteen or seventeen, walked toward Hannah and tucked her short, red hair behind her ear. She was small and unassuming, but in a flash, she shifted into Landon—sweet, caring Landon.

Hannah froze.

"Hannah, what are you doing? What is all of this?" Her voice was an exact mimic of Landon's. She even had his warm brown eyes and sandy brown hair. "We had that special moment on the beach the other night, and then I just don't hear from you again?"

To know about her and Landon's night on the beach, she must have been able to read minds. *Fuck off, witch bitch,* Hannah thought.

Insult played on fake Landon's face, and he immediately threw a punch. Hannah blocked the shapeshifter with her arm but recoiled from the heavy impact. The young girl not only displayed Landon's features, but his strength as well. Before Hannah could recover, fake Landon high-kicked the center of her chest.

Hannah's body plummeted against the hard, slate ground. Winded, she managed to stand back up. The fake Landon sprinted toward her. Hannah stepped to the side and grabbed the shapeshifter's arm.

"Turn back into your pretty-little-self," Hannah commanded, forcing her Siren's influence to fill her.

She wasn't sure if trying to compel the shapeshifter would work, as Mara's compulsion had proven to be undeniable. But she wouldn't be able to fight off these creatures for long, and this wasn't how she was supposed to die. "Stop attacking me. You don't want to hurt me."

Fake Landon transformed back into the little redhead girl and looked at Hannah apologetically. Hannah released her grip, and the girl stumbled back.

"I do not desire to hurt you," the girl repeated.

In that instance, Hannah knew that she was equally, if not more powerful, than Mara. The fact that her Siren ability could overturn the undying servitude instilled within one of Mara's creatures was a game-changer. She was unsure why her song to turn Mara's creatures away from the library didn't work, yet in this moment, her command was strong enough to sway their allegiance. Perhaps her compulsion by touch was more powerful than she ever imagined.

She looked to the altar. Mara's upper lip twitched as she grated her teeth.

There wasn't time to touch and compel all of Mara's creatures, especially when she didn't know what other supernatural abilities they contained. So, she took a chance.

She surveyed the witches, connecting her eyes to each of theirs. They appeared confused and angry and were seconds away from attacking. Hannah filled her mind with her alluring Siren song and hummed the entrancing melody, allowing it to blanket over the dark creatures before her. And just as her magic once provided her a spell from the old language when she was influenced by Mara's evil, she now felt as though her light magic was feeding her a spell—words to put to her tune.

"Though once you bowed at Mara Eden's feet,
   and acted as her malicious fleet,
   you now answer to me—my every command.
   Ignore her orders. Together we stand."

Her words danced along her melody like mesmerizing lyrics to a hypnotic song. It felt more condensed over a smaller number of witches—each note more saturated with her magic. Hannah's heart thudded against her chest as glowing light glazed over Mara's creatures.

The witches softened and relaxed their stances. Hannah was overcome by both a cooling sense of relief and an empowering surge of conviction. She had turned the tables on Mara and part of her wanted to sic her new soldiers on the black witch who forced darkness upon them. But that was not part of Hannah's plan. Besides, Hannah didn't want to control her fellow witches. She was not like Mara. She wanted them to be free. And now, more than ever, she felt Raven's spirit swirling within her.

"No," Mara cried. She raced to the edge of the altar.

The witches stood behind Hannah. While Callan looked confused and concerned, Mara was pure rage.

"You answer to me, you imbeciles," Mara shouted. "Kill her! I command you!" She screamed at her creations, but her words no longer mattered to them.

"If you want me dead, Mara, then you'll have to kill me yourself." Hannah's magic zipped through her limbs, and she felt electric at the power she possessed. She knew, however, that it would soon come to an end. While Hannah's magic may have been able to turn the witches away from their master, she didn't believe it could overtake Mara.

"Then that is exactly what I shall do." Black smoke emitted from Mara's palms, echoing with fearful cries, and the dark magic plumed against the cave walls.

"Do what you will," Hannah screamed over the sobs that spewed from Mara's haze. "I'm going to die anyway, but I know I'll be back."

At this, Mara retracted her magic. The shrieking smoke flew back into Mara's body, and her red glare burned into

Hannah's eyes. "You think you have outsmarted me? That you are more powerful than I? We shall see about that!"

Mara's threat both terrified and electrified Hannah. She thought Mara was about to do exactly as she had hoped.

"I shall do what I tried to do three hundred and twenty-six years ago. This time, however, I shall get it right. You shall perish today, Ms. Fenwick. And you shall never again see the light of day."

Hannah released a slow and controlled sigh, preparing herself for Mara's wrath. This was it.

She looked at Callan, and despite his resentful expression, she offered him a longing gaze. He awakened her to a whole new world—one where the unexplainable anxiety and adrenaline filling her body finally made sense. He provided her answers to a truth that burdened her for years. He helped her realize who she was and what she was capable of. If it wasn't for him, she never would have discovered her true feelings.

She mouthed three last words to Callan. "I love you."

His eyes widened, more with suspicion than anything else, but at least he would know how she truly felt once she was gone from this earth—once he was free.

"Silentium," Mara yelled.

Her lips fused together. Hannah knew that her time left was limited. Though she felt incredible pain and trepidation at what was to come, she was happy knowing that *I love you* were the last words she will have ever spoken. Hannah realized that Mara was silencing her so that she couldn't tamper with the spell about to be cast upon her, just as Raven did all those years ago. But it didn't matter. Intervening would defeat Hannah's purpose. And even though all was going according to plan, tears still slid down her face.

The witches walked forward, but Hannah stopped them. She raised her hands out in front of them and shook her head. Hannah reassured their confusion with a sincere nod, closing her eyes for a moment and then reopening them. They took a step back and followed her lead as Mara raised her hands into the air.

"Might you wait until your spell is properly prepared?" Callan whispered to Mara.

"History is not repeating itself, now, Mr. Delmonte, is it?" she hissed at Callan through clenched teeth. "Is there any reason you would desire me to spare this girl?"

"Absolutely not," he said. He glanced at Hannah, his eyes filled with dubious suspicion. He wished to protect Mara, not Hannah. "'Tis just—"

Mara cut him off. "Good. Then step aside. I shall finish this once and for all."

Callan nodded and treaded backward a few steps. He fidgeted with the hem of his shirt.

Mara took a deep breath and spoke:

"I call upon the darkest forces to undo what once was cursed.

The spell I cast upon Raven Harlowe, I now ask to be reversed.

Reborn only to die on her eighteenth year was not the dark intent.

But rather to cease rebirth at all, her soul forever in descent.

So now I break the destined cycle of Raven reincarnate.

And commit this Hannah Fenwick to a darker, wicked fate."

Hannah felt her magic writhe within her, panicking at

the black spell infiltrating her soul. She moaned at the discomfort she felt from the magic being cast upon her, but no noise came from her bound mouth. Regardless of her magic pleading with her to fight back, Hannah ignored the urge. She thought of her mom and dad. She could smell her father's aftershave and feel the grass beneath her feet as she walked barefoot through vineyards with her mother. It helped to know that she might be able to see them soon.

As Mara continued, Hannah noticed a pained expression on her face. Callan saw it too.

"Something is wrong," he said, walking to her side. "Please, stop this now."

Hannah knew she could count on Mara's stubbornness and arrogance. Her black magic was far too powerful for anything bad to happen to her.

Mara pushed Callan away and carried on with her spell despite the agony playing on her face.

"Strike her down and kill her now, I wish to wait no longer.

For with her death and last dying breath, I feel myself grow stronger.

Smother the light that burns within her, never again to see the sun.

Commit her to my dark command, and let this spell be done!"

Mara trembled and gripped the podium before releasing a nerve-piercing scream.

Hannah felt the need to scream as well, but with her lips fused shut, her cries echoed only in her mind. Her body trembled. The spell spread through her veins like poison. She looked at Callan. She wanted his vibrant green eyes to be the last things she saw.

Mara reached her hand out toward Hannah and threw a sphere of her swirling black magic at her. Like a bullet, it shot through Hannah's chest. She collapsed against the stone, every part of her going cold. She could feel her heartbeat slow to a dull thump. The swirling sphere of black magic bloomed above Hannah. Threatening. Furious. It wailed and descended upon Mara, consuming her whole.

It worked.

Hannah's heart stopped. Her body fell limp, her eyes vacant.

CHAPTER TWENTY-TWO

*C*allan stood on the altar and watched in shock as Mara's black magic turned on her. It plunged through her body like wild vines piercing through her. The tormented screams reverberated beneath her skin. Mara's bellow decrescendoed into aching croaks. The dark, rapid smoke finally released Mara's dead body, dropping it to the cave floor. The shadowy tendrils floated into the air and plummeted into the ground.

A black mist seeped from Callan's skin and rejoined the pluming smoke. Callan wailed as darkness ripped from his body, and his knees buckled. They slammed against the stone as inky vapors dissipated from his lips, chest, fingers. He gasped, placing his palms against the cool floor.

He caught his breath and hunched over. Mara lay dead beside him. Her eyes dulled to amber.

"You did it," he said. "You did it!" he repeated louder. "Hannah, you defeated her. How..." He turned his head to find Hannah, but his expression fell when he noticed her lying lifeless on the cold, stone floor. He scrambled on his hands and knelt beside her. He hoisted her upper body into his arms, cradling her head in the crook of his elbow.

The other witches seemed to be coming out of their compulsion and looked at each other, addled and dazed. The shapeshifting girl cried into her hands. The dragon witch looked down his arms, disgusted at the scales. The banshee sighed in relief. They were free.

"Go! Leave this place," Callan shouted.

The witches hugged each other, cried together, and rejoiced at their new-found freedom.

"Leave!" he screamed so harsh and loud that his voice broke. Pain filled his face and tears flowed from his green eyes. Though he was no longer under Mara's command, he was still a Siren and could compel them all to leave. With the unmistakable urgency and torture in his voice, however, he didn't need to. A few of the witches looked sorrowful at Callan cradling Hannah. Others widened their eyes at his temper. They scurried up the large, stone staircase, disappearing from the underground cave.

Callan shook Hannah in his arms. "Hannah. Wake up. You cannot be gone. This is not happening again." He ignored the tears flowing down his face and gently rubbed his hand along her pale face. "Open your eyes. I know you are still in there." His voice broke. He shook her again, harder this time, but her body remained heavy and limp. "Prithee, Hannah!" He held her close to his chest and kissed her forehead, his tears wetting her curls. He swayed back and forth as he hugged her small body, closing his eyes tight. When he opened them, he had a new resolve.

He placed her body back against the ground and hovered his hands over her chest.

"Mara Eden now dead, may her magic too disappear.

And allow this girl, Hannah Fenwick, return right now, right here."

Callan waited for his spell to work, but as the moments passed, his face twisted with frustration. "'Tis fine," he said. "'Twas not specific enough." He gathered her small, cold hands in his and squeezed them as he took a deep breath.

"With Mara Eden's death, may her darkness be erased.
The evil that she spread, be undone with great haste.
For if I could be saved from her wicked control,
Then so may Hannah Fenwick, reawaken her soul."

Hannah's eyes didn't open, and her body remained still. Callan continued his spell.
"Repair her magic and fill her with light.
And allow her blue eyes to once again shine bright."
Callan's rhymes became less eloquent—his mind unable to think clearly as he held a dead Hannah in his arms. This didn't stop him from continuing.
"I promise never to be tempted again,
And realize I'm weaker than other men.
But if you give her back to me,
Light is all I'll ever be."
He collapsed his head onto Hannah's chest. His entire body heaved in devastation. "I love you," he proclaimed, and pressed his lips against hers.
Nothing happened.
His shoulders sank. "I am sorry. I am so, so, sorry. The fault is mine." He breathed so fast that he could no longer speak.
He stood up and paced away from Hannah. He grabbed

onto the top of his head. His entire body trembled as if each breath spurred on the panic burrowing into his chest. His eyes fell on Mara's body, lying against the altar. His nose crinkled, and his eyes darkened. As he honed in on his new target—a place to focus his fury—his breathing became more controlled. He charged toward Mara.

Hannah gasped.

Callan froze in place.

He turned around.

Hannah's chest rose ever-so-slightly. He sighed, and joy filled his face.

Hannah opened her eyes. Her cheek rested against the cool ground, and her gaze connected to Callan's. She managed a smile.

CALLAN WAS NEXT TO HER IN A MATTER OF seconds, and Hannah could instantly tell that he was himself again.

"It worked," she said, her voice raspy and frail. For so long, she had felt that things just didn't work out for her. She had resigned herself to the fact that her life would be a series of unfortunate incidents. But her plan worked. It actually worked.

Callan crouched beside her and helped her sit up. He positioned himself behind Hannah. She leaned against his chest.

"How is this possible?" he asked. "My spells were useless. I know with certainty they did not do this." He didn't even try to hide the tears sliding down his face. Because unlike before, these were tears of happiness.

Hannah took a moment to catch her breath and feel the

ground beneath her. She wanted to make sure that she was actually alive, and not in some mirrored afterlife. But when she felt Callan's tears drip onto her cool skin, it was as if it hydrated her magic. She felt it stir within her, and she knew she was alive.

"For a witch who breaks the cycle of his or her own spell or curse may face the consequences of committing themselves to that fate," Hannah recited, taking a deep breath once the phrase left her mouth.

"What? Where did you hear that?"

"Raven told me."

Though Callan looked confused, it didn't take away from his delighted disbelief.

"I read it in her manuscript before I even knew who she was or that magic was real," Hannah continued. "Mara forgot that magic is its own separate entity. It holds all the power and simply flows through us. She needed to be loyal to it, and not the other way around."

Callan nodded at Hannah's words.

"So, when she broke my cycle of death and betrayed the original curse, she was punished."

"You are brilliant," Callan said.

"It was a shot in the dark, really. Raven's manuscript brought me back to that passage before..." She loved how happy he looked and didn't want to shatter his smile—she yearned for his smile.

"Before I dragged you here. Back to Mara." Callan's forehead creased as he furrowed his brows. Hannah could see him burdening himself again with guilt and it was the last thing she wanted. She used what little strength she had to twist her body so she could face Callan.

"You saved *me*. Don't you see that?" Hannah rested her hand on his tortured face. "If you hadn't sacrificed yourself to Mara's command, then I never would have broken free of her darkness." She gazed at him until she was sure that her words registered within his mind. "You are the strongest man I've ever known."

He smiled, and she kissed him. She ran her hands through his short hair, and he pulled her even closer with one hand behind her neck. They separated and gazed into each other's eyes.

Callan placed one of Hannah's out-of-place curls behind her ear.

"So, will Mara be reborn and cursed to die at her current age? Or is the Devil gone for good?" Callan asked.

Hannah shrugged, not really knowing the answer. "All that matters is that she's gone now and you're free."

"And you are alive," Callan said. "How did you know it would work?"

"I didn't. But someone very wise once told me that magic is mysterious. We can't possibly understand every aspect of it. We must accept that it is an unknown force. Otherwise, we'll drive ourselves crazy." Hannah smirked, taking great joy in getting to throw his words back at him.

"I love you," he said.

She remembered a time when she doubted how he truly felt, because of his old feelings for Raven Harlowe. But through this experience, Hannah had come to realize that they were one and the same. She had Raven's strength, passion, bravery, magic, and love for the young man kneeling in front of her. Though it took her a while to realize it, she now felt empowered and comforted knowing that Raven's soul lived within her.

"I love you too."

CHAPTER TWENTY-THREE

SIX DAYS LATER

*A*fter Bryce's funeral, Callan and Hannah returned to her dorm room. Amelia was so overcome by grief that she decided to go home for a couple days. Though he managed to keep it together during the service, Hannah could tell that Callan blamed himself for all the heartache and tears that poured over Bryce's coffin. He was, after all, the one who compelled him never to feed on another living being.

"He was a Vampire," Hannah said as she closed her bedroom door. "If you didn't do what you did, so many others could have died."

"I know," he said. "But it does not ease the guilt I possess."

They sat on the bed, and Hannah rubbed her hand up and down his back. She looked at her clock, and it read 6:00 p.m.

"A few hours more until you are officially eighteen years of age," Callan said.

Hannah scoffed. "Or a couple more hours until I officially die...again."

"Mara broke that curse. That is why she perished, and you are still here." Callan squeezed her hand.

"That was the intention, but we can't know for sure. We don't even know how I'm still alive."

"I have a theory," Callan said. He shifted on the bed. "Mara's new spell made it so you could never be reincarnated, correct?"

Hannah nodded.

"Well, that might mean that your magic could not leave your body after you died. It is connected to your soul. Therefore, if your soul never left your body, then your magic remained attached to it. And like I said before, your magic shall always protect you."

"So, you think my body died, but my magic didn't. And because of that, it brought me back to life?"

He nodded. "'Tis my hunch, at least."

Hannah smiled. "What you're saying is that I will never die? My magic won't let me?"

"I guess we must simply wait and see."

The clock on her bedside table glowed 6:02 p.m.

"What if you're wrong? What if the clock strikes twelve and I drop dead of a heart attack or brain aneurysm? What if I die without ever..." Her cheeks warmed.

"Without ever..." Callan repeated.

Hannah kissed Callan, parting his lips. She pressed her body against his until she forced him to lie back onto her bed. She straddled her legs on top of his waist and kissed him even more urgently than before. She slid her hand down his shirt and finessed his belt buckle with her fingers.

Callan moved her hand away from his pants and sat up, her legs still wrapped around him. "I desire this as well, believe me." He laughed. "But I desire to be with you out of love. Not out of fear."

"I do love you," Hannah said.

"I know you love me. I love you too. But I do not desire this to be something we do simply because you think you have a deadline. It should be a celebration. Not a possible farewell."

Hannah couldn't negate Callan's argument, because she *was* coming from a place of fear. What if in a matter of hours, her heart stopped beating again? She was already given a second chance at life, and she didn't want to waste it.

"I know," she said. She moved off of Callan and couldn't help but pout a bit.

Callan wrapped his arm around Hannah's shoulders. "You shall not die. Trust me." He kissed the side of her forehead.

"We aren't in the 1600s anymore. Maybe less *shalls* and more *wills*." Hannah offered him a smile. The clock blinked 6:06 p.m. All they could do now was wait.

The next few hours crawled by. In order to distract themselves, they went for dinner at the Harbor House cafeteria and walked aimlessly around campus. The entire time, Hannah feared that this might be the last time she would see all of this. The last time she would hear the ocean crash along the cliffs, smell the sea salt in the cool, fall air, or hold the hand of the man she loved.

Long after the sun went down, Hannah and Callan returned to her room. The clock read 11:52 p.m., and

Hannah could feel her heart beating fast against her chest. She couldn't tell if it was because she was nervous, or if it was the starting signs of a heart attack.

"I need to call my uncle," she said. She pulled out her cell phone and dialed. "Hey, Paul, it's me." Hannah had called her uncle since coming back to life, but they were quick and vague conversations. She didn't know what to tell him or how to express everything she had newly discovered since arriving at Bellcliff, so their conversations consisted of niceties and platitudes about being new to college life and how everything was going fine. With another pending death staring Hannah in the face, however, she needed to tell him something very important.

"No, I can't sleep. You know, birthday excitement and all. I just wanted to tell you something." She looked at Callan and smiled. "I have a boyfriend." The phrase sounded so juvenile, but there was no other way to spin it. "His name is Callan, and I'd love for you to meet him some day."

If Hannah died, perhaps Callan could be the one to tell everything to her uncle. He deserved some semblance of the truth. And if this was Hannah's last conversation with her Uncle Paul, she wanted him to know that she was happy and living a normal college life.

Hannah laughed into the phone. "Yes, he is very hand-some and very kind. You'd like him a lot."

Callan grinned.

"And I just wanted to thank you. For all you have done for me since Mom and Dad..." She nodded. "Yes, every-thing is fine," she said, feeling some tears well behind her eyes. "Just get emotional around birthdays." The clock read 11:58 p.m. "Anyway, I better go to sleep now. Love you,

Paul. Goodnight." Hannah hung up the phone and placed it on her bedside table. Tears tumbled down her cheeks.

"It will be all right. Come here." Callan pulled her into his arms. He trembled as he held her. This was exactly where she wanted to die—here in Callan's arms. She looked at the clock over Callan's shoulder: 11:59 p.m.

Her mind raced. Perhaps she should have spent the last few days trying to concoct a spell that would have guaranteed her survival past her eighteenth birthday. After all, with Mara gone, she was the most powerful witch left in the world. But after everything her and Callan went through, she was tired. She just wanted to be with him—experience life unburdened by the amazing magic she may soon be without. After they returned Mara's grimoire beneath the stone slat in the library and sealed it with a spell, Callan had convinced her to relax. She was certain that the book would be safe there, only accessible to her or Callan if they needed it, and so she forced herself to stop worrying. But now, when she was faced with her own mortality, yet again, she didn't feel ready to accept it. She finally knew who she was and had gotten a taste of what life could be like. It didn't have to be sad and tragic. It could be filled with self-discovery, adventure, and cosmic love. It could be magical.

Hannah buried her face against Callan's shoulder and squeezed her eyes shut, pressing a small tear down her freckled cheek. When she felt Callan's chest sink with a relieved sigh, however, she opened her eyes.

The clock blinked: 12:01 a.m.

Hannah exhaled, not even realizing that she had been holding her breath. Relief flooded her body, goosebumps crawling up and down her skin. Tears welled behind her eyes, and she couldn't help but beam with joy.

"How do you feel?" Callan asked, his eyes glassy.

"I feel...good." Hannah could feel the light she was converged with two years ago, a warm current beneath her skin. And though being turned into a Siren was a scar of darkness that she and Callan would always wear, it would challenge them to choose light every day.

Callan kissed her and pinned her onto the bed. Hannah wrapped her arms around him. She soaked in his scent and the love she felt in this moment.

Her skin glowed with tiny white orbs, drifting from her skin and sparking in the air.

"Can we celebrate now?" Hannah asked, a suggestive grin on her face.

Callan laughed and nodded.

She wrapped her legs around his hips and pulled his head closer to hers. They enraptured themselves in each other.

She pulled away and stared into Callan's beautiful green eyes.

This was her fresh start.

HANNAH STILL NEEDS YOU

Did you enjoy Awakened? Reviews keep books alive . . . Hannah needs your help!

Help her by leaving your review on either GoodReads or the digital storefront of your choosing. She thanks you!

ACKNOWLEDGMENTS

First and foremost, I must thank my family for always being supportive and encouraging, even when writing and getting published only felt like a pipe dream. Mom, you showed me that writing was something people could actually pursue; it didn't have to be unattainable to dreamers like me. Thank you for keeping me company at Barnes & Noble while I wrote that first book, proving to myself that I was capable. Dad, you never questioned my passion for writing. You only ever urged me to push myself and do my best. Furthermore, thank you for making movies an interactive experience. I don't think I would have become a writer had we not constantly tried to predict the major twists and turns of every movie we watched. Ryan, thank you for always playing with me as a child... even though I was always the one to die in our make-believe battles. Darren, you always gave me credit for following my passion, and that was more encouraging than you could ever know. Liz, I've always admired your determination and girl boss energy, and try to channel that into my own life.

Mal, you have read more of my work than anyone. Thank you for your time, encouragement, and honest feedback, which helped me grow with every project.

Cian, you are my most dedicated support, and there are not enough days in a lifetime to thank you for all the encouragement and love you have provided me. Whenever I questioned myself, you reminded me of my strength and determination. Whenever I was frustrated with the writing or editing process, you guided me back to calm and resilience. Whenever I felt stuck or unmotivated, you were patient, inspiring, and thoughtful. You have always lifted me up and acknowledged my talent...something I still struggle to recognize. So, thank you for being my unwavering partner and constant champion.

I, of course, need to thank everyone at The Parliament House Press, who without, my dream would not have become a reality. They believed in *Awakened* and shepherded me into their publishing family. Thank you to Shayne, Chantal, Kassie, Cindy, Malorie, Sophia, Erica, and the rest of the team who worked so hard on this book. You answered all of my questions and truly welcomed me with open arms. Similarly, the online writing and reading community have been wonderfully supportive and enthusiastic about *Awakened*. So, to everyone who participated in the cover reveal, release, and shared general excitement about this debut, thank you! You make a huge difference.

Earning my MFA from Boston University was instrumental to my knowledge of story and character development, so I would be remiss not to mention the wonderful program that helped shape me as a writer. Thank you, Scott, J.B., Debbie, and all my classmates.

Finally, I must thank those who creatively influenced me, even though they do not know me and will probably never read this. Veronica Roth, Victoria Aveyard, Suzanne Collins, Adrienne Young, Rebecca Ross, Kendare Blake, Shelby Mahurin, J.K. Rowling, J.R.R. Tolkien, and so many more. Your writing made my world feel large and full of magic.

ABOUT THE AUTHOR

Ciara graduated with her MFA in Screenwriting from Boston University where she worked as a writing fellow and later taught undergraduate writing courses. She now owns her own editorial business, *Ciara Duggan Editorial*, where she helps writers bring their stories to life from start to finish. She is also an editor and judge for Book Pipeline and Script Pipeline. Ciara resides in Connecticut with her husband, Australian Shepherd, and a never-ending pile of books.

THE PARLIAMENT HOUSE

THE PARLIAMENT HOUSE
WWW.PARLIAMENTHOUSEPRESS.COM

Want more from our amazing authors? Visit our website for trailers, exclusive blogs, additional content and more!

Become a Parlor Peep and access secret bonus content...
JOIN US!

MORE PARLIAMENT BOOKS

The Half-Class by Kayvion Lewis

Of Beast and Burden by Kelsey Kicklighter

Usher House Rising by Don Roff